THE WOMAN NEXT DOOR

BOOKS BY SUE WATSON

Love, Lies and Lemon Cake
Snow Angels, Secrets and Christmas Cake
Summer Flings and Dancing Dreams
Fat Girls and Fairy Cakes
Younger Thinner Blonder
Bella's Christmas Bake Off
We'll Always have Paris
The Christmas Cake Café
Ella's Ice Cream Summer
Curves, Kisses and Chocolate Ice Cream
Snowflakes, Iced Cakes and Second Chances
Love, Lies and Wedding Cake
Our Little Lies

THE WOMAN NEXT DOOR

SUE WATSON

bookouture

Published by Bookouture in 2019

An imprint of StoryFire Ltd.

Carmelite House
50 Victoria Embankment
London EC4Y 0DZ

www.bookouture.com

ISBN: 978-1-78681-894-2
eBook ISBN: 978-1-78681-893-5

For Lesley Mcloughlin, who knows all my secrets.

Have you ever had a secret that you couldn't tell a soul,
even the person you love? I have…

CHAPTER ONE

Lucy

I'll never forget the first time I saw Amber. It was late spring and she was driving down Mulberry Avenue in an open-topped sports car, with sun-burnished red hair, huge dark glasses, a low-cut top and those full, red lips. You had to look twice – she was just different from everyone else on our new estate of young mums and middle-aged empty-nesters walking their dogs. Built for families at all stages, Treetops Estate didn't attract any singles – let alone glamorous women in fancy cars. I was cleaning the windows inside and couldn't help taking an interest as she parked up outside Greenacres. It was the biggest, most gorgeous house on the estate, and just three doors down from ours. Along with ten other homes, it formed the fringe around a large crescent of grass – a vague nod to a village green on our suburban concrete jungle.

As I slowly wiped the windows, I saw her take her phone from her bag while climbing elegantly from the car. A flash of red as shiny black Louboutins hit the ground and crunched up the gravel towards the imposing white pillars framing the doorway. There was something about her that was vaguely familiar. Chatting on her phone, arms waving, she seemed to be having a rather heated conversation, and I was intrigued. Pacing up and down the drive, she eventually ended the call, throwing her phone back into the Prada handbag that probably cost a month's salary – well, a month of *my* salary anyway. She then took off the huge sunglasses to gaze around and as her face turned upwards towards my window our eyes met. I continued wiping, now with more enthusiasm, pretending I hadn't even noticed our new neighbour while feeling rather foolish and exposed. Then I began on the next window, where I carried on watching discreetly. I couldn't help it; she was fascinating.

Stepping up the two small steps to that big double door, she took out her keys. Tight skirt, short-sleeved blouse open at the neck, teeny-tiny waist. How jealous the women of Treetops Estate would be when the beautiful new neighbour turned up at their barbecues – and how cordially she'd be received by their husbands. I had to smile to myself. Her entrance was certainly a performance enjoyed very much by Dave from number 12. He was fortunate enough to have a bird's-eye view as he cleaned his gutters, his gaze wandering over to Greenacres as its new owner disappeared into her beautiful house. Dave went back to his gutters and I carried on cleaning my windows like nothing had happened… but it had.

TWELVE MONTHS LATER

CHAPTER TWO

Lucy

Amber downs her Prosecco, throwing back her head like a cowboy drinking whisky. In a matter of moments the glass is empty and she slams it down on the table with a smile. She seems slightly on edge tonight.

'More. We need more alcohol.' She laughs, lifting the bottle from a bucket of melting ice and filling our glasses. 'Lucy, drink up! You're lagging behind.' She holds the bottle over my glass, but I shake my head.

'I can't keep up. I'll just watch you,' I say apologetically, feeling rather boring. It's a Wednesday evening and I have to be up early for work in the morning. 'I can't teach multiplication with a hangover… especially to six-year-olds,' I add. 'It's a dangerous cocktail.'

'Oh, you don't realise how brilliant you are. Look how you worked out my phone bill the other day. I hadn't a clue.'

'It was quite simple really. You just had to work out the—'

'Yeah, yeah, but I didn't understand it,' she says, unable or unwilling to face anything as boring and mundane as a phone bill.

'You can do anything, Lucy,' she continues, throwing an arm around me. She's quite tipsy, which I always find funny, but I hope she isn't drowning her sorrows. She seemed quite down when I went to collect her and now she's all over the place. From experience, I know it will only take one more drink and she'll be dancing on the tables.

I sip at my Prosecco, and try not to worry, just enjoy her company, her craziness. We've been friends now for almost a year, yet it feels like we've known each other for ever.

'Ooh, he's a bit of all right, *and* he's got a friend,' she suddenly says, looking at me with raised eyebrows.

I roll my eyes.

'What?' she giggles at me, her hair moving like a shiny red curtain.

'You're abstaining, and I'm married, or did you forget those minor details?'

'I'm only kidding… or am I? You wouldn't be tempted to stray, would you, Lucy?' she asks, screwing up her bronze-flecked eyes, looking directly at me, playful, but knowing.

'No, I wouldn't. You're terrible,' I say, refusing to even take this on. I pick up our bottle of Prosecco from the ice bucket and share the dregs between us, shaking my head in mock outrage.

'Anyway, I'm not abstaining now. That was last week; tonight I'm back on the prowl.' She growls and makes cat claws with her hands.

Amber is so much fun. We see each other or talk on the phone most days, go out all the time – curries, drinks, the cinema – have girls' nights out, girls' nights in. I don't know what I'd do without her. Tonight she's brought me here to JoJo's, because I told her I've been feeling a bit down lately. It isn't anything serious, just that at forty-two, I've realised after a few bumps in the road that my life isn't turning out as I'd hoped – but then whose does? It's so sweet of her to bring me here to cheer me up, but I'd rather have gone to the cinema and eaten my weight in popcorn.

I watch her moving to the music in her seat; she's unable to sit still, looking around. She can never sit still. She's always scared of missing something. JoJo's is considered to be one of the best wine bars in Manchester with its copper walls and on-trend 'utility' light bulbs dangling helplessly from the ceiling. Amber's right at home here. It's what she calls 'buzzin'. And Amber loves 'buzzin'. But

I'm not like her, and when she suggested we come here, my heart sank a little. I didn't want to seem ungrateful, but I said, 'What about the new romcom at the Odeon?' But Amber had already made up her mind. She said I'd love it here. I'm trying.

I'm enjoying people-watching. This world is so different to mine, it's filled with over confident TV and advertising types with loud voices and big opinions. I'm particularly relishing the theatrical performance of the barman mixing bright cocktails, moving the shaker like a musical instrument, pouring effervescent, neon liquid from high into a Martini glass. I find the heavily accessorised, foaming cocktails absolutely fascinating. And against the soundtrack of jarring jazz and juicy conversations, I'm trying to filter nuggets of gossip when I see two women nearby looking over at Amber.

'That's her, isn't it?' one of them says to the other. 'Yeah, she looks older than she does on TV.'

I strain to listen to more, but sadly they are drowned out by other conversations about politics and audience figures. Damn.

I turn to Amber to see if she heard, but fortunately she's busy checking something on her phone.

'Should we order some food?' I suggest, when she eventually looks up.

She nods and I pick up a menu lying on the table.

'Oh, it's tapas…' I say, knowing she won't want this. We hate tapas.

'God,' she sighs absently.

'I *know*. Small plates and sharing are two things that should never be associated with food.'

'So right.' She puts her phone down, a look of concern shadowing her face, and I don't think it's related to the tapas.

'You okay?' I ask.

'Yeah,' she says, frowning at the phone, 'just work.' She looks slightly uncomfortable but isn't going to tell me what's wrong, so I pick up the previous conversation.

'Shall we go somewhere else to eat – a pizza place or something?'

'A pizza place? God, Lucy, what era are you living in? No one eats pizza any more, you're an unsophisticated heathen!'

'And *you're* a cheeky cow,' I say with a smile and we both start to laugh – we always end up laughing.

Her eyes are still laughing as her lips purse into a mock pout worthy of any film star, and I take a sip of fizz and purse my own lips slightly, mirroring her, which makes us laugh again.

'Shall we forget tapas and just get chips on the way home?' she says, leaning in conspiratorially.

'Yeah, let's do that. Good idea.'

She winks and goes back to her phone, while I glance around at the long-legged girls with bright orange cocktails.

'What are they drinking?' I ask.

After a few seconds she puts down her phone again and joins me, screwing her eyes up to see the drinks. 'Negronis.'

'Negronis?' I ask, but she's distracted again; she's like a magpie. She sees something glittery and forgets I'm here. I follow her eyes – she's looking over at some handsome guy with long hair wearing a white linen shirt. He's gorgeous. 'He's cute,' I say.

'Yeah, he is, isn't he? Actually, I know him. Harry's an old colleague.' She gives him a cutesy wave with her fingers and he waves back with a warm smile, his eyes staying on her long after the smile has faded. Men like that never smile at me in that way.

They're both still looking at each other like no one else is here and I watch this intimate but very public exchange. It's quite obvious these two have a history. There's a secret in their smiles. I reckon Harry's perhaps more than just a colleague – after all, Amber has quite a colourful love life. After it ended with her long-term boyfriend last year there have been no end of suitors. She's whisked away for fabulous weekends, expensive dinners and parties on millionaires' yachts. I imagine they're all worldly and rich. Good-looking too.

She doesn't have a regular boyfriend as such, not since she moved into Mulberry Avenue. Matt, my husband, reckons a lot of her dates must be men she's met on Tinder, but I said to him, 'Amber doesn't need Tinder. You should see her when we're out. She's a man magnet, she can have whoever she wants.'

She's now tapping her fingers on the table. She still seems slightly distracted, and I ask again if she's okay, but she dismisses my enquiries with a smile and, 'I'm fine,' but I'm not sure I believe her.

Watching her, I feel a little shiver run through me, and it isn't because I'm cold. I'm really quite warm, too warm. Amber says we're in for another hot summer, and temperatures are unusually high for early June, which the sweat on my upper lip is a testament to – even the prickly chill from my Prosecco isn't cooling me down. I sip on my fizz and glance through the window. The pavement is packed with summer people, enjoying after-work drinks in the late-evening sunshine, dressed effortlessly in cool, loose linens or long summer dresses. I note with envy that The only perspiration they are showing comes from their cold beer bottles. Meanwhile, I'm sweating profusely in my new Marks and Spencer jumpsuit. Nothing effortless here, just two words – fat and frumpy. It looked good on the hanger, and not too bad when I tried it on in the shop, but now I feel so out of place among these sophisticated media people. I wonder if I'd feel more 'in' if I was eight stone and drifting around in wedges and a maxi dress like Amber? She seems to be able to throw stuff together, brush her hair and, voila, she looks fabulous. Tonight she's wearing a cotton halterneck dress with her hair down around her slim shoulders. She reminds me of the film actress Julianne Moore, with her dark red hair and pale skin with a smattering of freckles.

I have similar colouring to Amber, but where her eyes match her red-brown hair and she has a golden glow, I'm the colour of milk, with blue eyes and ginger frizz. Even my freckles are ugly brown patches, not pretty little sprinkles like hers, and as for a long, halterneck dress, I can't pull it off. I tried a halterneck dress on during one of our recent shopping trips. Amber and I stood next to each other in the fitting rooms. She looked like a svelte summer goddess and me a short, fat woman with strange, hoisted breasts. Amber can just wear clothes in a way I can't – she looked so good in her jumpsuit when we went to the cinema last week, and I just had to get one, but this isn't the venue, and trust me, mine isn't the body.

Amber is still very much aware of Harry, the guy with long hair, and asks me if he's looking at her.

'Yes… and he's dribbling,' I add, which makes her laugh, and she throws back her head elegantly, all white teeth and red lipstick.

We sip our drinks as she bats her eyelashes, licks her lips at me. We both know this 'show' is for Harry – Amber can't rest until every man in the room has fallen in love with her. And they usually do.

'What's he doing now?' she asks.

'Oh my God, you're not going to believe this, but he's taking his clothes off…'

For a moment she looks surprised, then realises I'm joking. 'Lucy! I'm shocked! It's not like you to speak of naked men.'

'Oh, you might *think* you know me, but you really don't,' I say.

'I do. And the only man you've ever seen naked is Matt.'

'Yeah, okay, I can't compete with *you*.' I roll my eyes as she twiddles with the stem of her glass. All the time she's snatching glances at Harry. 'Look at you, you're like a rampant lion. Look out, Handsome Harry, Amber's gonna eat you all up,' I say in his direction. He can't hear, he's too far away, but this tickles Amber and we both start laughing at his new name.

'I'll tell him what you called him,' she says, pretending to beckon him over.

'No! I would die.' I laugh.

We're both giggling now, and I think how glad I am that we found each other. She's brought so much fun into my life. When Amber moved on to Mulberry Avenue, she was the antidote I needed to the other women on the estate, who talk for hours about different baby food brands and nappy bargains. From my mid-thirties, I'd begun to feel excluded as my friends all became pregnant and each month brought nothing for me. I was pleased for them – who couldn't be delighted that someone was bringing a new little voice into the world? – but the news was always bittersweet, because I longed for a baby of my own.

Now, at forty-two, despite extensive tests and a couple of rounds of fertility treatment, I've never experienced so much as a missed period. I'm okay, I deal with it, but an evening of in-depth discussions about the tantrums, fussy eating and toilet training of my friends' kids is not my idea of a fun night out. Consequently, I welcomed single, childless Amber, who thinks a 'baby bottle' is a mini bottle of Prosecco served with a straw.

'It's okay for you,' she always says, 'you've found your soulmate. I'm still looking for mine.' And she's right, I have found what I'm looking for in Matt. We've been married for ten years and I love him to bits. Despite her looks, career and her money, I really feel for Amber because all she really wants is what any of us want – someone to love who'll love her back, and I've got that. As for her ex, Ben, he must have been mad to walk away. I mean, how could any man not want to marry my beautiful, funny, accomplished friend? Men are, and always will be, a mystery to me.

Now Handsome Harry, who's been glancing over at Amber all evening, is wandering over, finally making his play. And what a performance. They greet each other like long-lost friends; she leaps up and he kisses her on both cheeks, then proceeds to touch her up for the next ten minutes. *What happened to #MeToo?* I think as, uninvited, his hand moves up and down her lower back. Then he tells her some story, which apparently is hilarious, judging by the way she's throwing her head back in laughter. I'm sitting at the table as they both stand engrossed in each other. Amber hasn't actually introduced us, and as I'm sitting down and at their waist level it's all rather awkward. She's touching his arm now as he whispers something in her ear. I love her, but I wish she wouldn't embark on a full flirting session while I sit here feeling like a voyeur.

My Prosecco glass is now empty, as is the bottle, and I'm struggling with the etiquette. It's not that I'm desperate for a drink, but I must look stupid sitting here all alone with an empty glass. Should I go to the bar and order us both another drink? Or would it be rude if I don't offer to buy Harry one too? And what happens now about us getting chips on the way home? I was rather looking forward to that.

I can't cope, and decide to head for the ladies'. I can kill a few minutes and Amber won't even notice I've gone.

Once in the cubicle, I look at the time on my phone and see it's already 11 p.m. and promise myself we'll leave by midnight at the latest. Amber made me stay really late last week at the Allegra Bar, just because she thought Ben might be in there, and I was working the next day. Tonight hasn't really gone to plan either; the whole point of the evening was supposed to be about Amber cheering me up, and yet here I am sitting alone in a toilet while she has a great time with Harry. It hasn't cheered me up at all. I knew I should have insisted on the cinema.

I check the time again and leave the toilet cubicle and stand next to a tall slim woman who's reapplying mascara. I wash my hands as she finishes her eyes and spritzes perfume, filling the air with the scent of chemical blossoms. I glance up at myself in the mirror. My make-up has all but melted off and my fringe is sticking to my forehead. Not a good look. Patting my face with toilet paper, I then put my head upside down under the hand dryer – a technique Amber uses to get instant hair volume. She always emerges from this looking like a supermodel, but another glance at the mirror tells me I look more like something from the *Lord of the Rings* trilogy. Wild-haired, blotchy-faced. Not pretty.

I feel like crap, so text Matt to say Amber's met a friend, and if they hit it off I might grab a taxi and be back soon. He texts back a laughing face and a heart, which makes me smile; we both know what she's like. I'm trying not to feel resentful, because Amber means well, but she's soon distracted, and ignoring me to flirt with a good-looking guy is not exactly my idea of 'fun'. But I'm being selfish. Whatever her flaws, Amber has a good heart, She's my number-one supporter and our friendship matters. So I might have felt a little left out back there, but I should stop feeling sorry for myself. I have a lovely husband to go home to and poor Amber has no one.

I can't hang around the toilets any longer, and in the hope that Harry has gone and Amber and I can resume our girls' night out, I head back to our table. As I approach, I see she's sitting back down and seems to be alone, which is good, but as I reach her, I can tell something's wrong. Her eyes are filled with tears, and she looks really upset. I feel for the chair and sit down, leaning towards her.

'What's the matter?' I ask, putting my arm around her protectively and trying to work out what's wrong from the expression on her face. 'Has something happened? Was it Harry, the guy you were talking to?' I say, looking around for him, remembering his hands all over her, his mouth on her ear. I wonder if, in my absence, he went too far, said or did something inappropriate, but she's shaking her head vigorously. Then she clicks on her phone and pushes it across the table towards me and, puzzled, I look at her while taking the phone, an irrational fear slowly creeping through my chest.

Still searching her face for clues, I drag my eyes from hers to look at the screen, where a text message sits waiting, throbbing. I can see a collection of words all placed together to create a message that makes the hairs on my neck prickle.

Beautiful Amber, I can see you flirting with those other men. If you hurt me I will hurt you. Are you scared? I like it when you're scared. It excites me.

CHAPTER THREE

Lucy

'Do you know who sent this?' I ask, gazing at the text on her phone.

She shakes her head. 'It's not nice, but it's just another weirdo; it comes with the job,' she sighs.

Amber is a TV weather girl on the local news and says she receives many 'love' letters, care of the TV station, from viewers asking if she'll marry/date/have sex with them, but this is different.

'I'm just a bit worried because whoever it is, he has my mobile number, and I don't know how he got it.' She's playing this down – she doesn't want a fuss – but I can see by the look on her face that she's petrified.

'Is there any signature, some kind of ID?' I ask, looking at the phone, pressing buttons as if suddenly the text sender's name and address will miraculously appear. 'Do you know who this is?'

'No, of course not. I haven't a clue.'

'Could it be someone you know playing a joke on you?'

'Do you think it's *funny*?'

'No, absolutely not.' I take a tissue from my bag and hand it to her. 'I didn't mean it like that, but why would someone suddenly do this, say these things… on a text, out of the blue?'

She takes the tissue from me and looks around, like the sender might be there watching. 'It isn't exactly out of the blue,' she says quietly as I strain to hear her over the music bashing my ears.

'What do you mean?'

'I had a few texts before, weeks ago now. They're the same… they're from the same person.'

'You mean threatening texts like this one?'

She nods and looks at me. She's trying to hide it, but again I see the fear in her eyes. 'Why didn't you tell me, Amber?'

'I just… I… I didn't want to worry you.' She looks around the bar, wrapping her arms around herself protectively, like *he* might still be here, watching her. 'I've told you before, it's being on TV, it attracts all the nutters…' she says.

'But you still have to take these things seriously.'

'No, Lucy, the opposite. You have to ignore them. They send a few texts, make the odd call and if you don't respond, never reply, then they get bored and—'

'These people don't get *bored*, they get dangerous,' I say, aware that I'm probably scaring her more. 'You have to change your number and only give it to a few close, trusted friends.'

'I can't do that. I've had it so long it's tied up with everything – work, the bank… Ben.' She looks at me, and a guilty shadow passes over her face.

'You're putting up with this because you're worried Ben might call you late one night and not get through, aren't you?' I can see by her face that this is exactly why she isn't changing her number, she wants to be totally accessible to him, just in case.

'Look, it's a nightmare having to change your phone number,' she says, clearly a little irritated that I know what she's thinking. 'I'm not cutting off people I care about because some weirdo is sending me texts Lucy. No, I'm going to just ignore them and delete them,' she says adamantly, tears wiped away, her strength returning.

I reach out and touch her hand. 'Amber, I just wish you'd told me, shown me the other texts.'

'I deleted them.'

'Why on earth would you do that?' I can't believe this. If I'd received creepy texts I'd be screenshotting them and calling the police. Right now!'

'I told you, the best thing to do is ignore and delete. Besides, I didn't want those... *words* on my phone. It felt like he was inside, made me feel dirty... infected. I had to shower the first time I got one.' She shudders at the memory.

'Just block the number then.'

'If I do that I won't know when he's stopped.'

'That's madness...' I start, but Amber will do what Amber wants to do, and I can tell by her face that she's determined for some reason not to block this number, so I let it go.

'Look, I'm fine, I was just a bit shaken because I got the last one a few weeks ago. I thought that was it, that he'd stopped. He's obviously bored tonight,' she adds.

'I think we should call the police.' I look at her with what she always calls my 'teacher face'.

'No.' She says this with such alarm it surprises me. 'Look, shall we just have another drink? I really need one.'

'Yes, of course. You stay here, I'll get them,' I say and go to the bar, where I wait an eternity for the young guy who's serving to notice me, but he's too busy chatting up the Negroni girls. I think of how different this scenario would be if Amber were here waiting to be served. We're the same age, but I just know this twenty-something guy would be at her service straight away; Amber is very visible – especially to men. That's why she gets so much attention, and it would seem not all of it is welcome.

I glance over to check she's okay, and despite her protestations that she's fine, she still looks worried. She's constantly looking around, because she knows whoever sent the texts saw her talking to Harry. The text accused her of 'talking to men', of being 'unfaithful,' and as she glances over her shoulder I feel a chill wondering if she has any idea who her stalker might be. There are the wealthy guys who whisk her off to lovely places; she's had liaisons with work colleagues – Handsome Harry and Ben-the-ex to name but two. And then there are the drunken one-night stands, but I doubt she'd remember most of them. Matt joked the other day that her bedroom has probably hosted half of Manchester since she moved in. I giggled at this – he had a point – but it doesn't excuse someone sending her threatening texts.

After being ignored for too long at the bar, I shout at the bartender. It's very late, and I don't even want a drink. I'm only getting them because Amber says she needs one. 'If you don't serve me now,' I say, over the music, 'I shall speak with your manager.'

He looks shocked, and one or two people turn round to see the dumpy middle-aged woman in the too-tight jumpsuit giving it to the barman. I can see by his face he didn't think I had it in me – well, watch and learn little boy.

Two glasses of Prosecco soon stand before me on the bar. I may not have Amber's looks and charisma, but I can use other, less seductive, means to get what I want. Being a primary school teacher, you have to develop a commanding voice for the noisy playground, which can also be useful in noisy bars.

I go back to Amber and put our glasses on the table – I didn't feel a bottle was appropriate now; too celebratory, given the circumstances. Amber nods in thanks and takes a large gulp of hers. I know she doesn't want to talk about the texts as it makes her uncomfortable, but I can't just leave it.

'Amber, think hard – do you really have no idea who's texting you?' I ask gently, sitting down opposite her.

She tears up, takes another gulp of her drink too quickly and shakes her head. I steady her with my hand, as if the shaking of her head will cause the tears to spill everywhere and if I can stop that I can stop the tears. I suddenly realise how stupid it seems that we aren't reacting to this, and as her friend I really should be doing something about it. So, silently, I take out my phone and unlock it.

'Lucy, what are you doing?'

'I'm calling the police.' I find the number for the local station and start punching in numbers.

'No, no, don't get them involved. I told you,' she says, putting her hand on mine, trying to stop me, 'I've had shit like this before and they're a waste of time. I don't want plods all over the place, riffling through my stuff, my life – half of them are on the payroll of the tabloids.'

Ignoring her protests, I dial the number and hold the phone to my ear. 'I'm not sure the newspapers would be that interested that a weather girl has received some weird texts,' I say, and instantly regret it as her face drops.

'Cheers for reminding me about my car crash of a career.'

I feel terrible, because Amber started as a weather girl on national TV many years ago, then tried her hand as a TV presenter. I remember being a bit of a fan twenty years ago; she was on TV a lot – just small presenting jobs – but one week I remember her on the front of the *Radio Times* as 'the one to watch'. She was heading for stardom, but then she suffered a personal tragedy when her husband died, and she wasn't on screen much after that.

Knowing her now, I'm aware how devastated she was when her life collapsed like that. Her husband's death wasn't straightforward. She had to take time away from work and before she knew it there were other 'ones to watch'. Now she's back as a weather girl on a regional television channel, where she started, and not where she'd expected to be at the age of forty-two. And I've just rubbed it in. Whatever I say now won't erase my comment, but I stop calling, put down the phone and try. 'Sorry, Amber, I didn't mean… you're not important…'

'So why say it?' she snaps, looking away from me. I can see that despite pretending it's nothing, she's shaken by these texts, and she isn't really cross with me. In her stress she's lashing out and just snapping at me because I'm here. It amazes me that even amid all this drama Amber's declining career still has the capacity to cut through bigger stuff and sting her.

'Amber,' I start, as calmly as I can muster, 'I didn't mean anything. I'm just worried about you. You've received a violent threat. He could be watching you now, he could follow you home. This is scary and I would never live with myself if something happened. Tonight he sent a threatening text. Who knows what he'll do next?' I pick up my phone again and make the call, still trying to placate her. 'I'm your friend, I care about you... Hello, is that the police?' I'm apparently on hold until someone can be bothered to pick up, which they do eventually. 'Hello? Yes, I'm calling because Amber Young, the weather girl on *Manchester Tonight*, is being stalked,' I yell down the phone.

Amber looks alarmed. She's asking me again to stop calling but I carry on. She's probably embarrassed that I'm shouting, but it's so noisy in here, I have to.

Eventually, I get through to whoever I need to speak to and the half-baked woman on the other end keeps asking if it's *me* that's being stalked and when I say no, she asks if I'm the bloody stalker! I yell down the phone 'NO I'M NOT,' and finally get the accurate information across and give Amber's details as she scowls across the table at me, and the woman makes a vague promise that someone will go round and take a statement.

'Can you be more specific, like *when* will someone go round?' I ask, rolling my eyes at Amber, who doesn't respond. She's obviously still pissed off I'm even making the call. 'Wednesday?' I gasp, when the call handler tells me. 'That's four days away. A woman's life is in danger. Can't you send an officer now? What if the stalker turns up tonight and climbs in through the window? If I call to tell you my friend's dying in a pool of blood will you still send someone on Wednesday and leave her to bleed out?' I'm quite pleased with this line – I heard it on *Midsomer Murders*. I like the way it sounds. Squelchy. Onomatopoeic. Terminal. Amber clearly isn't as impressed as me by my crime vocabulary. She's now rolling her eyes, but I refuse to give up on this. I want to make sure the police are taking this seriously, even if Amber isn't.

I wait for a response from the monosyllabic woman on the other end of the phone, but she doesn't answer for a while, then repeats 'Wednesday.'

'Well, if it *has* to be Wednesday…' I concede, and then the handler suggests a time and I clarify, 'Wednesday at three?' I know that Amber is on a late on Wednesday, so will be available, but she'll tell them it's nothing and she's fine. I'd like to be there to stress how serious this is, so I add, 'Could you ask the officers to arrive *after* three thirty because I'm a teacher and won't be able to get back until then. I need to be there with my friend… Hello? Hello?'

She mutters something I don't hear, then she's gone. Meanwhile, Amber's shaking her head and saying, 'Lucy, for God's sake, stop being so dramatic!'

'I'm your friend, and if you won't look after yourself, then I will,' I say, clicking my phone off and mustering as much authority as I can after four glasses of Prosecco. I realise I also can't possibly let her go home to that empty house of hers. I know I should really check with Matt first, and he won't exactly be delighted since he's not a huge Amber fan, but we can't leave her alone tonight. 'Come and stay with us tonight,' I implore.

'Are you sure?' is her response, which I interpret as 'thank God, I couldn't be alone tonight'. She's petrified really and just pretending it's all nothing, which makes me feel even more justified that I've done the right thing by calling the police.

'Of course I'm sure. Matt and I would never forgive ourselves if anything happened to you. I wouldn't want to go home alone after a text like that and I'm sure you don't.'

Amber looks genuinely scared now. 'I must admit I don't like the idea that he's been watching me, but when I go home tomorrow I'll make sure I sleep with a kitchen knife under my pillow.'

'Don't be silly,' I mutter. 'Everything will be fine,' I add, not completely convinced. I offer a reassuring smile and a pat on the arm before picking up my phone to call Matt. He sounds sleepy, but after giving him a very brief explanation, I ask him to come and collect us from JoJo's.

'Yeah, yeah, okay,' he says. 'I'm not sure which bar it is, can you stand outside and wave?'

I'm becoming anxious. 'Hardly, Matt, we don't want to draw attention to Amber if he's watching, do we? Look, just… just get here, and we'll find each other.' I click off my phone. 'God, why does it have to be so bloody complicated?' I say, exasperated. 'Why doesn't he just hear what I'm saying – my friend's being stalked, rescue us.'

She smiles. 'Stop complaining. You're lucky to have a knight in shining armour.'

I laugh and just hope Matt gets here soon on his trusty steed.

We finish our drinks and sit in silence until Matt texts to say he's outside. Relief floods through me and we head out into the night, where he's waiting in his little Toyota. I can see Amber looking around suspiciously, like someone might jump out of the darkness, so I put my arm around her as we walk to the car. She smiles and squeezes my hand, but doesn't look at me. She's on edge, her eyes darting everywhere; perhaps she's finally taking this seriously? I'm so tired I just want to go home and when I see Matt, I have this urge to throw my arms around him and kiss his face. But as I go to open the back door for Amber, I remember she has to sit in the passenger seat; Amber suffers from car sickness so always sits in the front.

Once home, I put the kettle on and Matt makes us all a cup of tea, which calms me down.

'Rehearsals went well tonight,' Matt says. A rather unsubtle dig at me for not asking. Matt's also a teacher, but you'd think he was Steven Spielberg, not the newly appointed Head of Drama at the local comprehensive.

'Sorry, but we had a few other issues to deal with,' I say tightly. It's not that I don't care. I always try to be an encouraging and supportive wife, but I also like to think I'm a good friend, and Amber needs me now. So instead of asking Matt about the latest news on the school production of *Bugsy Malone*, I encourage Amber to talk about the texts. I'm hoping that if we talk about it, Matt will pick up on the seriousness of this and support her too. I give him a look and he forces himself to show vague interest, for which I'm grateful, and I tell her we're both here for her and somehow she seems to open up as the three of us drink tea in the kitchen.

'You're right, Lucy, I should have told you before now. Thing is, I've been putting on a brave face and pretending it isn't happening.' She sighs. 'I'm scared to death really.'

She's sitting at the head of the table, with Matt and I either side. I'm holding one of her hands and the other is on my mug of tea, so I gesture with my eyes to Matt to take her other hand and support her too. In spite of her tears, I can't help but think some good has come of this situation, because Matt's felt obliged to sit down with us both and listen to her.

She's such a good friend to me. I wish he liked her, but Matt sometimes makes his mind up about people and won't be budged – 'She drinks too much, sleeps around and expects you to pick up the pieces' is his usual line about Amber. I can see why he might think that, but he doesn't know the Amber I do: she can be kind and supportive, she makes me laugh and keeps me company when he's too busy to spend time with me. He should be grateful to her. He gets to direct a performance of Year 10's *Bugsy Malone*, while Amber and I have a great time going out, or staying in. Before Amber I was always complaining to him about being lonely, but now, with Amber, my life is filled with stuff to do and I'm never lonely or bored. When we first met, Amber took me round the TV studio where she works. I met the news reporters and she introduced me to the make-up girl, who showed me how to apply concealer the right way. I sat in the studio and watched the evening news go out; it was fantastic, like nothing I'd ever done before. I took photos and told my pupils about it the next day.

The other thing people probably don't realise about Amber is how much of an amazing support she's been to me. Until Amber, Kirsty was my closest friend. She's a teacher at the same school as me and also lives on Treetops Estate. I still love Kirsty. But when I first told her that Matt and I couldn't have children, she cried like someone had died. I was already in agony and her reaction just compounded the pain. I know she didn't mean it, but God, it hurt. Like she saw me as broken. When I told Amber her reaction was so different, and so much more positive, if one can ever be positive about infertility.

'So what?' she'd said. 'Having a baby isn't everything. Think about it, you and Matt can do anything, be anything, go anywhere. Why would you have wanted to fuck that up with a kid who'll spend all your money and give you wrinkles?' It was classic Amber, and certainly provided a different viewpoint and put things into perspective for me. 'You're a teacher, Lucy,' she'd added, 'not just a mum with a couple of kids – you have thirty children in your class. You can *really* make a difference.'

Sitting in my kitchen tonight, I remember this. I owe her so much. And in spite of the horrible reason she's here with Matt and I tonight, I'm happy that I'm able to be here for her. 'I'm going to make up a bed for you we have a couple of spare rooms, it's no problem,' I say.

At this Matt nods, though I detect a vague shadow of reluctance, but at least he's being agreeable on the surface, for which I'm grateful. It's under sufferance, but he's doing this for me, and I smile affectionately at him over her head.

Later, in bed, Matt says how worried he was when I called him. 'I don't like the idea of someone out there with bad intentions,' he murmurs in the darkness. 'You shouldn't go out with her again. What if he's following *both* of you?'

'I'm sure he's not interested in me, Matt. And even if I could, I wouldn't abandon her now. I'm her friend. I can't just say "sorry, Amber, I'm not seeing you again because I'm scared of what's happening to you".'

'I didn't mean not *see* her. But perhaps not go out… in public, where whoever this is can follow her… and you. You could just invite her round here or something? I don't want to sound paranoid, but if you're in a bar or a restaurant, he can see you. He might be following her, watching both of you. Who knows what he'd do, and you could be caught up in it, Lucy.'

I'm touched that he's concerned for me, and I lift his arm off the pillow, pulling it around me while I rest my head on his chest. He soon falls asleep, but I lie there for a while in his arms trying to think of ways to cheer Amber up. Amber tried to cover her feelings tonight so as not to worry me, but I know my friend, and she was really shaken up. I decide I'll make her a cake and eventually find myself dropping off to sleep as I conjure up a recipe for a cake containing all her favourite things.

I would have made a fascinating anthropological case study. A feral child, left alone in the living room to be brought up by paternal TV presenters. My view of the world was formed early on by BBC values, TV catchphrases, and The Muppets. *But my favourite was the weather girl – always smiling, always fresh and pretty. I imagined she was talking directly to me – and only me. The weather girl appeared at the same time every evening. She always turned up and never, ever let me down – unlike everyone else in my life.*

CHAPTER FOUR

Lucy

The day after she moved into Mulberry Avenue I made Amber a cake. I'd racked my brains to try and work out why she was so familiar, and that evening we turned on the TV and there she was, Amber Young the weather girl. I have to say, I was delighted to know we had a minor celebrity in our midst, and couldn't wait to tell Matt, who was pretty unimpressed. 'Z-list,' he muttered. But I ignored his remark and set about welcoming her to the neighbourhood – and what better way to do so than with a cake?

I decided on something simple yet impressive for our TV weather girl – a home-made angel cake. It was moist and plain like a traditional angel cake, but given her celebrity status I added a glamorous twist by dressing it in meringue icing and strawberry ganache. It was challenging to say the least; the meringue icing was extremely difficult, and the strawberry ganache nearly gave me a stroke. Hot liquid, cold liquid, strawberry puree, all mixed at the right time in the right way. But as it was half-term and I was off work (Matt was busy with the local amateur dramatics group) and I didn't have anything else to do, I quite enjoyed baking. I found the process of mixing and whisking very calming, and looked forward to taking the results over to our new neighbour.

I knew who Amber Young was from TV, and I'd watched her more than once. I loved the way she smiled and seemed so positive even when she was predicting cold temperatures and snow. Before I'd met Matt, I'd lived alone in a flat, and I used to watch the news before I went to bed. The weather report came right after, and I remember Amber always ending her late-evening forecast by wishing 'a special goodnight to those who are on their own tonight'. I loved that. When I felt my most lonely, it just made me feel momentarily like someone cared. The cake was, in my own way, a little silent thank you for all those lonely nights.

When he came home the cake was resplendent on the kitchen counter and he thought I'd made it for him. I'd just finished perfecting the peaks of meringue when he wandered in and reached for a slice, which made me scream and slap his hand.

'For God's sake, Lucy, what's the matter?' he asked, all hurt.

'Sorry, babe, but it's not for you, it's for Amber Young. You know, our new neighbour. The weather woman? Who's moved in at number 13' I said.

'It's a bit over the top, isn't it?' he said sulkily.

'No, not really,' I responded, but allowed the doubt to bubble in. 'I don't think so anyway.'

'It looks like a *Great British Bake Off* showstopper.' He laughed. 'A Victoria sponge might have been enough.'

'Mmm, well, it's too late now, I've already made it,' I said, a little miffed.

'It's not. You don't have to give it to her. You could keep it here… I could eat it?' he teased.

'No. You eat enough cake, and so do I for that matter.' I stood back and admired the juicy strawberries dotted on glistening meringue. 'I always make new neighbours a cake,' I said defensively. 'It's about saying hello; it's the way we do things round "these 'ere parts".' I spoke in an exaggerated country accent.

Since we moved in three years ago, it has always been a joke between Matt and I that we've moved to the country, because it's a housing estate near parkland that was marketed to seem semi-rural.

Matt calls it 'pseudo-rustic' as it's hardcore suburbia a short drive from the city, but there are patches of grass and the roads are all named after trees. We often laugh about it, talking in 'country bumpkin' accents about 'them rolling fields', which don't actually exist here. We've been sold a rather nostalgic facade of village life – an imaginary escape from daily commutes, air pollution and a world where neighbours only meet on Facebook or Tinder. But despite Treetops being counterfeit countryside, I'd still choose it over the city any day – I love it here, and if it's good enough for the likes of Amber Young, it's good enough for me.

The morning I went round to welcome Amber with the cake, Matt was still after a slice.

'I really don't know why you're bothering,' he said, trying to put me off, hoping I'd abandon the confection in the kitchen and he could help himself.

'You're not having any, Matt, so no point in trying. I want to take a cake over. It's a lovely welcome and I always do it. I made a cake for Kirsty when she moved in down the road. And when Stella had her appendix out I was round there with a coffee and walnut before she was out of surgery.'

'Yeah, but they're different, they're friends. You don't even know this woman. She's some woman off the TV.'

'That's mean. I guess maybe I feel like I know her because I've seen her on the telly though. But I would probably say hi to her in the street.'

'And *she'd* probably think you were weird – a total stranger saying hi,' he murmured, chewing his gum while leaning on the fridge, arms folded.

I pushed him playfully out of the way and opened the fridge to take the cake out. 'You're only saying that because you want to eat it yourself,' I said.

'Me?' He put his palm on his chest, feigning mock surprise. 'I could just test it before you take it round to Mrs Z-List at number 13?'

'Matt, you're terrible. Amber Young's our new neighbour, and it's about time we had someone interesting move in, Z-list or A-list.'

I'll admit I was slightly awestruck by our new neighbour even before I met her. I wanted to know all about the other presenters she worked with on *It's Morning*, the show she used to be on when she was really famous years ago. I reckon Matt was vaguely impressed by her twinkle of celebrity too, even if he pretended otherwise. His ambition as a kid was to be an actor or presenter, and I'm sure that would extend to reading the weather if pushed. He'd wanted to go to drama school but was talked out of it by his teacher who said he needed something more secure – so he'd ended up teaching. As I always jokingly point out, if he'd become an actor he may never have met me, as we met at our first jobs in the same school. 'And that,' I always say, 'would have been a tragedy!'

But sometimes I feel for him. He has this huge passion for drama, and he's actually a really good actor and loves holding forth on the stage at presentation nights at school. I know he'd have loved a showbiz career and, even though it isn't for me, I can understand why someone might be drawn to the theatre or TV. I feel it when I'm with Amber, that remnant sparkle of faded celebrity; she wants to be noticed, be the centre of attention. And she usually is. Only the other day, we went into Marks and Spencer and I noticed people whispering behind their hands, looking her up and down. She stands out with her appearance alone, but I sometimes forget she's on TV, because it's not like she's properly famous, like she used to be.

She says she misses her life in London, and it sounds silly, I know, but I want her to feel settled here. I feel responsible for her happiness. It's the same with Matt – does he wish he was an actor or film director, instead of a teacher living here with me in our fake rural suburbia? I suppose everyone has regrets, wonders *what if?*

Anyway, with a freshly baked angel cake I went to find out about Treetops Estate's newest inhabitant, and to discover what her story was. After all, everyone had their reasons for moving here. Who knew what lay behind the floaty curtains and the well-groomed lawns of Mulberry Avenue? I hoped to get to know a bit more about Amber Young. So I kissed Matt on the cheek, picked up the cake and headed for number 13 – unlucky for some.

On arrival, I held my achievement proudly up to those white pillars like a sacrifice for a queen, standing in front of that huge grey-painted door. While standing on the doorstep, I looked down at the cake in my arms and hesitated; Matt was right – it was a little over the top. Less 'welcome to the neighbourhood', more 'welcome to Vegas', but it was too late now. I gave as firm a bang as I could with the knocker while trying not to drop what I now realised did look like an ornate celebration cake, and I waited for the door to open and for Amber Young to gush over the cake and be so grateful and touched she'd invite me in. But when the door didn't open, I guessed she hadn't heard, so I knocked again, louder this time. I waited, and waited, and with no luck at the front had a cheeky little walk round the back. If she caught me, I figured I could pretend I was looking for her, when really I wanted to see what the garden was like. She wouldn't mind. She always seemed so nice on the TV, and besides, who could be cross with a neighbour bearing cake?

I pressed my face between the slats in the fence and saw two glamorous wooden sunloungers sitting empty on perfectly placed decking. Obviously I'd checked out the house on the estate agent's website, but had wanted to see the garden 'in the flesh' because I'd fallen in love with it. The style was all understated elegance, with soft ferns and a natural wood accent, and I wondered what it might be like to sit on one of those sunloungers sipping chilled white wine on a summer evening with Amber Young.

I wandered back round the front; the nose of her sports car was peeping out from the garage, so she couldn't be far away. I was worried my meringue icing might melt, so started to walk back down the gravel drive towards home, but as I did, I turned back for one last look and saw a movement from an upstairs window. I may have been mistaken – it could have been the sun on the glass – but I was sure it was her, looking down at me. I can't explain the feeling, but despite the heat, I felt a chill and shuddered slightly, marching more quickly down the crunching gravel.

A few days later I popped round to her house again. I'd made another cake, this time something simpler, less extravagant, that wouldn't be too showy-offy or droop in the heat – a naked Genoese sponge. This time, after several minutes standing on her doorstep again, the cake was fine but *I* was beginning to droop in the heat and realised I was wasting my time calling on the new neighbour. I'm friendly, but I'm not crazy, and I was just turning to go home, call it a day and present the Genoese to Matt when, voila, the door opened.

'Oh, you made me jump,' I said, giggling nervously. It was a stupid thing to say. I had knocked and was waiting, so what had I expected? But I was thrown by her… presence. She was even more stunning up close – her make-up was perfect. Arched eyebrows, glowing skin, long black lashes and those full red lips. She was wearing a beautiful pink silk kimono, and her hair was caught up in glossy tangles. It was like she'd tried, but she hadn't – her look was a contradiction of effortless yet perfect.

'Can I help you?' she said, seeming vaguely irritated.

'Hi! I hope I haven't called by at an inconvenient…' She looked at me, slightly puzzled, waiting for me to explain myself, causing me to feel rather foolish. 'Sorry, I should introduce myself. I'm Lucy. I live here – number 7.' I gestured towards my house and her eyes seemed to reluctantly follow my hand. I expected her to relax at this, invite me in, understand that I was here for good not evil, but she was still looking at me like she hadn't a clue why I was on her doorstep. She wasn't about to embark on a neighbourly chat over cake and coffee; I'd misjudged this badly. Perhaps she wasn't like her lovely TV persona after all. I wished the ground would swallow me up, but I pushed on. 'I just want... wanted to say... welcome.' I smiled stupidly, suddenly turning into a six-year-old, holding up the cake like I was a pupil and she was my teacher.

'Thank you, but I don't really eat cake – it looks lovely though,' she added as a palliative.

'But *everyone* eats cake...' I started, smiling, hoping to win her over, but her eyes registered nothing.

'I'm always on a diet,' she responded coolly.

'Oh... me too.' I laughed. 'But it lasts until lunchtime.'

She smiled at this, like she was humouring me, and in my embarrassment I gave a little twirl, which was ludicrous. The look on her face was sheer bemusement and I had to keep talking to cover my awkwardness.

'Everyone here's very friendly,' I started. 'My friend Kirsty and I have organised a couple of events too: there's the annual summer barbecue, and we had a street party for the royal wedding, and we did a charity run – well, it was more like a charity *walk* in my case.' I giggled awkwardly. She looked slightly horrified at the prospect of people grilling their sausages in front of her house, but on I went through the pain barrier. A stand-up comedian who'd just lost her audience. I was dying out there. 'And... oh yes, we have the book club, on the first of every month.' I nodded vigorously, hoping she'd mirror this. She didn't. 'Next month we're at Stella McConnall's. She's number 9, Daffodil Drive,' I said, producing this like a moth-eaten rabbit from a hat. Why on earth would TV star Amber Young want to sit in Stella's front room discussing the pros and cons of the latest supermarket paperback? I hadn't intended to even mention the book club, but I guess I was vainly hoping if I offered her enough of a varied selection something might pique her interest. Apparently not.

'That all sounds... great,' she said, sounding totally unconvinced. 'Thanks so much for calling by.' She forced a smile from behind the slowly closing door, which she then shut in my face.

I was shocked at the abruptness and if I hadn't got the message, the resounding click as she locked the door confirmed that my new neighbour wasn't interested. Actually, it was worse than disinterest, it was as if she was locking her door to protect herself from me, like I'd spooked her with my sad cake and endless list of lame social events. Someone else had locked me out once before, a long time ago, someone I thought was my friend, and that hurt so much. The memory has lingered through the years, seeping into my happiness like a stain, and standing on the doorstep that day I was reminded that there's nothing quite so painful as the sound of a lock keeping you out.

In spite of this, I continued to stand on her doorstep, clutching my bloody cake like a reject from The Women's Institute. My hurt morphed easily and quickly into anger and as far as I was concerned that was it – the end of my reaching out. Amber Young could piss off with her fancy house and snooty attitude. And Matt and I would enjoy the cake, watching something on television that categorically wasn't that night's weather forecast.

CHAPTER FIVE

Lucy

When I got home, Matt comforted me while devouring the rejected Genoese, informing me through crumbs, 'I'll get my screenplay finished, we'll adopt a rainbow family and live in Hollywood, and when we throw big fuck-off parties and invite the old neighbours, she'll wish she'd been nicer to you.'

He could be so sweet – a bit naive and a dreamer, but sweet. 'Can we have a pool party? We'll need a place with a huge swimming pool,' I'd joked, 'and I'd like a place in the Maldives to escape to sometimes.'

'Absolutely.' He smiled, putting down his now empty cake plate, and wrapping both arms around me. I pushed my face into his chest, his T-shirt soft against my cheek, his body warm underneath, his musky smell familiar, comforting. I put my arms around his waist and as I looked up at him, he kissed me, and all the prickliness of rejection was smoothed over, my tender wounds bathed. And later that evening, in bed, I lay in his arms in the afterglow on tangled sheets and tried not to think about Amber Young and how she'd virtually slammed the door in my face. And locked it.

'I'm just angry at myself,' I murmured.

'Why? It isn't *your* fault,' Matt insisted, his hair messy and his eyes sleepy. I loved him like that.

'I shouldn't have allowed her to just dismiss me. I'm not good with confrontation. I avoid it after all the rows in my house. My mother was always so angry, and it's infectious, fills the air until you pick it up, but you don't know what you're angry about.'

'I know what you mean,' Matt murmured. 'It colours your life; my mum wasn't exactly a saint either.'

'Yeah, but now as an adult I worry I've gone the other way, and I'm too much of a pleaser.'

'Lucy, if by pleaser you mean kind, then yes you are – and you mustn't change. Other people are the problem, and just because they aren't like you, it isn't your problem, it's theirs,' he said, rolling over and stroking my face.

'I just sometimes feel like I have to be extra nice, like I have some making up to do, you know?'

'Yes, I do. But maybe stop always trying to compensate for being a tearaway as a kid – you're not that girl any more, and you don't have to keep apologising for who you are.'

'Yeah, okay, I'll stay positive and give her the benefit of the doubt. After all, there might be a reason why she was so off with me. I mean, her lipstick might have melted in the heat,' I said, trying to make light of it.

'Agreed. That would be tragic, but still no reason to be like that with someone who just wants to be friendly and welcome you,' he said, getting out of bed and putting on his dressing gown.

I wanted to discuss this further, to consider what might be eating Amber Young, but Matt closed any further investigation as he smiled hopefully and said, 'Babe, will you test me on my lines now?' He held out a dog-eared script.

I laughed. 'Have you given yourself a part again?'

He nodded in mock shame. 'The kids love it.'

'You love it more.' I took the script from him, reading it as he spoke his three lines.

Matt always liked to play a small cameo in all the school productions. Like Hitchcock in his films, Matt would suddenly appear, the only adult in a sea of young teenagers, and say a few lines. The kids all loved him, whistling and shouting when he bowed at the end. 'Go sir!' they'd yell, and he loved it just as much as they did.

Perhaps this wasn't the life either of us had planned, but in those moments, as the kids cheered, I hoped he'd found what he was looking for. I know he loves me, but sometimes I think he deserves so much more because he's such a good, kind husband. From the minute we first became friends, Matt rescued me in his own way – and once we fell in love, every day, every little hurt, every bleed of mine was willingly mopped up by him. I've reciprocated by supporting him too – neither of us had ever had too much love before. We'd never been first on anyone's list of priorities. But here we are now. We're through the difficult childhoods, the unhappy teens, and we're both happy and loved; all we'd ever wanted really. Sometimes it feels like we're both two frightened kids clinging to each other, but I thank God we found our other half to make us finally whole.

'I still can't believe she was so rude,' I muttered as I held the crumpled script adorned with pencil graffiti – vital words and reminders. 'I mean, why would someone be like that?' I knew I was probably taking this far too personally and needed to move on, but I couldn't understand her reaction. I would have been delighted if someone had brought me a home-made cake when I'd first moved in here.

'I don't know,' he sighed. 'Why does anyone do anything anti-social? Like you say, she might have her own issues… something to hide… Secrets?'

I laughed. 'Trust you to go all Gothic, you drama queen. She might just be a spoilt bitch.'

'She might.' He nodded. 'Or perhaps inside that house is a sex dungeon, and she's a part-time dominatrix…' He said this in an exaggerated German accent, which made me giggle.

'Enough.' I giggled. 'Stop teasing me. I can respect someone's privacy. I'm not going to pry…'

He gave me a knowing look. 'You? Pry?' He laughed and continued in the funny accent: 'You have ways and means of making them talk, Madam Metcalf.'

'Okay, okay.' I sighed. 'I'll admit I did want to find out more about our new neighbour. But now I don't suppose I ever will.'

'Forget her. Concentrate on me, I'm the important one in your life,' he said, and I tested him on his lines. Again.

When the monthly book club came around a week later, I almost didn't go, but Matt was working late and Kirsty cornered me in the staffroom, saying I was spending too much time alone. 'You're like a single woman,' she'd said. 'He's never home. You need to get out.' So I went along, and if I hadn't gone to book club that evening I probably wouldn't have become friends with Amber. And who knows how things might have turned out?

I'd originally joined the book club hoping it might provide some respite from the incessant baby/child chatter that filled the air here in our pseudo 'village'. But on my second visit, the conversation about books had been blurred by wine, and talk touched dangerously on children's themed birthday parties, and I almost fell asleep. By the third meeting they were threatening to share birth stories and I really couldn't cope. After years of scheduled sex and several rounds of IVF, Matt and I had finally found a way to live with our childlessness. And though we discussed adoption and fostering, for now we'd decided to see where life took us – even if, to be honest, there were days when it felt like life was taking us nowhere, and neither of us wanted to admit that. In the meantime though, as far as the book club mothers went, I didn't need my face rubbed in my childlessness and was definitely considering quitting and finding another hobby.

But that evening I agreed to give book club 'one more go', making Kirsty promise to step in if there was so much as a sniff of umbilical cord chat. 'If I'm bored I won't be coming along next month,' I said, not knowing that I would be anything but bored, and from that night on life would never be boring again.

Amber's arrival at the book club was a surprise to everyone, especially me. She 'landed' in clouds of perfume and enthusiasm, her gleaming red hair and quick chatter like a perfectly controlled storm, wild and swirling electricity emanating from her rapid hand movements. She oozed glamour and money, but in complete contrast to our previous encounter, there was now a warmth, a keenness to listen to others and show interest. How different this Amber was to the one I'd encountered on her doorstep. Perhaps I'd caught her at a bad time?

Awestruck, the rest of us sat on Stella's bland beige three-piece suite as Amber talked. We just drank in this stranger's confidence, her vivaciousness. We were captivated by that indefinable something that Amber possessed, and all leaned closer, like it might brush off on us like gold dust. She even seduced Sergeant Major Marjorie, the self-appointed leader of the book club, who made all the rules and disapproved of anyone who broke them. Tucking her long legs under her slim, well-toned body, Amber was quite at home sitting in Marjorie's usual chair while 'our leader' sat on the only remaining free seat – a small velveteen pouffe at Amber's feet. I had to suppress a smile at the sight of the queen of the book club in such a submissive pose.

Amber Young was familiar to everyone there as our one local celebrity. Not just from her recent work though. Back in the day when she was a rising star, there were reports that she was about to have her own talk show. Obviously her husband then died and she took some time out. I remember stuff being in the newspapers at the time, but it was over twenty years ago. I recall reading an article saying her husband's family had never liked her, which at the time I couldn't understand. She was so lovely on screen. If she was as cold with them as she had been with me on our first encounter, no wonder, but I was prepared to give her the benefit of the doubt.

That night at book club it felt like we were back at school and all vying for the new girl's attention, asking her all about her new job at the local TV station. Amber seemed happy to fill us in; she told us how she had once danced with George Clooney at a film awards dinner, hinted at an affair with a royal prince, talked about weekends in St Tropez, glamping in Devon with a Michelin-starred chef, and we gasped as she recounted a recent trip to Cannes where she stayed on a millionaire's yacht. Amber was committing a book club crime in not adhering to Marjorie's doctrine of talking *only* about the book – but she was getting away with it on charisma alone.

'Fabulous necklace, Marji!' Amber had said, love-bombing our leader, who was still sitting astride Stella's pouffe, and causing her to flush with pleasure. I smiled to myself. One could only imagine the scenes if anyone else had dared referred to her as 'Marji'.

Later, as we came to leave, I was aware of Amber standing close to me as we said goodbyes and thanked our hostess. We were at the peak of summertime, but it being a British summer, the evenings were fringed with chilliness, and while the rest of us made do with old cardigans and sweatshirts for warmth on the way home, Amber was swathed in acres of blush pink cashmere. She seemed to glow in the darkness.

'I'm really not sure how I got here,' she said, looking straight at me with helpless pleading eyes. Still smarting from our previous encounter, a mean little part of me wanted to tell her to find her own way back. But that isn't me. I find it hard to be unkind to people, so I just smiled and said, 'That's okay. I only live a few doors down from you. We can walk together.'

'Of course,' she said, 'you're the lady with the cake.' To her credit, she looked suitably embarrassed.

'Yes, that's me,' I said, waving goodbye to Kirsty, who lived in the opposite direction.

'This place is like a maze. All the houses look the same,' Amber said as we walked along.

'It takes a while to find the road you're looking for. I used to get lost most days driving home, but now I know this estate like the back of my hand,' I said, cringing at the pride in my own voice. I wanted to qualify this, explain that I did have a life, that I hadn't spent every evening learning the road structure, but I thought that might just make me sound worse. I wasn't quite sure what to say, and she seemed lost in her own thoughts so we just walked back in silence.

When we arrived at hers, I was about to say goodnight and continue on home, when she hesitated. 'Lucy, I feel really bad. I decided at the last minute to go along tonight, but I realise I should have let you know. After all, you're the one who invited me.'

'Oh, that's okay. I'm glad you came.'

'And thank you – for calling by that day. I wasn't… I wasn't… I was tired with the move, and not really up to chatting.'

'It's okay, I understand.'

'My partner… Ben, he was supposed to help with the move, but he's been so busy he couldn't, and it was a lot to do on my own.'

'Oh, I didn't realise. You should have let us know. My husband and I would have helped.'

'Oh, it was fine. I had removal men, just not *my* man,' she said sadly.

'That's a shame. Is he moving in soon?' I wanted know more after having had a glimpse into Amber's world at the book club.

'Yeah… yeah, Ben's moving in any time now.'

'Oh, lovely. Have you been together long?'

I remember Amber paused slightly before answering. 'Yes, years. Ben was the TV executive who gave me my first network job doing the weather. Until then I'd been doing freelance shifts on local TV and I went to see him – and he gave me the role. It was thanks to Ben I hit the big time back then and I'm working with him again now.'

'That's nice. Perhaps you'll eventually get that talk show gig?' I said, and could have bitten my tongue.

'That was a long time ago,' she said, and her face became closed off, as it had been when we first met and I stood on her doorstep with cake.

'Yes, it must be almost twenty years ago when you started on *Good Night Britain*,' I said, desperately trying to change the subject, but probably digging myself a deeper hole. Even I knew that ship had sailed. Amber was now in her forties. Her career trajectory had gone from network TV weather girl with everything at her feet to a job on local TV. All our horizons shrink as we get older. God knows mine have, but it must be particularly difficult when you're in the public eye – and once had such promise.

'Ah, that was my first on-screen job, before I got the job on *It's Morning*. Happy days.' She sighed nostalgically.

'I remember your saying…' And we both said in unison, in bright voices: 'A special goodnight to those who are on their own tonight.'

We laughed.

'Oh, Lucy, you're a superfan,' she said, then looked at me. 'I'm only joking.'

'Well, I'm definitely a *fan*,' I said. 'I lived on my own then and found it comforting late at night. It was as though you were talking to me.'

'Oh, that's so sweet,' she said, beaming. 'Hey, why don't you come in for a quick coffee?'

The invite took me by surprise and I wasn't entirely sure what I made of Amber. One minute she was open and warm, and the next distant and aloof, but I wanted to know more so of course I accepted, if only to see what she'd done to the house. She opened the front door and led me inside. The brightly lit hall was painted white and dotted tastefully with orchids and huge mirrors leaning against walls, apparently beautifully abandoned but no doubt strategically placed. The floor was pristine white stone and Amber slipped off her shoes and walked in bare feet ahead of me, through to the stunning white minimalist kitchen.

'So you met your… Ben in TV?' I prompted her, as she spooned freshly ground coffee into a cafetière.

'Yes. So I went for an audition.' She turned and leaned against the kitchen counter, holding the tin of coffee. 'Our eyes met over a clapperboard and the rest is history.' She winked and poured hot water onto the coffee, the steamy foam escaping the plunger as she pushed it down.

'Ah, how romantic…' I sighed, wondering where her husband had fit into all this.

'It was,' she said, seeming to brighten even more talking about him. 'But Ben was my boss before he was my boyfriend.' She hesitated. 'People can be very competitive, very jealous, in TV, especially the other women.'

'I can imagine.' I didn't blame the other women. I would hate to have to compete with someone like Amber. She continued to tell me all about Ben and how they'd eventually fallen in love – which I presumed happened after her husband's death. I just listened, sensing her vulnerability beneath the perfectly made-up surface of shiny lipstick and glossy hair, as she told me how she was once 'the golden girl', but not any more.

'Life in TV is all about being young and pretty – I'm worried about the future, what's going to happen to me. I'm in my forties now, Lucy, and not so young and pretty.' She sighed, moving into the sitting room with our coffees. I followed her into another stunning space, painted in shades of grey, with one huge painting that filled the wall. It was a beautiful swirling blur of red, pink, amber and orange, muted peaks of shimmering pink pushing through nebulous cloud. It must have measured eight feet by eight feet, and just pulled you in.

'That's beautiful… just beautiful,' I said, mesmerised.

'It's called Nepal Sunset,' she said, her eyes following mine to gaze on the painting. 'Can you see the peaks of the Himalayas poking through the clouds? Michael, my husband, and I travelled to Nepal. We were just students backpacking. We had nothing back then – we really roughed it,' she said. I glanced at her. She was staring at the painting and I could see she was back there. 'Years later, when we married, he bought this for me. Said it reminded him of our time there. We'd been so happy. He picked it up for nothing in a little gallery, but I think it's worth quite a bit now…'

'It's stunning.'

'It is, isn't it? I don't care how much it's worth in money; it means more to me than anything. It's part of me, my first love. My youth, you know?' Sitting on the sofa, she brought her knees up to her chin, like she was protecting herself. 'He said I was like a Nepalese sunset… bright and fiery, slow to settle.' She smiled sadly. 'I miss him.'

'I'm so sorry,' I said. The air was tight with emotion. I couldn't think of anything fitting to say, but couldn't resist asking, 'Your husband. What happened? If you don't mind me asking.'

'I'm sorry, Lucy, can we talk about something else?'

I was mortified, and just nodded, burying my head in my coffee cup. We both finished our coffees in silence and she suddenly stood up, stretched and began clearing away the cups. When she wandered into the kitchen, leaving me alone on the sofa, I realised I was being dismissed. I sat there feeling helpless and stupid. I'd offended her by asking about her husband. I'd ruined everything, including a potential friendship, with my insensitive questioning and I felt terrible, cursing myself, wanting to erase the last few minutes. I wanted to run from her house and go home to safety but was now stranded on the pale sofa in a sea of pink cushions as the sun set over the Himalayas. What on earth had made her react like that, though? As a wife I completely understood someone not being comfortable talking about their husband's death. I was sure I wouldn't. But it was over twenty years ago. Was she still upset all these years later now she was in a happy new relationship?

CHAPTER SIX

Lucy

'She's got a boyfriend,' I told Matt the morning after that first book club. He barely looked up from his script.

'Who?' he asked absent-mindedly.

'Amber Young. His name's Ben. She's all loved up. I can't wait to see him. I bet he's gorgeous,' I said, still wondering about her reaction the previous evening. Despite her gushing about the amazing Ben, it seemed there were still some open wounds left from her husband's death.

'Gorgeous or rich?' Matt said.

'Or both,' I said, hoping for a dinner invite once he'd arrived.

A week later, I still hadn't seen any sign of Amber, or her man, and was beginning to wonder if something had happened. Then, on bin day, she didn't put her bins out.

'I hope she's okay; in this heat she should really put them out,' I murmured to Matt as I peeked through the curtains. In my opinion, when people don't leave their bins out when they should it's often a sign that all is not well and something is amiss in the home. 'Perhaps I should have put them out for her,' I said, almost to myself.

'No, don't you go moving her bins. It's her funeral if she wants rats,' he said.

'Yes, but now I think of it, I haven't seen her for days. What if she isn't well?'

Matt didn't respond. He wasn't remotely interested, so I set off for work and discreetly looked at the house, seeing nothing but shuttered windows. I didn't have time to knock but planned to call round the following day, a Saturday.

I told Kirsty all about the bins, and she was convinced it was significant too. 'My mother's old neighbour didn't put her bins out and when they found her she'd been dead for days, slumped over the cat.'

'Oh God, I do hope she's okay,' I sighed.

Unlike Matt, Kirsty was as interested as I was in the comings and goings of our new neighbour and we talked about her quite a lot on our coffee and lunch breaks at work. I told her everything Amber had said about Ben but made her promise not to tell anyone because I didn't want Amber to think I'd been gossiping. I was secretly quite flattered that Amber had chosen to tell me – and I didn't want it going round the whole estate. But Kirsty was as keen as me to know if and when 'the boyfriend' was moving in. I knew she'd love to hear all about him, but I never told Kirsty about Amber's husband and the beautiful painting. Other than a lack of 'bin action' though, there was nothing else to share with Kirsty regarding the resident at number 13.

Then, the next day, just as I was mowing the lawn and contemplating popping over and knocking to make sure Amber was okay, I saw him. A good-looking man pulled up in an expensive car and, after talking for a little while on his phone, got out and strolled up Amber's drive. He knocked on the front door, leaned against one of the pillars, loose jeans hanging on his hips, big expensive sunglasses just like hers, and when the door opened, he went straight in.

Despite taking my time over the mowing, I didn't hear or see anything else until late that night when I leapt up at the sound of screaming outside. Matt and I were watching *The Ted Bundy Tapes* on Netflix with a bowl of popcorn and a bar of chocolate, and when I jumped up to look through the window he yelped with shock.

'Sorry, love,' I said, trying to see whose house the noise was coming from, abandoning Matt, Ted and the TV snacks. 'I think something's going on at number 13… Amber's house.'

'Why do we bother watching TV?' he grumbled. 'I mean, you've got all the entertainment you need at number 13.'

The screaming was definitely Amber. She was at an upstairs window hurling clothes, golf clubs and all sorts onto her gravelly drive, and the guy from earlier was picking everything up, piece by piece, narrowly avoiding a club to the head. Then, with an armful of belongings, he jumped into his fancy car and drove off – over revving the engine. 'He made a right racket. He didn't have to do that,' I said to Matt, having provided him with a running commentary on events from my perch behind the curtains.

'Just because they've got a fancy car,' Matt grumbled, 'think they're *all that,* people like her and him.'

I agreed with him. We might grumble sometimes, but Treetops is a nice area with lovely neighbours who respect each other, and cars revving loudly at all hours and people screaming obscenities felt very out of place. I'd happily said goodbye to all that when I left home. I didn't want it now. But I was intrigued.

'Forget them,' Matt said, making room from me on the sofa. 'Ted Bundy's just killed again.'

'It was definitely Ben,' I said to Kirsty on the Monday at school. 'And I reckon they're over.'

'Is he handsome?' she asked, loving the gossip, wanting to know every detail.

'From what I saw, he is, yes… and probably rolling in it too: expensive car, expensive-looking sunglasses, sure of himself. You know the type?'

She nodded. 'I can imagine. Pretentious like her too.'

'I wouldn't describe her as pretentious, but I think she blows hot and cold,' I said, defending Amber slightly.

'Yeah, well, more cold than hot if you ask me. I only met her that one time at book club, but she ignored me totally when I saw her in the street the other day.'

'Oh, she wouldn't deliberately ignore you, she probably didn't recognise you,' I said, doubting Amber had even noticed Kirsty. Her head was filled with Ben, or filming that evening's programme, or planning one of her glamorous getaways. 'Honestly, she's lovely, and her house is to die for,' I added.

'Mmm, so you've said,' she murmured. 'Quite a few times.'

I ignored this; I'd noticed that Kirsty was becoming quite mean and jealous where Amber was concerned. Back then I thought she would get over it and grow to like Amber, but if anything she's grown to hate her even more.

'So, she's been dumped by her boyfriend,' she said. 'Can't say I feel sorry for her. She probably cheated on him; I heard she likes the men.'

'I don't know anything about that,' I said, sure that Kirsty was just being nasty; she didn't know any more about Amber than I did. 'I just know she sounded very upset and angry, and I felt sorry for her. Who knows what happened?'

'Well, I don't feel sorry for people like that,' Kirsty replied. She didn't *want* to like Amber, and wasn't prepared to give her a chance – she was just jealous because she saw a woman who had everything and resented her for it. I realise now that she also saw her as a threat to our friendship; she thought Amber would replace her as my friend, and perhaps she has, but it wasn't deliberate. These things happen.

I felt disappointed by Kirsty's immaturity around the whole 'Amber issue' and I wasn't going to even listen to her bitchy comments, let alone join in, because I liked Amber. Our last encounter, when I'd quizzed her too much about her husband, had been difficult, but essentially that was all my fault, and I should have been more sensitive. Yes, it was strange that she was still so affected by his death that she couldn't talk about it, but I saw something Kirsty couldn't see because she was blinded by her envy. Since that night I had given it some thought and now, instead of seeing the beautiful woman in her gorgeous home, I saw a woman who appeared to have everything but had a vein of deep sadness running right through her. Her husband had died, and now another man had left, and I had a feeling that all it would take was one little tap and the beautiful, brittle facade would be shattered.

CHAPTER SEVEN

Lucy

'Who is he, what does he want… and do we even know he's a he?' I say to Amber the morning after JoJo's as we eat breakfast at mine.

Amber just shrugs. It's early, Matt's already left for work and I'm forcing her to eat poached eggs on avocado toast despite her protestations that she doesn't eat eggs.

'You eat eggs when they're foamed at the top of a cocktail,' I say, feeling like her mother as I point to the plate, a silent instruction to eat up. 'Just eat the avocado then?' I try, but she's just messing about with the food on her plate. Amber only ever does what she wants to do.

'It's been almost a year since Ben walked out,' she suddenly says.

'Oh wow, is it that long?' I say, remembering the night too well: the shouting, the low-flying golf clubs and guttural screaming from her bedroom window.

'Yes, it was a horrible time; it's been a horrible year since,' she adds sadly. 'I met Ben when I was just twenty-two. We've had our ups and down since then, but I think I'll always love him. He said he wasn't ready to commit,' she continues, shaking her head, wanting to talk through it, still desperate to work it out. 'Twenty fucking years I waited and then he tells me he doesn't love me any more – it's not me though, oh no, he has commitment issues. I mean, how many clichés can one man fit into a break-up speech?' she spits.

I try to console her, tell her she's better off without him, but hear my own clichés, stop talking and just listen. Apparently when he first moved to Manchester from London, the plan was they'd move in together, start a new life, even get married. 'I found our perfect home, on Mulberry Avenue,' she says, 'but when it was time for us to move in together he'd gone cold and rented a bachelor flat in the city. Can you believe it?'

I shake my head. However many times I hear this story, I still can't believe it.

'I had a feeling things weren't right, but I didn't listen to *my* feelings, just listened to *him* and heard what I wanted to hear. Lies,' she hisses. I'm surprised her anger is still bubbling after a year; she must have really loved him. I suspect she still does, which saddens me, because he is clearly a pig and doesn't deserve someone as special as Amber.

'You were obviously wasted on him,' I say. 'Amber, you wouldn't ever go back to him, would you? I worry he'd only hurt you again.'

'I don't think so. But I miss him like hell, Lucy. Okay, I've had a few dates, seen other men in the last twelve months, but it isn't because I'm over him, or moving on. I can't explain it. I feel like I'm looking for him in everyone I meet, except of course I don't, because it doesn't work like that, does it? There's only one Ben and no one else quite does it for me. Weird, isn't it?'

'Not really. I'm sure I'd feel the same if Matt and I split – I'd still love him, so I'd want to be with him. Sometimes I wonder what I'd do if I ever caught him cheating,' I say. 'I don't know what I'd do, and I don't want to be tested, but I'd probably kill them both.' I laugh. The thing is, Matt was my first proper boyfriend, and it's hard to imagine either of us being with anyone else. We met in our teens and I feel lucky we're still together. My marriage is so easy and uncomplicated. I still don't quite understand Amber's relationship with Ben. One thing I do know is that the solution to missing him doesn't lie in a million one-night stands, or 'dates' as she likes to call them.

'Perhaps you just need some time alone to get over him. Don't complicate your heart with other men?' I offer tactfully, but she isn't listening to my advice.

'I haven't told you this,' she says, avoiding eye contact, 'but a couple of weeks ago I bumped into him… Ben, outside JoJo's.'

'Oh?' I say, guessing the end to this story before it's even been told.

'Yeah. It was all a bit drunken; we didn't say much. I'd had a few drinks with the guys after work and was waiting for a taxi. He staggered out, apparently looking for one too. I asked if he'd like to share mine and he agreed.' She takes a sip from the mug of tea I've placed by her plate, the eggs and avocado now abandoned, knife and fork splayed across the congealing yellow and greying green. 'I assumed when the taxi stopped at mine that he'd just get out and come in with me,' she continues. 'I thought we'd just pick up where we left off, like we have in the past. But he didn't…' She looks at me with such hurt in those beautiful eyes. I can't believe he wouldn't want to be with her, and I'm angry at him for hurting her – and maybe even a little angry with her for letting him.

'Oh, Amber, you don't need a man like him! I mean, God, the idiot dumped you after you'd moved your life up here to be with him!'

'I know, I know,' she says, sounding defeated, 'but I can't help how I feel, and I thought he felt the same. So before I got out of the taxi, I kissed him goodnight, and he kissed me back… you know, tongues and…'

I nod, living the moment with her, remembering the first time Matt and I kissed like that.

'And for a minute I really thought…' She pauses. 'But he pulled away, lifted my hands from his shoulders like I was clinging to him and had to be removed. "Goodnight Amber," he said, like he was talking to a little kid. I felt like a fool, but Lucy, it broke my heart.'

She lets out a small sob. I've never seen her like this before. My heart goes out to her and I just feel so angry that a man like that can have this effect on a strong, independent woman like Amber.

'I'm sorry, Amber, he's a pig. He didn't deserve you. And there are so many more men out there – kinder, nicer men who stay for the long haul,' I add, thinking of Matt.

'I know, but it's crazy, isn't it? As hard as I try not to, I *still* love him. I watch him at work sometimes and have to stop myself from just going into his office and kissing him, full on the lips.'

I feel for her. It must be awful to be faced by the object of your affection all day every day and know it's one-sided, that it's over. 'If you see him every day, how on earth are you ever going to move on?'

She's staring down into her mug of tea. 'I don't know, but I have to stay at the studio. I won't get work like this anywhere else right now. And I really thought… *hoped* he might change his mind. Even after he finished it last year, I thought that seeing me at work every day he would crumble, like he always has in the past when we've broken up.'

I can only imagine Ben 'crumbling' over Amber; it's what most men seem to do. Apart from being extremely beautiful, she has this dazzling energy and those deep bronze eyes, quite mesmerising and intriguing, like they're keeping a secret. She's also very determined, and I imagine she's always got what she wants where men are concerned. Her looks and seduction techniques have obviously always worked in the past, both at work and play, but Ben seems to be the one that got away. I think she wants him because she can't have him. That's what women like Amber live for – the challenge, the chase – and he's certainly giving her that.

'Do you think he's playing games with me?' she asks.

'In what way?'

'Well, is he playing hard to get?'

I doubt that very much, but don't want to hurt her, so put my lips together and my head to one side with a 'maybe' look.

'He's been without me for a year,' she carries on, oblivious to my opinion anyway. 'He's seen that the grass isn't greener and maybe he still wants me... or why would he share a taxi and then play hard to get?'

'I don't know, Amber. I've only ever been in a relationship with Matt and we're pretty transparent. I don't know what you and Ben are like; perhaps he *is* playing hard to get,' I offer. She clearly thinks he is – or wants to think he is – and though I want to be honest I don't want to shatter her illusions totally, and what do I know? I don't know the moron. 'Would you expect him to do that – to pretend he doesn't care when he does?' I ask, trying to play the therapist and throw her question back at her.

'Perhaps.'

'Well then, he might be,' I say, not really believing this myself, but I haven't a clue, I've never even met him. People are strange, as the song goes, and who can ever understand the workings of the human mind when love's involved?

Amber smiles at me, squeezes my hand. 'Thanks Lucy.' She looks hopeful and I don't want to hurt her, but wonder if I should be a little stronger in my condemnation of him.

'If he *is* playing games,' I start, not wanting to give my friend false hope, 'you have to ask yourself: do *you* really want to be with someone like that?'

'Oh, I don't know. Men! Let's not talk about it,' she says. 'It makes me angry now just to think of him.'

'Okay,' I say, surprised at this sudden cut in the conversation. I can't help but feel there was more to this relationship than she's letting on, but knowing Amber it could be a while before she tells me. If ever. 'Let's just hope that one day soon you'll be able to kiss him goodbye... metaphorically, I mean. And *not* with tongues.' I giggle.

She laughs. 'Never with tongues. He's not good enough for my tongue,' she says.

'Let's leave it there, shall we, Miss Young? That's quite enough about tongues, thank you,' I say, playing the teacher for her amusement.

'Okay, Mrs Metcalf, whatever you say. There will be no more suggestions of smut in front of Miss this morning.'

'And talking of me being Miss, I have to get to work,' I say, picking up her still-full breakfast plate and throwing the contents in the bin.

Her face drops. 'Oh, Lucy, I've just had a horrible thought – I'm not at work today, and if I go home… what if *he* knows where I live?'

I have to say, I'm glad she's finally taking the stalker seriously.

'You don't have to go home if you'd rather not, sweetie,' I say. 'You're welcome to stay here – Matt and I will both be at work all day, but you'll be quite safe. Even if your stalker – whoever he is – knows where you live, he'll hardly know you're staying three doors down.'

She looks relieved. 'Thank you so much, Lucy. It's just for today… I guess I suddenly feel a bit creeped out.'

'Of course you do, and you're welcome to stay here. I only wish I didn't have to rush off,' I say, putting on my jacket and grabbing a pile of books to take with me. I'm already in danger of being late, and if the traffic's against me I'm likely to miss morning registration; I've never been late for work. 'You relax, eat whatever's in the fridge, watch the telly… Oh, and there are lots of books…' I'm heading out of the kitchen, grabbing my keys with one hand while looking for my phone.

'Lucy… I just realised I'm in your pyjamas…' She stands up expectantly, and I turn and notice how much better they look on her, like a different pair.

'Yes… That's okay, have a pyjama day.' *Why is she looking at me like that? What does she want me to do? I'm going to be late.*

'I would rather go and get my stuff…'

Oh God, I can't let her go home alone, given what's going on, but I don't have time for this. Knowing Amber, she'll want to shower and put on a full face of make-up before she can step outside of the house. I can't find my phone anywhere, and I feel hot.

'Okay, we can….' *Where the hell is my phone?* 'We can… go to your house together later after I've been to work… and you can get changed and… Have you seen my phone?'

She shakes her head, oblivious to my stress as I try to retrace my phone 'steps'. I had it first thing because I checked the news and commented to Matt about the chance of a teacher's strike.

I'm now lifting newspapers and tea towels. 'I'm sure I last had it in the kitchen,' I say, and I ask Amber to move so I can check under her chair, but she's in her own little world and I have to say her name a couple of times before she even reacts.

'Sorry, Lucy, I'm miles away,' she says, and I feel bad making a fuss about my missing phone when she's got bigger things to worry about. 'But the thing is, I couldn't possibly wear pyjamas all day. And if *he* were hanging around… I mean, what if he knocked on the door and… and I needed to run?'

Where the hell is my phone? Shit!

'I'll just have to go to work without it,' I say, almost to myself.

'Sorry, I'm being silly and selfish,' she suddenly says.

'No, no, you're not, it's just that…' *I might actually have a heart attack.*

'Lucy, you're angry with me and I don't blame you…'

'No I'm not.'

'There's me feeling sorry for myself and you've got to get to work. I'll be fine back home, honestly. I'll go now.'

'No, no…' I get up from the floor, where I've been surveying the whole surface area for my phone.

Amber's now taking her bag containing last night's clothes from the chair and I feel terrible. I've spent the last few minutes completely ignoring her, oblivious to her fear and anguish.

'Lucy, I'll be fine,' she's saying, but tellingly she isn't looking at me.

'Absolutely not,' I insist. And that's when I come to my senses and realise this isn't about me being late for bloody work, it's about me being there for my friend. 'Sod work,' I say, relief flooding through my veins at having given myself permission to step back and not have a coronary. I take off my jacket and abandon the so-far-fruitless search for my phone. 'The teaching assistant can cope for an hour. So I'll be late and miss registration and assembly – it's not life and death,' I add, in an attempt to convince myself as much as Amber, but deep down I know it's the right thing to do. So we leave the house together, and I push all thoughts of being late from my head. For now.

'I love blinds at a window,' she's saying, as we walk down the drive. She's still wearing my pyjamas after I convinced her she looked gorgeous in them and we're chatting about number 11's new blinds. 'They give good solid cover – I'm glad I have them. No one can peer inside when I'm on my own.'

'You don't *have* to be on your own,' I reassure her. 'You can stay with us whenever you like, for as long as you need to. When she doesn't answer, I look at her, but she seems to be gazing ahead and I follow her gaze. There's something on her doorstep. 'What's that?' I ask.

'I'm not sure,' she says, sounding scared.

'It might be a gift from someone… Ben?' I offer, knowing this is what she wants but at the same time doubting it – why would he suddenly send a gift now, after a year apart?

As we get closer to the doorstep, I can see it's a small, oblong box, wrapped in flowery wrapping paper and tied with a large pink bow. We look at each other, and I think we're both thinking the same: it may not be from a friend.

'Looks pretty,' I say uncertainly, as we both stand staring at it.

'Would you mind… picking it up?' she asks, and I hesitate before bending down to touch it. I look back at Amber, who's now white with fear, then lift it with both hands.

'It's surprisingly light. Could it be jewellery?' I say, gently shaking it as she steps past me like it's contagious and opens the front door. She goes inside, and I follow her, grabbing the door with one hand while holding the box with the other.

She quickly turns the alarm off and we go through into the kitchen, where I put the gift on the counter.

'You know… it might genuinely be a gift,' I say, nodding.

She just shakes her head. 'Who would give me a gift out of the blue like this?'

'I don't know…' I gesture towards the box. 'Are you going to open it?'

'No.' She speaks quietly, her fear tangible.

'Shall I?' What can I do? One of us has to, and we always knew it wouldn't be Amber.

'Would you mind?'

'No.' I'm feeling very jumpy as I reach for the pretty pink parcel, like it might be a bomb, or a bracelet. A gift or a gun. I approach it like a plaster and rip the paper off quickly in an effort to cause less pain. Under the wrapping paper is the closed box, and it's very pretty: pale pink, painted with pictures of tiny birds and blossoms. It reminds me of the kimono Amber wore when I first met her at her door. 'It must be from a friend,' I say. 'This box is very you, isn't it?'

She just looks from the box back to me, wanting me to get on with it I suppose. So, in silence, I push my nails under the flap to open it and reveal an abundance of pink tissue paper.

'It's like pass the parcel,' I joke lamely, pushing both hands into the pink paper and moving them around. Then I feel it – a cold dampness on the ends of my fingers, and I hear myself scream.

CHAPTER EIGHT

Lucy

'What?' she's saying loudly, her voice filled with panic. 'What is it, Lucy? Tell me.'

I don't answer. In my horror I put the box down and move away, but I know if I don't open it neither will Amber. So I go back and pull out more tissue paper and more; it's never-ending. And then the final piece reveals what my hands had touched – the body of a tiny dead bird, covered in blood. I look at Amber, her mouth half-open, her eyes moving slowly from mine to 'the gift' and back again. I look down at my hands, red and damp with blood.

The silence is deafening.

She's looking at me and a tear is crawling down her face like a long, silvery insect.

'Opening that box has to be the creepiest thing that has ever happened to me,' I say to Kirsty in school later that day. I have filled her in on everything that has happened since yesterday, and she just keeps saying 'No… I don't believe it,' and by the time I get to the dead bird, she's open-mouthed.

'She wanted me to throw the bird away,' I say, explaining that in the aftermath of the unwrapping, I'd scrubbed my hands, put the bird back in the box and, despite her protestations, left it in

Amber's fridge. She was absolutely horrified and said she didn't want it in the house, let alone her fridge.

'It's evidence, we can't just throw it away,' I said, and after helping her pack some essentials (Amber's definition of the word and mine differ slightly – a silk eye mask, scarlet underwear, three bags of make-up and a box of meditation discs are not something I would *need*), we headed back to mine. Once there, she asked me to wait with her a little longer.

'I'm just so nervous, I keep thinking he's watching me,' she said, so I stayed a few more minutes, and made her a chamomile tea. She didn't want to be left alone, but having spent half the morning calming her down, I really had to go into work.

'It was like something from a horror movie. The tissue paper was covered in blood. No note, nothing, just the dead bird – it was vile,' I tell Kirsty. It's now afternoon playtime, and we've just boiled the kettle for coffee and she's spooning granules into our mugs as I take the milk from the mini fridge.

'Oh my God, that's terrible. What did Amber do?'

'She cried… Well, we both did – you know what I'm like. I cry at anything,' I say, pouring the milk into our mugs. I'm trying to keep it light. Just hearing myself tell the story of what was inside the box is so creepy I don't want to freak Kirsty out.

'You cry at bloody *Coronation Street*,' she agrees, as we walk with our steaming drinks to a corner of the staffroom where we can chat without being overheard. 'So, has she any idea who…?' Kirsty's settling into her chair and I pull mine closer.

On second thoughts, I don't need to hold back. There's no chance any of this will freak Kirsty out; she's positively salivating.

'No, she hasn't a clue. At first I thought it might be from Ben – remember, I told you about him, her ex-boyfriend?'

Kirsty nods eagerly while sipping her coffee and, in her enthusiasm, almost causes a collision between mug and teeth.

'But now, I don't know. I just can't see him getting involved after everything,' I say knowledgably, like Amber Young is my subject on *Mastermind*. 'I mean, they've been apart for a year now, and as much as she'd love to get back with him, I'm not convinced he feels the same ...'

'Really? You don't think it could be him?' she says slowly, screwing up her eyes like she's considering this deeply. 'I'm not so sure – stalkers are often ex-boyfriends, and you've said yourself it was a strange relationship...' she adds, taking another sip.

'True, and it's not out of the question – she told me they'd shared a taxi the other night, so perhaps he is back on the scene? She loved him to bits,' I say. 'He promised her the earth and gave her nothing, and she spent twenty years waiting for him.'

'I don't think she waited around too much if the doorman at Allegra is to be believed.' She smirks, dying for me to ask.

I don't give her the satisfaction. Amber has never made a secret out of the fact she has 'dalliances', so I'm not joining in with Kirsty in judging her for that.

'Anyway, the police are coming over on Wednesday,' I add, a tantalising caveat that causes Kirsty's eyebrows to raise, which I note need shaping – something I'd never considered before Amber. She dragged me to her beauty therapist in town, and Olga's taken ten years off me with a reshape and a monthly hydrating facial. I've booked an appointment with Amber's hairdresser too – I love the way he does her hair, and the colour is 'to die for' (as Amber would say).

'The police?' Kirsty's saying, surprised.

'Yes, I called them from JoJo's when I saw the text. And we can tell them about the dead bird now.'

'Ooh, get you – in the posh wine bars. I notice you didn't invite *me*, did you?' she half-jokes, putting down her mug on the arm of the chair. I feel really awkward.

'Sorry, it's just... Amber asked me at the last minute... Sorry,' I repeat, feeling suddenly quite bad that I left Kirsty out. The thing is, Amber and I have a friendship that doesn't really include Kirsty, and it would be difficult to try and bond us all. And to be honest, I don't think Kirsty deserves to be invited along on my evenings out with Amber. She's so mean about her and she'd be horrible to her face too. The last time we got together was at Christmas, and Amber mentioned that we'd been to a spa and started laughing with me about how we were so slippery after our massages that we almost fell in the pool. I was silently willing Amber not to talk about it because I hadn't mentioned the spa day to Kirsty, but sometimes Amber misses the social cues. Kirsty's face was like thunder, and she made digs about 'best friends at the spa' for ages afterwards. And now she's making me feel bad that I went to a wine bar with Amber, and I'm irritated with her for producing all this guilt in me.

'Oh it's fine, I was only joking,' she says. But we both know she wasn't.

'Anyway, she got the text while we were in JoJo's,' I say, to take her mind off her petty resentment and focus on the story. 'So I called the police straight away, and then I called them again this morning when she got the… gift.' I shiver at the memory of the poor little bird, all stiff and cold and bloody.

'Shouldn't have bothered with the police,' she says. 'They're too busy dealing with *real* crimes.'

'Well, they're going to be at Amber's Wednesday afternoon,' I say, refusing to take on her comment. 'I wish it was sooner, but they insisted they couldn't come until Wednesday.'

'Told you. They don't do anything. She'll be lucky if they turn up.'

'I'll make *sure* they do. I'm leaving class early and I'll be with Amber to give them all the details and show them the bird too – they might be able to fingerprint the gift wrapping. I've kept that.'

'You'll be lucky – they won't bother with fingerprints or DNA or whatever. It's not like she's been murdered.'

I can't believe Kirsty's callousness. 'No, but who knows what *might* happen? It might be just a text and a dead bird on the doorstep now… but it can lead to… really horrible stuff.' I can't bring myself to say it.

'Lucy, you need to calm down. If it isn't her ex it's probably just some local oddball,' she says. Then she suddenly realises what I said. 'You can't just leave your class on Wednesday. You won't get permission, will you? I mean, it's not like she's family or anything. Surely she can speak to the police on her own?'

'No, I need to be there, to be objective and give a rational account, and they won't refuse me time off for something as important as this,' I insist, a bit peeved that Kirsty isn't embracing the drama as much as she was before. I suppose it's all a bit too real for some people to handle. Kirsty loves hearing all about it like some people love watching detective dramas, but when the real police are called it becomes a little bit uncomfortable. Then again, it's about Amber, and though she loves the stories I tell her, Kirsty always tries to put Amber or the situation down, and that's not going to change anytime soon. It makes me think Kirsty doesn't really care about Amber and the fact she's in potential danger; she just wants all the juicy gossip. So it's a good job Amber's got me, because I'm a true friend and I'll be there for her, however bad things get.

Later that day, I call Amber from the school landline. I'm lost without my phone, especially at a time like this, and I'm relieved when she answers.

'Oh, Lucy, I'm so glad you called. I just feel so scared,' she says, when I ask if she's okay.

'There's no need. Matt and I want you to stay as long as you want,' I say, knowing I'm not really speaking for Matt. I haven't been able to let him know Amber didn't go home as planned this morning because of the 'gift'. As I don't have my phone, I can't text him either. I could call his school on my school's landline, but I'd have to ask someone to fetch him and I'm not sure of his timetable, and I don't want him to be dragged out of a class – it's too complicated to explain in a snatched conversation. Plus, it's difficult for me to talk, especially if Kirsty's earwigging. Anyway, Matt's so busy with the *Bugsy Malone* production at the moment, he probably won't even notice if she's there or not tonight. Besides, even if he doesn't like Amber, he wouldn't begrudge a scared friend of mine staying over for her own safety.

'I'll be home soon. Shall we have one of our girls' nights in?' I suggest to Amber, in an attempt to cheer her up, but she just grunts on the other end of the phone. I know it sounds a bit trite, but I don't know how else to make her happy, apart from turning up later with a big bloody cake and Ben leaping out of it.

I put down the phone, having promised a great evening ahead, to which she mumbled something about being tired. I guess she thinks she doesn't want to watch a romcom marathon accompanied by baked goodies and face masks and anything else I can think of. But I honestly can't imagine a better way to spend an evening – I mean, a girls' night in with beauty treatments, Jennifer Aniston and a dozen cupcakes? It doesn't get better than that.

When I arrive home I tell her to close her eyes and as she does this, I 'unveil' our outfits for the evening. They were selling off some unicorn onesies in the party shop down the road, and I couldn't resist. They are cute and pretty, but quite ridiculous and her face when I take them out of the bag is a picture.

'I know, I know, they are CRAZY.' I laugh. 'But they were dirt cheap, only slight seconds, and it would have been rude not to – anyway, we could do with a laugh,' I giggle. One is bright pink, and the other is a lovely shade of lavender, and as she screams in mock horror she grabs the lavender one, despite me holding the pink one up against her.

'But this one's oozing sophistication, don't you think?' I say, because I don't really like the pink one, and I think it's going to be too tight for me, but I want to make her happy.

'Don't you dare say a thing,' she warns, her eyes laughing as she climbs into the lavender unicorn, pulls the hood over her head. I can't stop giggling as I attempt to squeeze myself into the bright pink unicorn that's at least a size too small for me, and I wonder at how she can look so good. In a unicorn outfit.

'I'm in the middle of hell,' she says, taking the Prosecco from the fridge. 'A crazy person is texting vile threats, sending me dead creatures covered in blood and wrapped in pink paper… and what does my best friend do? She makes me dress like a unicorn.' She laughs.

'Oh stop complaining, let's get our face packs on and start the film,' I say ushering her into the living room.

'Not Jennifer Aniston. Again,' she says as I press play.

'What? But you loved *Just Go with It* last time we watched it.'

'Exactly. I've already seen it. I know what happens,' she says. I help her with her face mask, but it keeps falling off because she insists on drinking continuously, which causes the wet paper mask to drop each time she takes a sip, and makes us both break down with laughter. It's going to be a great night. I bought a 'fine dining' pizza from the supermarket, two bottles of Prosecco – Amber's favourite – and a box of cupcakes from the bakery department – my favourite.

'Well, there's one thing this costume will be useful for. This can be a test – if he gets in touch and mentions my outfit, I'll know that he's been watching me tonight,' she says, wobbling the unicorn's horn up and down, her face mask slipping again.

I'm just taking a sip of Prosecco, and at the sight of her wobbling horn and drooping mask I laugh, causing bubbles to hit the back of my nose and the fizzy wine to come gushing out. This in turn makes Amber laugh and we are hysterical. Amber then throws herself across the sofa and starts posing model-like, her horn now drooping, and I think I'll never stop laughing. It's only when Matt walks in that we manage to compose ourselves. He'll be late all this week as he's doing extra rehearsals – it's the school play next week.

'Hi, babe.' I smile as he wanders in.

'What the hell?' he says, laughing, incredulous at the sight of two grown women dressed as unicorns in his living room.

'We're having a girls' night – trying to cheer Amber up,' I add, so he knows this is all for a good cause and I haven't gone mad. But after a day with thirty noisy six-year-olds, who could blame me for turning into a unicorn by home time?

Matt wanders over. He's shaking his head and, as I'm still wearing my sticky mask, kisses me on the ear and nods at Amber. He's smiling, but not exactly being welcoming, and I've still got to break it to him that she's probably staying for at least one more night, but I'll explain later. I don't want to mention the dead bird at this juncture; I'm trying to make everything pleasant for her. Unsurprisingly, it's really freaked her out – she doesn't need Matt questioning her forensically like she's the bloody guilty party. Last night Matt forced himself to be nice to Amber, but they aren't friends and I can't make him like her. Actually, it feels like both Kirsty and Matt have a real problem with Amber, and I just don't understand it – why can't my friends and my husband all like each other? It would certainly make my life easier and I wouldn't feel I had to constantly defend Amber every time she comes up in conversation.

Matt disappears into the kitchen and I follow him to ask if he's seen my phone anywhere, but he hasn't.

'Perhaps you left it at school?' he says, turning on the kettle and gathering the ingredients to make himself a cheese sandwich.

'No, that's why I asked. I couldn't find it this morning so didn't take it to school.'

'Okay, it'll be here somewhere. I'll help you look tomorrow.' He picks up the plate with the sandwich on and a mug of tea. 'I'm so tired, babe. I'm going to take this to bed.'

'I'll be a bit longer,' I say, gesturing with my eyes towards the living room where Amber's sitting. He nods and heads upstairs, saying he'll see me later in bed.

I go back into the living room, where Amber and I continue to watch the slow burn as Jennifer Aniston and Adam Sandler's characters fall madly in love in Hawaii.

'It's so romantic, isn't it?' I say.

'Yeah, I suppose so.' She's already downed most of the first bottle of Prosecco, so I go to the fridge for the other one, open it and fill her glass. I'm still on my first glass – I don't like to drink too much on a school night, and besides, I'm more interested in the cupcakes, which are quite delicious. 'To be honest,' she continues, as I go back into the sitting room with her glass, 'I'm not really a romcom girl.'

I'm disappointed at this – she told me she 'adored' romcoms last time we had a girls' night, and I realise she probably only said that to please me.

'What would you like then? A horror? A thriller?'

'No thanks. I'm having enough of that in my real life.'

'Do you want to talk about it? It must be really scary for you.'

'Lucy, it's so *bloody* scary.' Her eyes fill with tears and she pulls off the sticky paper mask she's wearing, dropping it on the sofa next to her. I think about how the moisture will soak in and leave a greasy mark for ever and ever, but she's talking and crying and it would seem insensitive to say anything, or try and move it. 'I haven't felt scared like this since I was a kid – a teenager.'

'Why were you scared then?' I ask, moving to sit next to her and discreetly picking up the sticky mask, holding it in my hand.

'Oh, my stepdad, he was vile. He was one of mum's boyfriends, not *even* my stepdad, but I hated him. He was with her for a few years. The others mostly only hung around a few nights.' She sighs.

I understood. I didn't exactly have a happy childhood either.

'What happened?' I ask.

'He met Mum when I was about ten. He hated me, used to hit me, but on my thirteenth birthday… he started… touching me.' She seems to recoil at the memory.

'Oh God, Amber, that's terrible.'

'It was horrible. I still have nightmares – his face leering over me, his breath on me… just horrible.'

'Did your mum help? Did she stop him?'

'She didn't know. She was a mess and I knew if I told her she might not believe me anyway, and if she did he'd leave – and he paid the bills.'

'You've never told me any of this before…'

'I worried you'd think I was disgusting.'

'No, no, of course I don't! You were a child. God knows I blame myself for things that happened when I was younger – I had a difficult childhood too. But we have to remember we were kids.'

'But it made me what I was, it *made* me…' She looks up at me, and I get this feeling that for the first time ever I'm seeing the real Amber. 'Mum got a job. She did shifts and we were left at home with him. Things got worse for me, but I don't remember much of it. I learned how to fly away, pretend I was somewhere else in my head. I put up with it for a long time, but in the end I just could handle it. I told my mum, and there were horrible fights and eventually he left. But Mum couldn't cope on her own, so I ended up in care.'

'Did you ever have any therapy?' I ask.

'You're kidding? I fought my way through the next few years and when I was sixteen I was spat out of care and had to find a life.'

We talk some more and I feel like I'm beginning to finally understand her, like she's lifting a curtain, showing me a little of who she is, and why.

'Thanks for listening, Lucy,' she says later. 'I never really had a best friend before, and I know I'm not the easiest, cuddliest person. I guess all those men traipsing through my mother's life left their footprints on mine. I've never really been easy with people, especially strangers, and I don't invite them in, because I know they can hurt me.'

'I know that too.'

'But you reached out to me. You were persistent... bloody persistent, with your cakes and your texts and your calls asking if I'd like to meet up for coffee. But I needed that. If you hadn't reached out, I would never have become your friend.' She smiles, and then she says, 'You know, I think you've found the other side of me.'

My heart melts a little. I sometimes think she can be a little thoughtless (the wet paper mask carelessly dropped on my sofa is still in my hand), but perhaps it isn't thoughtlessness. She's just got a head full of hurt and worry and she doesn't have space consider the small things. But she does have a heart, and she's finally opening up to me.

But then it happens again, that shift. The curtain's back and I can't see her any more. 'This is all too depressing, and it's supposed to be a fun night – will you paint my nails?' she asks, and I know there will be no more revelations tonight.

The next morning I knock on the spare bedroom door with a cup of tea for Amber. I have to get off to work and can't be late again, but just want to make sure she's okay before I leave. She calls me into the room and after only two nights it doesn't feel like mine any more – her clothes are strewn over the back of a chair, her make-up in chaos on the dressing table, brushes and bottles exploding from her toilet bag. The room smells of her, warm musk battling with sharp citrus – a total contradiction, and very Amber. She has made this room her own, and I feel like I'm the guest, in a good way. I'm glad she's settled in. I gaze over at the bed where she's still half-asleep, last night's eye make-up blurred, her hair tousled.

'Thanks, lovely Lucy,' she murmurs, when I tell her I've brought tea. She wafts her hand at the bedside table, and I place it there, knowing by the time she comes round it'll be cold.

'I'm just off to work,' I say. 'Make yourself comfortable. There's food in the fridge. See you tonight.'

'I won't see you later – I'm working.'

'Oh, I didn't realise. You can come back here after work – you don't want to go back to an empty house late at night.'

'I won't...' She emerges slightly from under the covers. 'I have a sleepover.' She smiles.

'You mean, with a man?' I feel a little put out that she hasn't mentioned this before.

She nods slowly, her eyes still closed.

I try to fight the waspy sting of irritation. I know it's unreasonable of me, but I can't help it.

'You never said.'

'I know, babe. He only got in touch late last night.'

'Who is he?'

'If you must know, it's Ben,' she mumbles from the pillow.

'Oh. Do you think that's wise?'

'I'll find out when I'm in his bed.' She giggles.

I don't giggle back. 'It could be him, you know?'

'Oh my God, Lucy. It isn't Ben,' she says, and pulls the covers over her head so she doesn't have to engage with me any more.

'I just hope you're right,' I say, unable to hide my disapproval. I can't help thinking she's playing with fire and that she'd be better off here with me and Matt. Ben will just lead her on until she's at another dead end and then he'll break her heart again. Then again, what do I know? I don't know him at all, but sometimes I don't think I know Amber either.

I made my own fun. I'd talk to myself, make a sandwich from whatever was lying around the kitchen, then, when it got dark or I was scared, I'd take myself to bed. I wasn't given hot milk and a goodnight story, because Mum worked late, then stopped by the pub for a few on her way home. Sometimes she'd bring 'a friend' with her and he'd stay over. I thought that's what everyone's mother did.

CHAPTER NINE

Lucy

The next day at work, I ask my classroom assistant Diane to take over for the last ten minutes so I can leave early.

'This has to be kept secret.' I speak in a low voice. 'My friend Amber, you know Amber Young, who does the weather on TV?' At this she nods. 'She has this situation… well, it's a stalker and I have to be there with her to see the police. He keeps texting her and on Monday he even left a dead bird on her doorstep.'

I stand back and wait for the gasp, but there isn't one.

'Oh yeah, Kirsty told me about that,' she says. 'Of course I'll stand in. You get off whenever you like.'

I can't believe Kirsty opened her mouth, that was supposed to be confidential and I only told Diane myself because I wanted her to do me the favour. I thought I could trust Kirsty but I'm not sure any more – and judging by Diane's reaction to my revelation, I reckon Kirsty implied to her that I'm exaggerating the whole stalker thing. Maybe I'm being paranoid, but it feels like Kirsty is almost making people take sides, I sense the cold shoulder these days from quite a few of the other staff. These are people who once seemed to like me but I'm convinced Kirsty's been telling everyone I've upset her. But Kirsty's real problem lies with Amber - only yesterday she accused me of leaving the book club and abandoning my friends just because Amber had decided she didn't want to go.

'You follow her round like a lost puppy. She's just using you,' she snapped, but she's wrong. How could Kirsty ever understand mine and Amber's friendship, it's like trying to understand someone else's marriage, you have to be there to know. I don't follow her around, I happen to enjoy her company, and Amber isn't using me, she *likes* me – and there's a *big* difference. We're good friends, we support each other and I won't just abandon Amber because Kirsty's feeling pushed out and being immature about it. I have enough on my plate without worrying Kirsty's childish resentment influencing my friends and work colleagues. I'd be tempted to send her a text telling her not to be so silly but I still haven't found my phone and feel so cut off. I've hunted through the whole house. I even recruited Matt to help and bring fresh eyes to the search, thinking it must be somewhere obvious that I'd missed.

'Is it looking at me?' I said, but he searched everywhere too, even upturned the sofa and stripped the cover – and nothing. I know I had it last in the kitchen, so it has to be in the house, but if it doesn't turn up in next couple of days I'll have to order a replacement. Then, on top of this, Matt keeps asking how long Amber's staying and when she's going back home. He asked again this morning.

'I don't know,' I said for the umpteenth time. 'When is her stalker going to stop stalking? I don't know, therefore I don't know how long she'll stay – funnily enough, Matt, I can't see into the future.'

'Yeah, but she must have other friends… family?' he said.

'Yes, and tonight she's staying with one of them, her ex Ben,' I snapped.

'So while we're supposedly keeping her safe here, she goes off with her ex as soon as he whistles. What if he's the—'

'He isn't apparently,' I said, trying to stay calm. Hoping Matt wouldn't ask me how I know Ben isn't the stalker – I don't, but Amber seems convinced.

'So how long is she staying with him? For good I hope?'

'Matt, I have no idea what's happening with her ex, but she's relying on us, and if she asks if she can stay here we have to be there for her. How would you feel if something terrible happened to her because she was in that big house on her own one night and he decided to pounce? First a dead bird, next…' I couldn't even bring myself to complete the sentence.

Don't get me wrong, I love Matt – but he is so involved with his school drama commitments, he often isn't home until late, so it makes me angry that he objects to my friend staying over. He's had to spend a lot more time involved in school business since he got the promotion, and in the past few weeks has been full-on with the school play. When he isn't rewriting the script and worrying about casting he's had to spend whole weekends in his office upstairs marking papers and planning lessons. If Amber wasn't around I'd have to eat on my own, watch TV alone and potter around just waiting for him to materialise. So whenever she asks if she can stay over I'm going to bloody well say yes.

Kirsty once said that she and her husband had talked about our marriage (which annoyed me a bit; I don't like the idea of my life being dissected over their evening meal).She said they both felt like Matt and I had become distant with each other, and that he'd withdrawn when we discovered we couldn't have children.

'Me and Pete think Matt might be grieving for the family he'll never have,' she'd said. At the time, I didn't really want to hear it. I wasn't handling it very well myself and Matt and I both needed to come to terms with it in our own way. We didn't need the well-meaning advice from the obscenely fertile Pete and Kirsty, who had two healthy, happy children and the option of more any time they wanted. Matt and I don't talk about babies these days – we don't really talk about much come to think of it – but I sometimes think about what Kirsty said, and I just hope Matt's not bottling up his feelings. When everything's sorted with Amber, I'll take time to sit down with Matt and see how everything is with him. But for now she's my biggest concern and I'm hoping Matt will understand.

When the school bell goes at 3.15 p.m. I run straight out of the classroom to my car. I don't want to be late for the police. I almost bump into Kirsty going the other way down the corridor. 'Got to fly,' I say in a friendly voice, but she makes a point of deliberately ignoring me. Childish. But even in my rush, I turn and feel a frisson of sadness, promising myself that when we're through this and I know Amber's safe I'll reach out to Kirsty. Friendship is important to me – it means everything really, because our friends can mean more to us than family.

I drive from school like the wind and almost have an accident, but when I get to Amber's they've already interviewed her and have left.

Amber is pretty monosyllabic about the whole thing, says she's told them everything and they are going to keep an eye on her property.

'That was it?' I ask.

'Well, they talked about getting the alarms up to date…'

'Okay, and so you're going to do that?'

'Yeah, I've booked an alarm guy to come and do a check,' she says vaguely.

I am so disappointed. I was hoping for a proper chat with the police, especially after the bird on the doorstep. I wanted to get their take on things; I'd even made notes with the dates and times of the texts and calls, based on what Amber had told me. Though Matt said he felt it was a little over the top when I produced my 'evidence' at breakfast. 'You're going to make a fool of yourself waving that in their faces,' he snapped. He was in such a grumpy mood. Typical that the police should get it wrong and turn up too early, even though I'd specifically asked them to come after three thirty.

*

It's been a week since the police visit and Amber's mostly been staying with us, except for the night she stayed with Ben. 'It was fine,' she said, when I asked, but she didn't want to talk about it, so I don't imagine it was all *that* fine.

She's staying over with us again tonight and we've had a great time. She hasn't had a text in over a week, and she looks happier, brighter, more chilled than I've seen her for a while.

'I told you, if I ignored it long enough, he'd just go away,' she says as I clear up the dinner plates and stack the dishwasher.

'I hope you're right.' I smile at her sitting at the table and feel like I should reassure her more. 'In fact, I'm sure you're right,' I add, although I'm not totally convinced. I read a lot of true crime books and love a good documentary on TV, and rarely does a stalker just walk away. They are obsessed, and obsessions don't just disappear into the ether, something Amber doesn't quite seem to appreciate. But I don't want to spoil the evening by scaring her with my doom-like prophecies when she clearly wants to forget it all and just enjoy herself.

Earlier, Matt cooked for us and, despite being a little stressed about tomorrow's first night of the school play, he was funny and charming and made us laugh. His cooking was delicious too, and he's promised to show Amber how to make dauphinoise potatoes. She said the ones he made us tonight were, and I quote, 'Better than sex, but a lot more fattening!' This made Matt smile. She's such a flatterer, and though he isn't delighted to have her, I think he's accepted our house guest for now.

Matt's gone to bed now, so we've moved into the sitting room and taken a sofa each, both with a glass of wine and our feet up. I'm glad she's here. I wondered if she might decide to go home as she hasn't had any more creepy texts this week, but she seems happy to stay. And I'm more than happy to have her around. I love her company.

As it's late, we've had a few glasses and she's relaxed. I pluck up the courage to ask her about Michael, her husband. As we're now best friends, I should know what happened.

'Were you happy with your husband?' I ask, sitting up from my reclined position on the sofa and topping up our glasses of red.

'Yes, but it was a difficult time, when he died.'

'I can imagine, and you finding him…' I recently put his name and 'death' into Google. As it was so long ago, there wasn't much, but I was surprised to see it was suicide, and poor Amber had discovered his body.

'Michael was depressed,' she says firmly, like she's making a point.

'Do you know why he killed himself? Did he leave a note?' I couldn't find anything on Google, no reason, nothing.

'It was my fault,' she says. I'm shocked and for a few seconds I don't know what to say, how to ask what she means. But I don't need to, because Amber goes on to offer an explanation.

'I was having an affair,' she suddenly says into the silence.

Wow, I didn't expect that. I'm surprised at her honesty and feel bad for even asking, but at the same time I was curious.

She nods. 'He told me he was going to end his life, but I didn't believe him.' Then, as if she realises what she's just said, she turns to me, her eyes dark and cold. 'I've never told anyone that I was having an affair when Michael died, you must *never* repeat it.'

'I wouldn't dream of telling anyone. You know you can trust me,' I say, glad she felt able to confide in me.

'I do… I do trust you, Lucy. I… It's just I've never been able to trust anyone. I've always felt like the moment I do, I'm taken advantage of. Even Ben. But Michael was different, like you – he seemed to actually like me for me. No hidden agenda, no gold-digging or using me to further his own career.'

'Do you feel that Ben did that?'

'I didn't realise it at the time. Michael and I had married young. We met when I was seventeen, married by eighteen. I was trying to escape my home life, my mother.' She pauses. 'When I met Ben I was only twenty-two, and married, but he opened up a big old world to me, made me see that there was so much more to life than staying home every night, and Michael suddenly seemed boring.' She looks at me sadly. I see a hint of regret in her eyes and feel so sad for her.

'You must have been very unhappy at home to want to run away and marry so young,' I say, probing, wondering what had happened.

She nods, but doesn't seem keen to elaborate, just carries on talking about Ben. 'He was my boss, a few years older, and he seemed so worldly, so sophisticated. He still does.' She goes off for a few seconds into her own little 'Ben' world and all I can think is that she'll never be over him.

'Ben told me I was amazing, and with his guidance I could go anywhere, do anything, even host my own chat show. I believed in him, and for a while I even believed in me. I was completely seduced by Ben and by this life he was offering me, something I'd never imagined myself being capable of. All the time I hated myself for what I was doing to Michael, I still do. But I loved Ben, and even though we tried, we couldn't stay apart for long. Ben was obsessed with me as much as I was with him.'

'Obsessed?' I say.

'Yeah, you know how it is,' she says, like I would know how it feels to have a man obsess over me. 'I still loved Michael in my own way, but I was a teenager when we met, he was my first real boyfriend, and I suppose I was ready for something more,' she said, with a sigh. 'That was Ben.'

'So you told Michael?'

She nods, her eyes filling with tears, and again I'm struck by how much this still has an instant emotional impact on her over twenty years later.

'Michael's death was tragic... He was so young, but I was young too, and God, I had fallen madly in love with Ben, and even though nothing had happened, not really, I'd decided the honest thing to do was to tell Michael. I told him it didn't mean I didn't love him, but I couldn't in fairness stay with him. But then he...' She wipes her eyes with the back of her hand and seems to disappear for a few seconds. 'It was all so horrific. And after that, if anyone had found out about Ben and me, and that we were the reason Michael killed himself, we'd be blamed and our careers would have been ruined too. Ben said I was going to be a big star and we'd put so much into this. Things were just starting to take off for me. So we decided to end our relationship and keep things on a professional basis.' She looks up to the ceiling with a sad smile. 'I think that plan lasted a matter of weeks, and we were back together.'

'That must have been very hard for you,' I say.

'It was, and it wasn't helped by the fact that Michael's family suspected we were having problems in our marriage, but I just denied everything. I felt so guilty, the fact that I broke his heart will stay with me for ever... but I keep it inside. It isn't "out there", where they can crucify me.'

When she was the pretty TV weather girl I recall there was interest in her young husband's death and remember photos of the two of them. I was struck at the time by their beauty, the photos of their wedding, of the two of them smiling, with so much ahead, and then the starkly contrasting shots of Amber walking down a road in London alone, looking sad and tearful.

'When he died, Michael had a little money,' she's saying, 'but he changed his will, stipulating that his family should receive everything, except the sunrise painting... which he left to me.'

We sip our wine and I can see now why the painting means so much to her. It's all she has left of him.

'Lucy, if I tell you what happened with Michael, can I trust you?'

'Yes, of course.'

'You promise you'll never tell a soul?'

'No, never. I promise. You have my word.'

So she pours herself another glass tells and tells me all about Michael's death, and the part she played. I just listen, and when she's finished I don't know what to say. I find it hard to process what she's just told me.

'I've never told anyone the real truth,' she says. 'Do you think I'm terrible? Do you hate me now?'

'No, I could never hate you,' I say, and mean it. 'Secrets are secrets for a reason, usually because they're something we're ashamed of, or we're scared if they get out we'll be judged, hated or worse. But I'm glad you trust me enough to share it with me – and I'm touched, I'm really touched. I'll never say a word.'

She hugs me, genuinely pleased that I'm not judging her for what she just told me, and I feel closer to her in this moment than I've ever felt to anyone.

'So now I've told you my deepest, darkest secret – you tell me yours,' she says, and so I take a deep breath, and tell her my secret.

CHAPTER TEN

Lucy

Today I've come straight to Amber's from school to see if she needs a lift to the studio. She spent last night at her own house, said she felt we needed our space, and despite me insisting we didn't, she wouldn't budge and stayed at hers. I would have called her but *still* haven't been able to find my phone. Matt and I have searched high and low and come to the conclusion that it must have been accidentally thrown out with the rubbish. Anyway, I had an email to say a replacement is winging its way to me, and it can't get here soon enough. I don't come over to Amber's much, mainly because these days she's usually at ours – but since finding that horrific package on her doorstep, I'm wary.

As I climb from the car, I'm really on edge remembering the gift, wondering if he's still obsessed, still lurking somewhere near, watching. I can't help it, I feel like someone's going to jump out at me and I keep looking behind me, feeling really exposed. I've got myself into such a state just walking up her drive, I think I must be imagining it when I see something moving behind the back wheel of her car. But as I walk closer, I see two legs, the feet clad in red-soled shoes, and my heart does a lurch. It's definitely her – or, God forbid, her body. There's no one else I know who can afford Louboutins. Blood thunders through my head as I dash towards the car. Oh Jesus. I gasp in horror, my heart thumping in my chest. She's on her knees, slumped forward almost under the back wheel. My heart's in my mouth as I slowly bend down to get closer to her. Something terrible has happened, but I can't even begin to imagine what it might be. There's no obvious sign of blood, but I can't see the front of her so she could have an injury to her head or chest. I try to say her name, but nothing comes out. I gently touch her back, and for a second she doesn't move and I hear my own voice making sounds I don't understand.

At this she jerks up, causing me to scream in fright, which causes her to scream, and we're now both screaming at each other on her drive.

'LUCY,' she yells, grabbing me to help her up, her stockings all laddered from the gravel, but with no signs of blood or injury. 'What the hell are you doing sneaking up on me like that?'

Tears of relief spring to my eyes. 'Thank God you're okay.'

'Of course I am. But you scared me to death coming up like that – I thought it was... well, you know.' She looks down, unable to finish the sentence, starts wiping gravel dust from her skirt. 'Don't you ever creep up on me like that again,' she says harshly, and laughs, but there's no mirth. She's using it to cover her irritation.

She's been quite prickly lately and I know it's because she's scared – but I wish she wouldn't take it out on me. 'I'm so sorry. I wasn't "creeping up on you",' I say. 'I just saw you lying there and... Sorry I scared you.'

'It's fine, it's just that I wasn't expecting you. Sorry, I didn't mean creeping in a weird way, I just meant... Oh, I don't know, just ignore me. I was in a world of my own and you gave me a fright, that's all.'

'It's okay,' I croak, swallowing the shock and threat of tears; it hurts when Amber's angry with me. 'What were you doing down there anyway?' I ask, resenting her reaction now and allowing a wave of anger to wash clean the hurt.

'I'm... Nothing really. Just looking at the car. I thought someone had scraped it when I parked it up in town.'

'Who? Him?'

'No,' she says, irritated again, dismissing my comment with a flutter of her hand.

'No point looking down there – if someone *had* scraped your car it wouldn't be near the tyre,' I point out. 'It's *here* where the damage would be.' I run my hand along the bumper. 'I can't see or feel anything.'

But she isn't listening, she's now marching towards the house, so I follow her.

'What makes you think someone scraped your car?' I'm asking as I try to catch up.

'Nothing… I just thought…'

'It's him again, isn't it?' She probably doesn't want to worry me, but I want to know what's going on. 'Have you had any more messages?'

She shakes her head and looks away. I can't help but wonder if there's something she isn't telling me as she opens the front door and I follow her into the hallway and close the door behind me.

'Do you think he's been hanging around your car? I knew I should have been here for that police interview. I bet you just played it down, didn't you? "Oh I'm fine, it happens all the time – it's nothing, officer." Well, a dead bird in pink wrapping paper isn't *nothing*, Amber!' My voice is raised. I'm in her face. I need her to realise what this is.

'Calm down, Lucy. I gave a statement, but didn't make a drama of it. I'm handling it, okay?' We're standing in the kitchen now and she's drumming her fingertips on the counter. I can feel the tension – she's as scared as I am, just in denial.

'Look, he's already turned up at your home to leave the parcel. If you think he's vandalised your car, what else is he capable of?'

'I don't know, but I wish you'd just stop talking about it.' She turns and picks up a cloth to wipe the already clean surface – she has a cleaner come round three times a week, so the place is spotless. She's obviously trying to avoid this conversation, but why? Clearly, she's not telling me everything. It must be something to do with the car; why would she be lying on the ground checking underneath?

Then it hits me. 'Oh. My. God. You think *he's* put a *tracker* on your car?'

'No I *don't*, Lucy.' She throws her hands in the air. 'This is not an episode of *The Wire*. People on Mulberry Avenue don't have trackers put on their cars.'

'Who knows what goes on here?'

She rolls her eyes and throws the damp cloth into the sink. 'Stop making out something's going on when it isn't.'

'You stop making out nothing's going on when it *is*!' I snap back, and we look at each other and I notice the glimmer of a smile.

'You're impossible,' she sighs.

'No, *you* are.'

'No, *you* are.' And we both start laughing. We can never be angry with each other for long.

'You know,' I say, pretending like this just occurred to me, 'the more it happens, the more I'm beginning to think it might be someone you know…'

'Well it isn't Ben, if that's what you're thinking.'

'You can't rule him out – have you seen anything of him since…?'

'Since last week? No, but there's a chance he might call. He might come over. I caught him looking at me yesterday at work. I know that look,' she says, her eyes going all misty.

'Just be extra cautious. Stay with us and if Ben calls you can always meet him here.'

'I don't know, Lucy. You and Matt have been very kind, but I feel like I can't intrude on you any more.'

'Amber, you aren't intruding, you're a friend. We love having you over. I hate to think of you alone here, scared to death at every little noise in the middle of the night. I understand you want to live your life, and if you want to spend time with Ben – or anyone else – it isn't ideal or romantic meeting up in your neighbour's house. But I just don't think it's wise to be on your own at night in your house until we know this weirdo has stopped.'

'But I haven't had a text in over a week and the alarm has been checked and now it's working…'

'Amber, he may not try and get into your house, he might just watch. What if he leaps out one night when you're out? Within seconds you could be lying in the gutter on a dark, empty road… or God knows, he could do that thing burglars do and short circuit the alarm. You aren't safe until they've got him.'

'Lucy, you're scaring me,' she says.

'I'm sorry, but you need to take this seriously. You haven't heard from him for over a week, but he might just be sitting in his dank little flat somewhere making plans. This is exactly what he wants – for you to think that he's stopped so that he can catch you out.'

But again she rolls her eyes. She's had creepy texts, a dead bird, and he's maybe done something to her car, but it's like nothing seems to touch her. I wonder what it would take for her to be *really* scared.

'I can't believe the police aren't going to put a trace on your phone, or that they haven't wanted to talk to your friends, exes… admirers?' I start, and glimpse the ghost of a smile and wonder if she thinks I'm faintly ridiculous for taking this so seriously. I know she thinks I'm overreacting, but she doesn't realise just how bad this could get.

She heads out of the kitchen and I follow her into the hall. She makes her way upstairs and, halfway up, turns to me.

'I'm off to work soon, Luce. Got to get ready now, so I'll see you tomorrow?'

'Sure I can't give you a lift?'

She stands for a moment looking annoyed. 'I can't ever just say no to you, Lucy, because you just won't take no for an answer.' She then seems to realise how this sounds and tempers it with a giggle. 'I was only joking!' she says, and we both know she wasn't.

Sometimes I wonder if Kirsty might be right and Amber picks me up and drops me at her whim.

She leans over the huge bannister and looks down on me.

'Hey, Lucy, I'm sorry if you're upset. I think this is getting to you more than me. What can I do to make it better? I know, is there anything girlie on at the cinema this week? We should go, do the popcorn thing?' She gives me a big smile.

'I'll check the listings,' I say sulkily, though secretly I'm quite pleased – there's a new Emma Stone movie out and it looks hilarious and romantic. 'Okay, I'll get off now, but be careful.'

'Okay, okay. I'll make sure I leave the studio with a male colleague,' she says. 'Someone big and butch and handsome.'

'Anyone in particular?' I bite back.

Her face lights up. 'Who knows…' she says, throwing me a crumb, letting me peep into her world. She often does this: opens up a little chink of light, a little sparkle of something just to intrigue me before closing it shut again. It can be quite frustrating, but I keep coming back for more, because it's a lot more than most people get from Amber.

'Do you think you'll ever be over Ben?' I ask.

Still leaning on the bannister, her face turns all dreamy.

'I don't know.' She looks at me almost defiantly. 'I can't lie, I still sometimes wonder if things might—'

'Would you take him back?' I hope not. He isn't good for her. I just know he'll break her heart again.

She looks up at the ceiling for inspiration, stretches out her arms and brings them back down onto the bannister, leaning on them, swaying softly. 'If I did, it would be on my terms. I'd be in the driving seat, and this time I'd want the fairy tale. I want what you and Matt have.'

I soften at this. 'Ahh, that's sweet,' I say. Though privately I think she might be being unrealistic. We're such different people to her and Ben.

'You and Matt have this lovely ease with each other, a mutual, supportive, loving thing – I envy you.'

I'm touched and a little surprised by this. Whoever would have thought that Amber Young would be envious of little old me?

'Yeah, Matt and I are happy,' I say, then I pause to reflect, 'but sometimes – I know it sounds mad – I feel lonely, like he just cares about what play he's involved in that week. I think about your exciting life in TV, the way you can click your fingers and have any man you want… and I envy you too.'

'The grass is always greener,' she sighs. She's right. We often look over at a friend's life or a neighbour's house and wish we had something they had, but we don't know what goes on behind closed doors.

'So, I'll see you later… that is, on the TV?' I say as I walk to the door.

'Yep, you'll see me after the late bulletin tonight.'

'You're going in very early if you're not on till that late.'

'Yeah, I'm going in early because I'm doing… other stuff.'

'Ooh, is it something special? Are you doing that on-screen reporting they keep promising?' I know it's her dearest wish to do reporting and presenting like she used to, so stop and wait for her to tell me all about it, but she doesn't.

'Oh no, nothing special… I'm just working on something behind the scenes… Anyway, bye babe. See you later.' And she disappears upstairs, leaving me to let myself out.

I walk back home knowing something doesn't add up. Is she just keeping things to herself because she doesn't want to worry me – or is she lying? And if she's lying to me – why?

I wasn't a typical teenager. I didn't socialise, never went to school discos, didn't hang around on street corners with the rest of them. I was at my happiest after the evening news, lulled to sleep by the safety and reassurance of nightly weather reports, moving gently from cold to warm from sunny to cloudy. If it was sunny, she took all the credit, but if rain was forecast, she prepared viewers with a polite apology – like it was her fault it would piss down all over bank holiday weekend. I loved the weather girl. She was always there for me – unlike my slut of a mother.

CHAPTER ELEVEN

Lucy

Later that evening, Matt and I watch Amber delivering the late weather forecast on TV. As always, it feels surreal to see my best friend on screen. So near and yet so far.

'She looks good tonight in that blue top,' I murmur.

Matt's busy with a script for the local amateur dramatics group – as if running a school drama department isn't enough! He's only half watching Amber as she predicts the next day's late summer weather.

'Yeah. Blue's good on her,' he has to admit, but I sense Mr Nasty coming in. He'll want to follow this up with a criticism or perhaps another comment about when she'll be moving back to hers, so I step in before he gets the chance.

'Amber was saying today that we have a great relationship.'

'Who does?'

'You and me, dipstick!'

'Oh, *that* relationship,' he mutters. As usual he's engrossed in what he's doing, but that doesn't stop me continuing the conversation.

'She's doing well to hold everything together. So calm on screen, but underneath she's really going through it,' I say, adding a little drama to get his attention.

He looks up. 'What do you mean?'

'Her car's been scratched – I think it's her stalker… I reckon he crashed into it deliberately.' Okay, I'm laying it on a bit thick, but I have to so he takes it all more seriously and doesn't dismiss it as 'some nutter'.

'What, you mean crashed into her car with *his*?' He looks doubtful.

'I don't know. When I popped over earlier, she seemed convinced that someone had either scratched it or bumped it.'

'Have there been any more wildlife deliveries? What did the police say about the feathered friend in the end?' he asks rather flippantly. It might be funny to him, but it isn't to Amber.

'Who knows what they said? She hasn't really told me.'

'Do you think she even actually spoke to the police?' He's still only half engaged; his mind's clearly on his script.

'Of course she has – they came on the Wednesday afternoon. I told you, I was pissed off because they didn't wait for me…' Has he not been listening to anything I've told him about Amber's situation for the last couple of weeks? This whole thing has made me realise Matt doesn't seem to take anyone else's problems seriously.

'So you've only got her word that she's spoken to the police?'

'I suppose so.' I turn to look at him. 'What do you mean?' I ask.

'I don't know… I just wonder if she might have called them and asked them not to bother. Perhaps she doesn't *want* the police involved… or maybe she has something to hide?'

My stomach twists slightly – I hate to admit it, but he has a point. She didn't want me to call them from JoJo's and there's no proof she gave a statement. Even if she did, I don't know what she told them – that's if they even turned up at all. But then again, she's my friend, and I shouldn't be so mistrustful. I just wish Matt wasn't so negative about her. It makes me question what she says and does – and then I doubt her too.

'I doubt she has anything to hide. It's probably because she just didn't want a fuss,' I say, irritated that Matt doubts my friend. This is the person who gives me more time than he does, the friend with whom I share dinners, drinks, sleepovers and secrets.

Without her my life would feel quite empty now, so I just wish he'd stop using every opportunity to put her down, because she really doesn't deserve it.

He puts the pencil he's using to his mouth. It reminds me of the way he held Sherlock Holmes' pipe last Christmas in the Manchester Drama Society's version of *The Speckled Band*. Being a thwarted actor, Matt sometimes likes to play a part and it really grates on me. He takes the pencil away. 'Lucy, what I'm thinking is… is there really a stalker, or is it Amber *pretending* there is?'

'Don't be so stupid.' I don't want to hear this. 'Of *course* there's a stalker. Why would she lie about something like that?'

'I don't know.' He raises his eyebrows in a disbelieving way. 'Seems to me that she isn't happy unless everyone's looking at her. Amber has to be the star. Like the other night… going on about her glory days in telly, and how she went out with royalty, and everyone had a crush on her.'

I laugh. 'Matt, now you're exaggerating. She was explaining how hard it is for women who work in TV. She said men expected to sleep with her for work – she never said they had *crushes* on her. That's quite different.'

'Well, that's what it sounded like to me,' he says, and is soon back in his am-dram world of script marking and scene setting.

Amber had talked quite a lot about her career that night, it's true. She'd told us about the different people she'd worked with and the fun they'd had. But she'd also described the sexism, the unequal pay, the unwanted attention and propositions made by male colleagues. I'd found it fascinating, and assumed Matt was enjoying it too. Perhaps I was so swept up in it myself I wasn't aware that he was bored?

'I think she was trying to distract herself by chatting about her work, but I could tell she was also thinking about the texts, and being watched. She *was* upset, Matt. I thought she might cry at one point.'

He shakes his head. 'Well, if I'd just had a text like that, or received a dead bird, I reckon I'd be sitting in my bedroom clutching a knife, not bragging about who I could have slept with and laughing my head off about some prank played on a news reader in 1998.'

'People deal with things in their own way. God, Matt, you always try and belittle things that happen to other people. You say that Amber wants to be the star but no one's got a bigger ego than you… always putting people down,' I snap, incensed at how he's being so dismissive.

But – typical Matt – he just shrugs and carries on leafing through the script like I'm not here. I know what he's doing. He knows ignoring me when I'm annoyed and want to discuss something really winds me up. I want to talk through our disagreements, but he wants to sulk through them. That's what our marriage has become: a competition about who can quietly hurt and irritate the other the most. When did that happen?

'You're trying to dismiss this whole thing because it isn't about you,' I say, refusing to let him win. 'Let's face it, Matt, you'd love a bloody stalker. You'd dine out on it for years, tell all the little teenagers at school, pretending like you're a real actor with a deranged fan!'

I know I'm being mean, but I'm angry and want to nip this constant Amber-sniping in the bud. I'm absolutely sick of it. I battle with Kirsty's sly remarks at work and Matt's comments at home. At the very least, I don't want Matt making dubious comments suggesting she's not all she seems the next time she's here. Which could be tonight when she returns from work. She won't want to go back to hers late and alone, and she has her own key so she'll probably come back here. I just don't want Matt making any comments about how long she's staying over the bloody toast and marmalade in the morning.

'I know you value this friendship, but you're always defending her – you're like a tiger mother,' he says, irritated.

'Only because you're being so unfair, Matt. Yes, perhaps I do overreact, but I'm bloody angry.'

He continues to look at his script as he delivers his killer blow: 'Perhaps it was for the best that we couldn't have kids.'

I am shocked rigid. And in an instant I'm fired up. He's lit the touchpaper, and I can't help it – when he looks up from his script, I lean in and slap him hard in the face. I've never done anything like this to Matt before and I'm as shocked as he is. I pull back, and we both look at each other, startled by my actions. I stand up from the sofa, aware there's a red hand mark already forming on the side of his cheek. 'You get really nasty, really quick, these days, Matt,' I say. 'Perhaps you should take out your frustrations somewhere else – not on your wife. I don't deserve that.'

He looks at me, but I can't read his eyes. He knows what he said hit right where it hurt and even now he's probably regretting it, but it's too late. I'm also regretting my own reaction; the slap was too far and I hate myself as much as I hate him right now. There's a cocktail of resentment and shame whirling around my stomach and I can't look at him, so I pick up my cardigan, pull it around me protectively and go upstairs to bed. Once there I cry quietly for the children we never had and for the marriage, which feels like it's disintegrating under the weight of our disappointment. And I cry for myself, and how my life turned out, the sadness and regret from my past still living in the present. Perhaps I *would* have been a tiger mother, but that doesn't mean I'd have been a bad mother, just a caring one. I can't redeem myself, but I might have been able to erase the past and blot out my own childhood by creating another one.

Later, I hear the front door bang. I sit up, wondering where he's going. I hear the car start and look at the time: almost midnight. For the next hour I keep climbing out of bed, pacing the room and looking through the window to see if his car's back. Once, after a big row, he parked round the corner all night – I was absolutely in bits worrying about him: had he been involved in an accident, had he moved out, was he with another woman? I knew in my heart none of these were probable, but nor did I think he'd park round the corner and sleep in the freezing cold just to hurt me. Who knows the lengths nice, normal people will go to when they've been hurt? I imagine he's just gone driving around to let off steam tonight, but the longer he is away, the more I worry that this time he really has had an accident.

It's almost 2 a.m. when I hear the door bang downstairs, and with all the racket he's making I assume he's trying to wake me up. I don't know if this is just another way of making me angry, or if he wants to wake me up so we can make up after that awful row, but I'm still not ready for that. I can be quite stubborn and I need a night's sleep before we can be us again.

When he eventually comes into the bedroom, I pretend to be asleep. I'm not ready to discuss what happened tonight. I'm still hurt and angry. I also feel bad about the slap and he'll probably want to talk about why that happened too. I don't. Matt will be calm by now but I'm still stinging and am likely to shout and lash out and I'm filled with self-doubt about control and emotion, slipping back to a place I used to be, where I can't trust myself.

Once Matt's in bed and safely asleep, I lie there a while and after an hour or so I've worked through my feelings and my anger and irritation begin to melt. I love Matt, he's my husband, and one of the very few people in my life who's ever loved me.

I roll over and curl my body softly around him; he's back and we're safe and in our bed – it's the best feeling in the world.

CHAPTER TWELVE

Lucy

The morning after our row, I wake up and Matt's asleep in bed next to me. I feel so bad about the night before and when he wakes he looks at me, kisses me and says how sorry he is.

'Me too,' I say. 'I was worried about you, just driving off into the night. Where did you go?'

'Amber called. She was stranded at work; I had to collect her.'

'Amber? Oh no, was she okay? Why didn't she ring me?'

'Apparently you didn't answer… It was late.'

I check my new phone at the side of the bed: five missed calls. I'd put my phone on silent after storming upstairs after our row.

'She came out of work and one of her tyres had been slashed,' he says, and I'm pleased to see that for once he seems concerned about Amber's predicament.

'Oh my God, I knew it! I told her he hadn't gone away. Did she call the police? Did she see anyone? Was she upset?'

'Don't know. She just wanted to get home. She was tired; we didn't really talk.'

'Thank goodness you picked up your phone,' I say. 'God knows what might have happened if you hadn't rescued her.'

He smiles at this; I think he likes playing the knight in shining armour – it doesn't matter who the damsel is that's in distress.

'I feel like a bad friend. I'm supposed to be there for her and haven't even checked my phone since last night,' I say. I'd been so angry and upset with Matt, I hadn't given Amber a second thought.

'She wanted you. I think she was disappointed when I offered to go. I don't make the same kind of fuss as you.' He laughs. 'I just said, "Okay, I'll come and change the tyre," but when I got to the studio there was a load of hassle because the security guard wouldn't let me into the car park. Even when Amber told him I'd come to help her, I still had to fill in loads of forms. They gave me a temporary pass – like bloody Fort Knox. It's a regional TV studio, not the BBC – ridiculous really.'

'Oh, babe, thanks for going. Sounds like a nightmare. You should have woken me. I'd have come with you.'

'I didn't want to wake you... Let's face it, things were a bit tense between us last night.'

'Sorry, about—'

'It's okay, I shouldn't have said what I did. I deserved a slap.'

He puts his arm around me and we lie together for a few minutes, regrouping.

'She shouldn't have gone home on her own last night. Did you invite her to stay here?'

'Yeah, yeah, but she said she'd be okay. I went over there when we got back, made sure she was safe.'

'Ahh, that's so lovely of you, thank you.' I kiss him. Perhaps he'll stop being mean about Amber now they've had a chance to bond? 'Amber thinks I'm making more of it than there is,' I say. 'But a slashed tyre? Surely that's serious enough for her to admit there's a real problem?'

'She knows; she was scared last night, but you know what she's like.'

'Mmm. She brushes it off.'

'Yeah she does, but she also loves the attention it brings from you. She's like a child constantly putting her hand up so the teacher will notice.' He smiles at this. I hadn't seen the dynamics quite like that – I felt it was me always trying to get *her* attention, wanting her to notice me. I'm flattered he thinks differently. 'Sorry again… about what I said last night.' He touches my face with the back of his hand. 'You know I'm gutted we didn't have kids.'

'I know. But you really hurt me when you said that, Matt.'

'I'm sorry. It was unforgivable of me – you'd have made a great mum.'

'I think I would have too… but I can see what you mean, about me being a little bit overprotective… especially with Amber,' I say, as his hands pull my nightdress up over my thighs.

'A *little* bit protective?' he murmurs into my neck. 'Anyone would think you were in love with her the way you go on.'

'Oh God, Matt, what a thing to say!'

I move thoughts of Amber from my head and my bed as Matt gently moves on top of me. I feel his need, his longing. We haven't made love in a while – it hasn't been easy with Amber around. But here, now, he wants me so much. I feel desired, loved. I can feel the hurt, the open wound from our words the night before, beginning to soothe and heal. Sex is the perfect poultice for pain. And when it's over, we kiss again and say we're sorry again and we are us once more. We're Lucy and Matt, the couple from number 7 – the teachers with the lovely home and no kids. That's our story. I realise I'm a bit much for Matt sometimes, but with no babies to care for there's a lot of love with nowhere to go. I just need someone to soak up the excess because sometimes my feelings overwhelm us both. Thank God I have the kids at school to care about – and, of course, I have Amber to talk to.

We spend the morning in bed. Matt brings me coffee and toast and we remember again why we're together.

'This is nice,' I say, and while everything's so good between us, I decide to open up to him a bit about how I've been feeling.

'I know you're busy with the production, but when you're up in your office working on scripts and stage directions, I sometimes feel a bit like you've forgotten me.'

'I'm sorry – you know what I'm like, I love what I do. Without drama, who knows where I'd be now?'

Matt never knew his father, and his mother died when he was only fifteen, and he always says if he hadn't had drama and the theatre he'd probably have been a mess. Like me, he had to turn his life around at an early age to give himself a chance, and sometimes I think that's what drew us together. We were two lost children looking for somewhere safe, and for someone who would love us.

'I need to give you more attention, I know that. I love you Lucy,' he says, and in this moment I feel so lucky. We've weathered the storm of loss, and now we're adjusting to what we are and coming through the other side. Of course there will be ups and downs, but nothing we can't handle together.

'I love you too.' I smile. 'It's good to have you to myself, not sharing you with your latest production… for the next few minutes at least!' I joke.

'You know it's important to me though, don't you? Drama is the only thing that helps me escape all the day-to-day worries. Maybe it sounds silly, but I need it in my life.'

'Yeah, I know, but don't let it take you over. You become so engrossed, it's like a bloody obsession. During the rehearsals for *The Speckled Band* last Christmas I barely saw you… I thought you'd run off with the woman playing Sherlock Holmes' housekeeper.'

He laughs. 'Did you see her?'

'Don't be mean. I'm sure she's a lovely person.'

'I promise I'll try not to let it take over. I do get carried away, but you have to promise you won't let *your* obsession take over either.' He smiles.

'What?'

'This obsession with Amber. When you're not with her, you're talking about her and worrying about what she's doing… or thinking her so-called stalker's hiding in the bushes.'

I groan; not this again. Why didn't he believe her?

'I'm not obsessed, I just like her; she's interesting… fun.'

'Famous?'

I process that and realise there is some truth to it. 'Yes, I suppose I do quite love the fact that she might have once slept with a royal prince and danced with George Clooney on a yacht in Cannes, but that isn't why I'm her friend. I like her because she's funny, and kind, and has time to listen. I like having a non-mummy friend who makes me feel like I can do anything. I've just felt so much more confident since I became friends with her. She's good for me. And don't refer to the stalker as a "so-called stalker" – he *does* exist, Matt.'

'Yeah, but as I've pointed out before, no one's actually *seen* him, have they?'

I shrug. 'Last night you had to rescue her when he slashed her tyres!'

'Yeah, but given the hassle security gave me to get in the bloody car park, you have to wonder how the stalker got in without a pass.'

'So you think it might be someone already there… someone who has a pass? A work colleague?' I suggest.

'That would be my guess.'

When he's gone to work on his script, I think again about Matt's insistence that no one has ever seen this stalker. But he obviously does exist – I've seen a text and was there when she found the dead bird, and now Matt's seen the slashed tyres and I think he's coming round to at least knowing someone's out there and that he isn't a figment of Amber's imagination. There are other things, though, that I'm not sure are real. I think Amber might tell some little white lies. She told me a couple of weeks ago that she was off to Cannes again with friends for the weekend, but I swear I saw a woman at the window upstairs *after* she'd driven off to the airport. Amber left at 6 p.m. and I know her cleaner visits on a Monday and Thursday morning, so that doesn't explain it, and the next day there were two Prosecco bottles in her bin that hadn't been there the previous evening. Was it Amber, and therefore was she lying about being in Cannes to make herself look good – and if that was the case what else is she lying about? Because if it wasn't her, who was it? And why did she leave early for work yesterday – the day of the tyre slashing – and wouldn't say why? She also told me the police had been before I arrived on Wednesday, but she didn't to want to talk about it and there's been no more contact from them. As Matt said, has she really spoken to the police or just told me she has? And if so, why? I'm sure all these things are insignificant and can be explained quite simply – but sometimes I feel like she might be hiding things from me. Amber certainly has her secrets, and being the sort of person that I am, and her friend of course, I can't help but be curious.

On Saturday morning I call her to see what time she wants to meet to go out for our usual Saturday afternoon retail and coffee therapy, as we call it. She doesn't pick up, so I leave a message, then I text her to ask if she's okay because she doesn't always check her voicemail. She's obviously busy because she doesn't get back to me, and as Matt's busy writing I give Kirsty a call. She's a little frosty at first, but after I've warmed her up and told her some slightly scandalous school gossip about the prim music teacher and the head of English, we are somewhat more bonded and she agrees to meet up for a sandwich in the pub, where an hour later I'm filling her in on the latest dramatic events in Amber's life.

'Her tyres?' She's chewing on her prawn mayo baguette and looking very doubtful.

'Yes… slashed to ribbons, Matt says.'

'Well, Matt's a bloody saint. Pete wouldn't have gone out in the middle of the night to fix someone's car.'

'Yeah, well, I think it broke the ice with them. Matt seems to have come round a bit,' I say, disappointed with my roast beef on brown and wishing I'd had the prawn too.

'So where is she today? Don't you two usually spend Saturday shopping together?'

'No,' I lie, wondering how she knows. If and when we're talking, I rarely tell Kirsty about what I do with Amber. I know it only upsets her and it isn't worth it.

'I wonder who hates her enough to slash her tyres?' she's saying, clearly relishing this.

'No one hates her. It's clearly him, the stalker. And he doesn't *hate* her! He's obsessed, crazy for her.'

'He must be crazy to be obsessed with *her*.' She laughs, and I realise that, try as I might, I don't enjoy Kirsty's company like I used to – I never imagined she could be so mean. I ignore her remark and change the subject, but inside I'm angry. Amber never says anything nasty about her, but Kirsty seems hell-bent on turning every little piece of information about Amber into something barbed. I find it uncomfortable, and once we've finished our sandwiches I tell her I have loads of marking to do and we head off in separate directions.

Once home, I check my phone and the landline, but there's still no communication from Amber, so I call her again. I suddenly feel guilty that instead of checking she was okay first, I just went out with Kirsty. 'I'm worried about you,' I say to her voicemail. 'I can see your car outside the house so wonder why you aren't responding to my calls and texts.' I remind myself this isn't unusual, in fact it's classic Amber. On several occasions I've rung and left messages, texts, and ages afterwards she eventually gets back to me saying she couldn't find her phone/dropped it down the loo/had no signal. The Wi-Fi and phone signals aren't great here – it's a bit of a black spot – so perhaps she has sent me a message or tried to call? Perhaps I'm just worrying about nothing.

It's three hours later when I call her and she finally picks up.

'I was having a nap,' she says.

'Oh, sorry, did I wake you?'

'Kind of, but I didn't want to stay in bed all day, so probably just as well.'

'I had coffee with Kirsty,' I volunteer, for something to say.

'Nice. Was Matt working on his play?'

'No, he went off to the gym,' I say. 'He announced this morning that he's going to work on his body as well as his mind. He's swapped one obsession for another,' I add, trying to start a conversation, but it seems she's in one of her moods.

'Look, Lucy, I'm not being funny, but I have the most awful headache and I just need to sleep.'

'Oh, I'm sorry, I'll let you go,' I say, hurt. I thought our friendship was beyond her dismissing me when it wasn't convenient. She did this when we first met. She can be so chilly sometimes, and I'm supposed to be her best friend.

'Thanks…'

'I could call round later? We could get a takeaway and watch a film?' I say hopefully, refusing to let her dismiss me so easily. 'Matt's out tonight – still up to his neck in sodding *Bugsy* at the moment.'

'Perhaps… Look, can I let you know? Thing is, my head is pounding. I really need to sleep. Let's talk later, yes?'

'Oh, okay. I'll let you get some sleep.'

'Thank you.'

'Would you like me to pop round to make you some chamomile tea? It helps with headaches. It's very soothing.'

'That's so lovely of you – but I'm incredibly tired, and not much fun. I think I might just turn off the phone, put my feet up and chill.'

At least that rejection was a little more polite, less chilly.

'Okay, well, if you need company…'

'I'll call you, yes, definitely.'

And she clicks the phone off. I know she says she's got a headache, but I can't help feeling put out that she clearly doesn't want me to go round. We're friends, and even if you're not well and want to chill, you can always chill with a friend, and I could have made her some restorative chamomile tea. Her loss I suppose.

I spend this free time doing some overdue marking, but can't stop my mind wandering back to conversations I've had with Kirsty, and though I try to push them away I find myself wondering if she might be right, that Amber just picks me up and drops me at her whim. She's happy to spend evenings with me when she's too scared to go home, makes me late for work when she gets horrible 'gifts' and needs me there, but today she doesn't need me, and I know I'm oversensitive, but I can't help feeling a little bruised.

If the evening's weather forecast predicted rain and cold, that was good news. I could run home, close the door and put the TV on straight after school. No one would be hanging around street corners; even school bullies hated rain. If the weather was warm, they'd all be out, like worms coming up for air. I hated other children – and they hated me.

CHAPTER THIRTEEN

Lucy

'Have you seen Amber?' I say to Matt on Monday morning.

We're having breakfast… well, I'm popping toast in the toaster and he's making coffee, both rushing round like headless chickens getting ready for work.

'No… I haven't seen her. Why?'

'She's just been a bit funny this weekend. She didn't want to meet up Saturday afternoon, said she'd let me know about a film and takeaway here, but never called me back. Then yesterday I called her and she said she was busy and didn't ask to stay over either… I think she's being a bit funny.'

'What do you mean, "funny"?' he says, sitting in front of a slice of toast but not eating it.

'Just a bit moody. You know how she is… Was everything okay with her, when you changed her tyre?' I've been thinking about it and Amber and I haven't actually got together since then, and I don't want to wind Matt up but I wonder if he offended her in some way. Perhaps he was a bit off, gave her the feeling of being unwanted?

'Of course, she was fine,' he says absently, pouring us both a coffee.

'Was she chatty? Did you talk?'

'Yeah but was after three by then and we were both really tired, and I think we both just wanted to get some sleep. It took me ages to fix that tyre.'

'I know bloody hell, Matt, you were gone more than *three hours* – Amber would've been better off calling the breakdown people.'

'It would have taken just as long by the time they'd got there,' he says, sounding slightly offended by my implication that another man might have done a better job. He gets up suddenly, kisses my cheek and heads for the door, and is just about to leave when the landline rings. He's hanging around by the front door to see if it's for him as I answer it.

I cover the phone with my hand. 'It's Amber,' I say, surprised and delighted to hear from her after the AWOL weekend. He rolls his eyes and I turn away to talk to her.

'Hi, sweetie, you okay?' I ask.

'Oh, Lucy, I don't know what to do… Something really weird happened.' Her voice is trembling, like she's about to cry.

'What… what's happened? Tell me,' I say, looking over at Matt. He shoots me a look back, and from the way the blood drains from his face I think it's finally sinking in with him just how serious Amber's situation is.

'I was woken up this morning by the sound of water running,' she says. 'I thought it was a leak, some burst pipes or something. But then when I went into the main bathroom both taps were full on.'

'Oh… Do you think it's a plumbing problem?' I say, relieved we're back to how we were – no awkwardness, no chill coming from her on the other end of the phone.

'No, because after I'd turned those taps off, I heard a noise downstairs, but I couldn't see anyone, so I made a cup of tea. It was only 6 a.m. though, so I went back upstairs and when I got up there the taps had been turned on in my en suite too! Lucy.' I hear the shiver in her voice. 'He's been in my bedroom.'

'Oh my God, no!' I say loudly, making Matt start slightly. He's looking at me, desperate to leave but intrigued and asking a silent 'what?' but I just shake my head at him. I don't have time to repeat what she's saying. I'll tell him once I'm off the phone.

'And that wasn't all. I turned them off,' she continues, 'and I could still hear running water, so I went downstairs again and it was the kitchen taps this time *and* the downstairs toilet. Full on taps just gushing.'

'Now, are you sure you didn't leave them on?' I say in the calmest voice I can muster.

'No, I didn't leave them on. Definitely not. Lucy, it's creeping me the fuck OUT.'

'Come over here now,' I say. 'He might still be there.'

'No, there's no one here now, and I've turned off all the taps. I'm so scared I can't move, Lucy.'

'I'm on my way, sit tight,' I say, and click off the phone, grab my bag and briefly explain the situation to Matt.

'It's probably something technical,' he says. 'If I had time I'd go round and have a look.' But I'm glad he doesn't because he wouldn't be able to help. In all honesty, Matt doesn't have a clue about plumbing, but like so many men, pretends that he does. 'Call a plumber out – the water pressure's probably up… or down,' he adds before leaving.

When I get over there, she's a mess, and looks like she hasn't slept all night. She's been crying and she's shaking and for the first time since the dead bird I see real fear – this has really freaked her out. There's no one else to look after her and clearly this is going to take a while, so reluctantly I call the school to say I'm going to be late. I'd never been late for work in my life until I met Amber, and now I've been late twice in as many weeks, and it doesn't go down well. But what choice do I have? Amber is like family and you drop everything for family.

'We should get a plumber in,' I say when I get there. I can't see anything wrong with the taps, but then I'm no expert. 'With any luck it might just be a technical problem… not a… not *him*.'

'But the taps in my en suite were on. He must have…'

'Not necessarily. It could just be your water pressure,' I suggest lamely, repeating Matt's theory, which was no doubt plucked from thin air.

She shakes her head, which is currently in her hands as we sit up at the kitchen counter island. 'Lucy, I've googled it, and can't see anything about taps just coming on in the night.'

'It could be ghosts,' I try and joke.

'Thanks. If I wasn't scared before I am now. It's a brand new house anyway,' she says, a glimmer of irritation infusing her words. She isn't in the mood for jokes, and I don't blame her. She's going through some kind of hell. I need to be more sensitive.

'I'm sure it will be fine. We'll get a plumber out and he'll put our minds at rest, I'm sure.'

She sits there, pale and listless, and when she doesn't move I take it upon myself to search for a plumber.

Eventually, after many fruitless calls, I find a plumber who can come out today, but he can't be here until 5 p.m., and as Amber's on the late shift she'll have gone to work by then.

'No problem,' I say. 'I can let him in when I get back from work, stay with him, then lock up after and set the alarm.'

She looks so relieved, I think she might cry again, so I put my arms around her.

'It will be fine,' I say into her ear, not totally convinced.

'You're such a good friend. I don't deserve you, Lucy,' she says, and bursts into tears while I hug her and just let her cry it out. After a little while, I find her some tissues, make a cup of green tea and she sips it slowly, which seems to calm her down a little, but her fear is still palpable.

'I'd better get to work now,' I say reluctantly. 'I hate to leave you, but I also can't leave a class of thirty six-year-olds with my teaching assistant – they'll destroy her.' I laugh, and Amber summons a faint smile.

'So you'll be okay to let the plumber in?' she says, looking up from her mug of steaming tea.

'Yes. I've got those keys you gave me for emergencies in the drawer at home, so I can easily let him in and make sure everything's okay.'

I hate leaving her, and as she waves from the door, I wind down my window and remind her to double-lock the door when I've gone. This has really knocked her. She's been scared before, but always managed to temper it with a little bravado, but now she isn't even trying. She seems so fragile, so vulnerable. Given all the creepy things that have been happening, it seems this is the final straw. And whatever Amber has said in the past about it being nothing to worry about, and part of the job, if the plumber can't find the answer, she's going to have to face the difficult truth. This isn't some random nutter – someone is stalking her, someone who knows where she lives and who's been in her house as she sleeps.

When I arrive at Amber's later after work, the plumber's as good as his word, and turns up at five. I tell him what happened and he looks at me like I'm mad when I ask if he's ever come across taps just turning themselves on throughout the house before.

'No,' he says.

'Would someone actually have to turn them on?' I ask, already knowing the answer.

'Yes.' He isn't going to elaborate. Instead he says, 'I'll get the radiators bled first, then look at your water pressure… then I'll replace the washers in your taps… and if that fails…'

'Yes?'

'Call a priest.' He laughs and turns away.

I make Chris, the plumber, a cup of tea with the requested three sugars, and imagine the horror on Amber's face. She's always dieting and working out; her body is great for someone in their forties, and she puts it down to low sugar. I don't point out the gallons of Prosecco she consumes on a regular basis when she tells me sugar is evil.

So Chris bleeds the radiators, checks the water pressure, then fiddles with the handles of the taps in the kitchen, undoes one of them, looks up it, then screws the top back on and says, 'Nothing wrong with those. All the washers are new. I reckon you've definitely got a poltergeist… or someone's playing tricks.' He laughs, but it makes the hairs on my neck stand up.

I pay him and thank him for his expert plumbing/psychic diagnosis and let him out through the front door, double-locking it when he's gone. I head back down the hall wondering what it's like to be Amber Young alone in this big house by herself. I then realise if I'm doing 'a full Amber' I need to be barefoot, so I kick off my shoes, not caring where they land. As I walk around the house, you could hear a pin drop. I'm not used to this level of silence. I usually have a radio on, or Matt's singing or saying lines, but this is the quiet side of the crescent, with no kids playing out front. Amber's brand new windows and doors must keep the sound out – and in.

Despite being alone, I'm quite enjoying myself; it makes a nice change being here. Matt's working late – fresh from his success with the school play, he's directing the local amateur dramatics tonight. His head will be filled with lines and stage directions, and he won't even know I'm not home, so with no reason to rush home I sit on one of the big white sofas and leaf through Amber's glossy magazines. This is the kind of house you see in *Hello*, and I sit with my feet under me, like Amber does, imagining the magazine photo. I pose like a film star… okay, a soap star… a reality star perhaps?

I soon forget about the possibilities of stalkers or ghosts and make myself a cup of coffee using Amber's lovely cafetière. I carefully spoon in the ground beans and pour the scalding water on top, leaving the filter for a few minutes the way she does. I do a couple of twirls while I wait; the underfloor heating reminds me of paddling in warm water as a kid.

When it's ready, I drink coffee from her favourite cup and wonder what she thinks about, how she feels when she's alone in this perfect white space. She probably thinks about Ben, the one that got away… for now. But knowing Amber, I wouldn't be surprised if she wins him back; she's one of those people who always gets what she wants. I remember girls like her at school: long, shiny hair, skinny frames, a million suitors. I was never one of those girls. I was never asked to dance, never even asked out until Matt came along.

But who needs a man when you live somewhere as lovely as this? Every little detail has been thought of, from carousels inside the kitchen cupboards so you don't have to reach, to blinds on the ceiling windows. As Amber says, 'you get what you pay for', and I know this house must have cost her a fortune. It's the biggest on the estate. Mine and Matt's is one of the smaller, less luxurious models; we could never afford something like this. Running my fingers along the paintings in the hallway, I study the brushstrokes closely, putting my face right up to the pictures. I've never done this while Amber's around – she'd probably laugh at me, but I have this urge to touch everything, to own it.

I stop by the sunset painting, and gaze through the shades of sunset, from orange to pink to palest yellow, and a suggestion of snow-dusted mountains, shimmering in a melting amber sun. I can only imagine the bittersweet beauty of Nepal, a land ravaged by poverty, earthquakes and human conflict. I'd love to go there one day. I've always wanted to travel the world, see other places, other people, work with children who need education, support, survival. But for now I'll just enjoy the painting and imagine what it's like to watch the sun set over the Himalayas, as Amber did all those years ago.

I move through into the hall, and wonder about the other rooms. Considering we've been friends for a year now, Amber's never shown me the whole house.

'I never tell someone everything about me,' she said once. 'That way they can't hurt you – always keep a little bit back.' When I asked for 'the tour' – cheeky I know – she didn't take me on, but I think I have earned a little peek now here and there. After all, I'm her friend, I'd never hurt her. And we shouldn't have secrets.

First, I investigate the lovely dining room (which looks like no one has ever eaten there), with a solid white table and chairs in the centre, the only colour a splash of pink on one wall. I sit on the chairs, feeling like Goldilocks, trying them for size, picking up the beautiful bowls adorning the sideboard and imagining a dinner party. Me, Amber and Matt all sitting around this huge table enjoying a takeaway and Prosecco, while Amber shares the latest stories from behind the scenes in TV land. It might happen one day.

Then I leave that room, closing the door carefully, and cross the hall into what Amber always refers to rather grandly as 'the library'. But I'm stunned – it is just like a library, with wall-to-wall bookcases and one of those ladders that's on castors and moves around the room so no book is out of reach. I place my palm on the spines, lift them from their shelves and open them, flicking through the pages with my fingers, breathing in the words, the dust and nostalgia. They aren't in alphabetical order, they're in clusters of colour – how very Amber. It's all about how things look; she probably hasn't read any of them. I smile at my eccentric, outrageous and perhaps a little shallow friend. Then just as I'm about to leave the library, I think I hear something drop; it startles me.

I wander back out into the huge hallway. It's probably nothing, but I stop for a few seconds to listen for any more sounds. I can't hear anything else, so decide to resume my self-guided tour, but double-check the front door is locked before I snoop any further.

Then I walk slowly to the sweeping staircase, and I can't explain it, but I have the feeling I'm not alone and turn round suddenly, holding on to the bannister with both hands in case anyone's there and I have to make a run for it. I stand very, very still, telling myself it's just my imagination. I wait and watch for a long time, and nothing. There's no one here; I'm being silly. I laugh loudly to myself – a kind of fake bravado to make me feel brave, when really I know in my heart I should just go now. But I have this urge to walk slowly up Amber's sweeping staircase, feeling like Norma Desmond in *Sunset Boulevard.*

'I'm ready for my close-up, Mr DeMille,' I mutter under my breath. But as I climb the stairs, my head high, feeling like a film star, I have the horrible feeling I'm not alone.

CHAPTER FOURTEEN

Lucy

Five hours later, I've never been so scared in my life. I'm sitting in a police station trying to explain everything, but I've never had to make a witness statement before, and despite seeing it happen on *Inspector Morse* and *Midsomer Murders*, this doesn't feel the same at all.

I've told DCI Manyon about the dead bird and the texts and the slashed tyre, but I don't think he's convinced. He just keeps looking at me with doubt in his eyes.

'So, tell us exactly what happened tonight, Mrs Metcalf – in your own words,' he asks now. He is sitting opposite me, a small tablet in front of him, with a notebook and a serious face.

'Okay.' I clear my throat, but no one offers me a drink of water, so I start, trying to remember what happened. 'The plumber left. I was in… the library I think… yes… when I heard something.'

'Something?'

'Yes, like someone had dropped some cutlery… a knife perhaps?' I offer, but he doesn't react. 'Then I remember standing in the hallway. I was looking up at the high square glass ceiling that pushes up through the house. There's this trendy chandelier that hangs down, very Amber,' I add as an aside, but he just sits there poker-faced, and I glance at the female detective who's joined us and is now also sitting opposite me. I hope I might get a little 'sisterhood' from her, but she doesn't flinch, making me feel even more nervous. 'So I went upstairs…' I say.

DC Manyon shuffles in his seat. 'Upstairs? Why did you need to go upstairs?' He seems irritated.

'To… check the taps were off.' Okay, I told a little white lie to the police, but it sounds better than admitting I was snooping around my friend's house, which sounds very dodgy.

'Oh.' He writes something down. 'So you checked the taps and came back downstairs?'

'No… not exactly… I went into Amber's bedroom… to check the taps in her en suite. And I honestly wasn't poking around or anything…' I add, immediately realising this may sound like I'm protesting too loudly.

I don't mention the beautiful pale pink silk robe hanging on the back of the door and how, as my hand glanced past the softness, it reminded me of my mother, causing my heart to twitch a little. I also don't mention how I couldn't resist taking it down and wrapping the Amber-scented pool of material around me. It felt wonderful, and I padded over to the huge mirror leaning against an almost blush-stained wall. Aware of my bare feet sinking into the softest wool carpet, I stood there, and I don't know what I expected to see in the mirror, but instead of slim, beautiful Amber with her shiny red bob and perfect, long neck, I was looking at a short, chubby woman with frizzy ginger hair. Even blush silk couldn't turn this sow's ear into an Amber silk purse, so, defeated, I took off the robe and put it back on the hook. But it kept falling off and in the end I had to jam it over the hook and hope Amber wouldn't notice. I'm thinking about all this when I remember where I am and I realise both officers are staring at me in anticipation of what I'm going to say next, so I bluster on.

'I was going to leave there and then, I really was, but something caught my eye. A photo of a young Amber in a frame by the side of her bed. I picked it up and looked at it. It must have been taken when she was on TV all the time, at the height of her fame

– all dressed up with her boyfriend Ben. They were a gorgeous couple… They aren't together now,' I add.

Manyon shifts in his seat and I wonder what he's making of this. Will they haul Ben in to be interviewed? In my opinion it's not the worst thing they could do. What I don't tell them is that when I put the photo back, I dropped the damned thing, and it hit the skirting board, cracking the glass right across the middle. I almost died, and put it back, but whichever way I stood it up that clean sharp line with little cracks emanating from it went right through the picture. I felt sick at the thought of her ever discovering I'd been rummaging around in her bedroom.

I also don't mention to Manyon and his mate that I opened her bedside drawer, partly because it makes me look weird and also because I don't think it's relevant. I don't know why I did it. Why do we do anything like that? Why do we look at other people's Facebook pages, people we barely know? Friends of friends of friends? We just want to look at other's lives, see how they do things, what it tells us about them and compare their lives to our own. Me opening up Amber's drawer was probably more primal – it was like when you're a kid and your mum says 'don't do that' and you're suddenly filled with this compulsion to do whatever it is you know you shouldn't.

I feel hot just thinking about the way I opened the drawer and looked through her stuff. At first there were no real surprises, just the usual detritus of women's bedside drawers and, coming to my senses, I felt ashamed at what I was doing and quickly tried to shut it. But for some reason I couldn't close the bloody thing and had to push my hand right to the back to see what was blocking it. I grabbed and pulled out a folded, glossy magazine which had got caught up and had to pull at it to get it out so I could close the drawer again. Obviously I looked at the magazine, which was dated only a couple of years back and was open to a page full of glamorous photos of some big TV event. That explained why

Amber had kept it – she must have attended the event – but on closer inspection I couldn't see any photos of her. Then I spotted Ben, looking handsome in a tux… and at his side was a beautiful blonde woman, but when I read the caption, I had to sit down on the bed. 'TV executive and recipient of the award for Best News Programme, Ben Bradshaw, with his wife, Geraldine'. I couldn't believe it.

'And then…?' DCI Manyon's looking at me, and I'm trying to make it seem like I'm telling him everything, but I'm not. I found something else in the drawer and had to stay in the bedroom for at least another ten minutes trying to compose myself before I heard the noise. But no way am I telling them.

'I was just leafing through a magazine on her bedside table when I heard a noise again downstairs,' I say, changing things slightly to save my embarrassment and shame – and perhaps Amber's too. 'And on the way out of the bedroom my eye was caught by something on the mirror of Amber's dressing table. My heart started beating so loudly I thought whoever might be downstairs might hear it.'

'And what was it you saw?' Manyon asks.

'Scrawled in red lipstick – *her* red lipstick – on the mirror, were two words: "fucking slut"!'

He's now writing this down, and the other detective is nodding slowly, like I just told them something really boring.

'Go on…' she says.

'So I'm standing in Amber's bedroom when I hear another noise downstairs and this time I wasn't mistaken. It was a clattering noise again and it was coming from the kitchen. I was really scared,' I add, thinking about how my chest was thudding so hard I thought I might actually have a heart attack. 'Then I thought it might be the plumber. Perhaps he'd forgotten something, but he wouldn't just come back in without knocking – and besides, I'd locked the front door before I went upstairs.'

Both detectives nod.

'Then I realised that if someone else *was* in the house, they must have come in *before* I locked the front door. They could have been there all the time, all day even.'

'So what did you do?' Manyon asks.

'Well, at first I couldn't move. I was so scared.' In truth I was also very embarrassed – I went cold just thinking that as I'd been dancing in her kitchen, posing on the sofa for *Hello* magazine, ferreting around her bedroom and twirling around in her bloody robe, someone was there. And they were probably watching me. 'Then I left the bedroom and was halfway down the stairs when I decided to make a run for it. I took the stairs two at a time and lunged at the front door. I pulled at the handle, but it wouldn't budge and then I remembered I'd double-locked it and in my terror my fingers just wouldn't work to unlock the door.'

'So what did you do?'

'Well, I don't know what happened, but I swear I felt movement behind me, so I turned around, but whoever it was had moved, possibly into the sitting room. I stood there for a few moments by the door. Then I heard footsteps in the kitchen. I know I wasn't mistaken; I definitely heard someone moving from the kitchen into the sitting room, which backs onto the garden. I thought I might never move again. It felt like time had stopped.' My upper lip was damp with sweat as I waited in thick silence, hearing nothing, but knowing I wasn't alone. I swear I heard breathing, but perhaps it was my own? 'Then I made a very slow move into the kitchen, trying not to let my heels touch the floor and make a clicking noise.'

'At this stage you've still seen no one, only heard noises?' Manyon asks, and I see a look, a moment, a nuance pass between him and the woman. I suddenly feel unsure of this situation. Is he doubting my account?

'Yes, I heard noises. Someone was there, I'm absolutely sure.' He doesn't respond, just looks at me, like he can see what I'm thinking, but I continue, hoping to convince them with my colourful descriptions. 'I spotted the Sabatier knife block sitting on the kitchen counter and with one eye on the open doorway into the living room, I reached for one. To my horror I saw that there was a space where the biggest, sharpest knife usually sits – I almost screamed. I was so worried someone might be standing behind the wall of the sitting room waiting to stab me. So I stood for a few seconds, gathering all my breath and courage and strength. Then, I grabbed the second largest knife and dashed through the French doors…'

'I thought the doors were locked?'

'Well they were, as far as I knew. Whoever had been in the house must have let themselves in and out this way. I don't know, I didn't stop to check, just ran through the back garden, clearing the back wall in a way I didn't think was possible for me – strange what you can do when you have to.'

'Indeed, Mrs Metcalf, it is.' His voice is as expressionless as his face. I don't think he believes anything I've told him, and it's making me feel quite paranoid.

'Anyway, I didn't stop running until I arrived home, falling in through the back door, straight into the kitchen, sweating, crying and breathless.'

'Is that when you phoned the police?'

'Yes… well, my husband, Matt, did. Luckily he was home. He'd forgotten his costume for the play and had popped back for it – I've never been more relieved to see him. "What the hell?" was all he said, and as I slammed the back door behind me, leaning on it with my body weight, I just remember screaming "call the police"!'

'Is that everything? There's nothing else you want to tell us about that you think might be significant?'

'No,' I lie. I can't tell them about what I found in Amber's bedside drawer, but I can't stop thinking about it.

Just as I was putting the magazine back, I saw something wrapped in a tissue, tucked into the side of the drawer, by her rolls of tights. I'd just had one hell of a shock about Ben being married to someone else, and knew I wasn't ready for any more of her secrets. I should have closed the drawer then, but in my mind I thought: *Amber is my friend. She stays in my house, we spend a great deal of time together – and therefore I need to know what's going on.* After all it could have been drugs or something. If she could lie about Ben, what else could she lie about? And I'm ashamed to say I couldn't stop myself, I just reached for the folded tissue and slowly unravelled it, holding my breath, dreading what I might find. I can't justify what I did. I knew I shouldn't be looking through her private things, shouldn't have even been in her bedroom, but still, I couldn't stop myself. I heard myself groan as the contents fell to the floor. A pregnancy test. And before I even looked, I knew it was positive.

CHAPTER FIFTEEN

Lucy

It sounds selfish, but when I found the pregnancy test, Amber wasn't my first concern. All I could think about was how sad it made *me* feel, and how was I going to face the spectre of my best friend's pregnancy and birth, something I'd yearned for myself for so long. I didn't worry about how as a single mother Amber was going to cope, nor did I even think about the fact this baby was probably going to be without a father, because it didn't look like Ben was exactly free to take *that* role on. Even if it wasn't Ben's child, then the alternative was that this baby would most likely be the product of a sordid one-night stand from Tinder, or not even that, someone Amber had bumped into in a wine bar. What a horrible mess!

I sit in the police station going over and over everything in my head, feeling completely at sea, but trying to appear to be a reliable witness – and I'm not sure I pull it off.

After my difficult witness statement that was, I'm sure, full of holes, Manyon is keen to point out again that no one actually saw this intruder, no one knows who left the dead bird and, apart from one text from an apparently untraceable number, there's 'very little evidence' to work on. They are also quick to remind me of at least two occasions when I've phoned up to report what DCI Manyon refers to as 'an *alleged* stalking activity'.

I am exhausted. I've been through physical and mental torture, the police seem to think I'm a lunatic and on top of all that I've discovered my friend has been keeping things from me. *Big* things. I understand that it's her business and I have no right to expect her to tell me everything about her life, but her ex-boyfriend, the man she talks about constantly, is *married* and she's *pregnant*. She hasn't told me either of these things – and I've told her everything. All *my* secrets. God, I blush to think what I've said to her during our heart-to-hearts – I've even revealed private bedroom stuff, things I wouldn't even tell Kirsty. But it looks like she's lied to me from the beginning about Ben – a quick google on my phone earlier confirmed he and Geraldine have been married for thirty years. *Thirty!* And what's more, they are the proud parents of three children!

I'm sitting here now with a scalding cup of tea in the waiting room in shock, going over all this in my mind. If she hasn't told me any of this, then what else hasn't she told me?

I have to stop thinking about Amber and her complicated life and think about myself and my current situation. I've been here for hours and I'm beginning to wonder if I should ask for a solicitor, but I'm a witness, and thinking about the TV detective dramas I've seen, I'm sure asking for a solicitor would make me look guilty. But guilty of what?

Mind you, I'm guilty of not telling the police everything. Matt knows about the pregnancy test though. After he'd called the police, he sat with his arm around me waiting for them to arrive. I was shaking and he was gently rubbing my shoulder when he suddenly said, 'Is that what I think it is?' I looked down to where his eyes had landed. I was still clutching Amber's pregnancy test.

'Oh… no… This isn't mine…' I said, embarrassed.

'I thought for a minute they'd been wrong, at the clinic.'

'I wish. Sorry, babe… it's Amber's.'

He turned to me, his face white. He looked so disappointed, so upset. 'Is she… is Amber…?'

'Looks like it.' I glanced down at the white plastic strip in my hands, felt the urge to cry again.

'So why do *you* have the test?'

'I... found it, just... lying about her house...' I gestured to the floor, implying it had just been there. I couldn't tell him I'd been looking through her stuff; I was so ashamed.

'Did she tell you... that she was?'

I shook my head, trying to hold back the tears, thinking what an idiot I was. 'She doesn't know that I know. I just found it... tonight.'

'What the hell, Lucy?' he said, pulling his arm from my shoulder to face me. 'Throw it away. If she ever finds out you kept it... Jesus, it would look strange.'

'I didn't keep it, I just forgot I had it. I was so scared I just ran and...' Whatever I said, he was right, it did look strange, so there was no point in trying to explain it. I just got up and threw it in the kitchen bin.

DC Manyon eventually announces that he will be in touch, and I'm allowed to go home from the police station. Matt collects me, and as it is 6 a.m. and I haven't slept all night, I call into work and take the day off. All I want to do is sleep, and process everything that is whirring around my head over and over. I lie on our bed, snuggled in the soft, mint-green bed linen, the window open, floaty curtains wafting in the late summer breeze, and drop off. But less than an hour later there's banging on the door, which startles me. After the previous evening I'm totally wired and aware that whoever was in Amber's house last night might have seen where I ran to. He knows where I live. So with pins and needles at the ends of my fingers, I stagger down the stairs, throwing my dressing gown around me.

Cautiously, I look through the little squares of frosted glass on the door to see if I can make out who it is, but I can't. So I only open the door slightly, and put my head out – that way I can either bar his way or run. But as I open the door, I see who it is and immediately stiffen. Amber.

I was hoping for more time before I saw her. I'm still not sure how I feel after discovering that she'd lied to me about Ben, never told me he was married. It's just another thing in a growing list of things that I feel she isn't being honest with me about, not least of which is that she's pregnant.

She's holding a huge bouquet of flowers in every shade of pink, and I think she looks like a bride, and my resentment softens slightly.

'Oh, Lucy, I feel so terrible, it must have been awful for you,' she starts, and the concern on her tear-stained face seems genuine. She's obviously upset by the whole thing too – it must be freaking her out that there was an intruder in her home, whether she was there at the time or not.

I step back from the open door for her to walk in, and she comes through, putting the bouquet on the kitchen table and turning to hug me, hard.

'You are such a good friend. You were doing me a favour, and then this happens…'

'I know… It was terrible,' I say. 'I haven't slept… Have you spoken to the police?'

'Yes, yes, I came home very late last night and they were at the house. They told me everything. I feel so… responsible.' She walks around me and puts the kettle on. 'Tea?'

I nod. 'Please.'

'I haven't slept a wink worrying about you,' she's saying, putting teabags into the cups, and I think how comfortable she is here, how it's like a second home to her. How much I've opened everything up to her – my home and myself. And I can't help feeling betrayed that she hasn't been open with me.

'You shouldn't feel bad. It isn't *your* fault some madman's after you,' I say, still feeling slightly prickly and knowing that until I address the issues, I will continue to feel like there's a wall between us.

'It's usually you making tea for me,' she says, bringing two mugs to the table, sitting down and resting her hand on mine, looking into my face. 'Are you okay, sweetie? You look exhausted… Are you still upset? The police said he didn't hurt you, but you thought he might?'

'Yes, I did… It was terrifying,' I say. 'And I think he had a knife.'

'A knife?' Her hand goes to her chest.

'Yes… He must have taken the biggest one from your knife block because it was gone. I picked up one too, but think I must have dropped it when I ran.'

'Oh yeah, the police found that.'

'Did you notice the big knife was missing from your block?'

'No actually. But I think it might have been missing a while…'

'I mentioned it to the police, but they didn't seem to take anything I said seriously. You should report it missing; it could be him that's taken it.'

'Yeah… yeah I will. But it doesn't matter now, as long as you're safe.' She's smiling, rubbing her hand up and down my arm and looking intently into my face. I conjure up a way of introducing the Ben situation, but can't admit I'd found the pregnancy test, because that means admitting I went through her stuff.

'Amber… I… I came across something. It was in an old magazine at the doctor's.'

'Oh… the doctor's… Are you okay, sweetie?'

'Yes, I'm fine… It was just a health check. But in the magazine, *Hello* magazine actually, from a couple of months ago, I saw a photo of Ben. He was receiving an award.'

She gently pulls her hand away from mine. 'That was ages ago,' she says, and clearly doesn't want to talk about it, presumably knowing exactly where this conversation is heading. But this time I'm not prepared to leave it just because it's making her uncomfortable – she can't be my friend and lie to me about important stuff. I want to know, so I tell her what I'd seen in the magazine, and before she can deny it or make up some story, I say, 'I googled his name, Amber. There's plenty of stuff about him online… and about his wife Geraldine.' I spell it out. 'Why didn't you tell me?'

She didn't expect this confrontation, this questioning – not from me anyway. I'm the carer. I don't have difficult conversations with Amber. That isn't our dynamic. I'm the one who smooths everything over and makes her happy, but she knows I'm not going to let this drop now.

'Yes… okay, I should have mentioned that he's married, but it's in name only. Geraldine and Ben live separate lives. They have for years. They'd already separated when we first got together… Their kids were little then and…'

'I'm not making a moral judgement, Amber, I just feel hurt that you didn't tell me.'

'I'm sorry. We're friends… best friends, and I *should* have told you, but how could I? I didn't want you thinking bad of me – like I say, it isn't like I wrecked their marriage, but sometimes it's hard to convince other people. You're kind, understanding. I suppose I didn't want to test that… or our friendship.'

'But it wouldn't have. You know me, I'm not fickle, and I'm loyal – *too* loyal sometimes. You made up all this stuff about him moving in with you and talking marriage… then inexplicably it just ended. You never said it was because he was already married…'

'What I told you is true. He said, "Find us a home and we'll move in together," and we *were* talking marriage…'

'But he already *is* married!'

'Yes, but she knows all about me. She was okay with it… Ben said she understood how much he loved me but begged him to stay for the kids, until they were old enough to understand… What could he do?'

We sip our tea, both with our own thoughts, and I try to put myself in her shoes. It all makes sense really. I can see that from Amber's perspective this was her boyfriend and she was going to marry him. She just missed a bit out, I suppose, and after all she'd been through with her husband, she was probably scared to tell anyone she was having a relationship with a married man – estranged from his wife or not. I can't imagine anyone being as understanding as Geraldine, his wife, though – I wonder how she really felt about her husband, the father of her children, living a double life with his weather girl?

'So Geraldine was really okay with it all?' I ask.

'Oh yes.' She's nodding vigorously. 'Ben told me it was difficult sometimes, but they both knew they'd come to the end, even then. Apparently she said, "I know you have to be with her, but please be discreet, just don't embarrass me," which is why we kept our relationship secret from everyone. Except you, Lucy… I didn't lie to *you*, I told you about Ben. If anything, I lied to everyone else, denying anything was going on. People I worked with might have guessed, made snide comments, but only you knew the truth.'

I'm beginning to thaw. I can see that in some ways Amber has been more honest with me than anyone else.

'So was Geraldine aware you were talking marriage?' I ask, intrigued by this woman who apparently was happy to hand over her man.

'She said when the kids were old enough to understand, then they'd divorce so we could be together,' she says.

'How old are the kids now?' I ask.

'The eldest is twenty-three, the youngest seventeen.' She drops her head. So this is why Amber had found a new house for the two of them – because the kids were old enough to be told. 'This was supposed to be our new life together. After all the promises, all the waiting, I was going to be his *real* partner instead of the one he kept hidden while he played happy families. Just when I thought we were going to be together openly, permanently, he told me he and Geraldine were "going to give it another go". *Another fucking go*,' she says, shaking her head, like she still can't quite believe it.

'Oh, Amber, I'm so sorry.' It's now my turn to put my hand on hers across the kitchen table.

'Those first few days after I'd moved in, I was just waiting for him to move in, but he kept making up excuses. I was lonely, really fed up, staying in every night on my own, just waiting for him to call… but he didn't, so I came along to the book club.'

It all made sense now. 'And it was after that he told you?'

'Yes, that's when I threw his stuff out of the window.'

'I remember.' I smile and we both giggle a little at the memory. 'But you've seen him recently, haven't you?'

'Yes, I'm sorry to say I gave in and we've slept together a couple of times. I'd heard he and Geraldine had finished… again. That she'd found out he was seeing someone at work and she'd thrown him out. I assumed this was all about me.'

'But if she knew about you all along and was fine with it, why did she throw him out?'

'My thoughts exactly. I can't help but wonder – maybe he never actually told her, and he was lying to both of us. It makes me sick.'

'What a charmer.'

'Yeah, well, I've never been very good with men. My mother was the same, always looking in the wrong places for her happily ever after. My biological father was married to someone else. I never met him, never wanted to, and I doubt he ever wanted to meet me either – I was a huge mistake, an embarrassment.'

'Don't say that.'

'It's how I feel, like I'm an embarrassment – not worthy of anyone decent. I always said I'd never live her life. Mine would be different, so I went to college and I married lovely, safe, caring Michael. I thought I'd landed on my safe harbour, but I can't be trusted, and as soon as the bad boy came along, I was hooked. I fucked up my happily ever after just like she did.'

'It's never too late, Amber. You're only in your forties. You're so attractive and fun; you have so much to offer. You deserve someone kind, who loves you for you.'

She gives a mirthless laugh like that's never going to happen. 'Those guys are already taken.'

'So where are things now… with Ben?' I ask, hoping she'll tell me about the pregnancy.

'Not good. He was still apart from Geraldine, and I still thought we would get back together until about a month ago. It was the night my tyre was slashed. I was leaving work, just getting into my car, when I saw them… Ben and the new girl from accounts. She's only in her twenties, far too young for him… but I saw them kissing.' She's gazing ahead, reliving the moment. I see the pain in her eyes. 'And then last week I heard they'd moved in together… He can't have known her more than a few months – I waited for over *twenty* fucking years, and all for nothing.' At this she bursts into tears and I get up and hug her, rocking her like a child.

'You must hate him.'

'I wish I did, but he's such a huge part of my life. I will always have feelings for him. I told you, I don't have an off switch when it comes to bad boys; I don't know when to get out. I always hang around for them to keep sticking the knife in.'

Eventually I sit back down, still holding her hand as she lets the last of the tears fall.

'I wish I'd known,' I say. 'Sometimes we can't see things for ourselves; we need an honest friend to shine the light for us, even tell us things we don't want to hear. You were flailing around in the dark, love, and he was stringing you along. Seems like he's lied to just about everyone.'

'I know, I know, but some relationships don't stand up to scrutiny. I wanted to hear what I wanted to hear… for twenty sodding years.'

'So… what now?'

'I don't know…'

I still want her to tell me about the pregnancy. We need everything out in the open so I can be there for her and we have no secrets from each other. So I tell her how I feel, hoping this will prompt her to share with me what's happening in her life.

'Amber, I feel hurt you kept all this big stuff to yourself. It wasn't good for you. And as your friend I feel like we were playing some weird game of friendship poker, and all the time I was showing my hand while you were hiding yours.'

'I'm so sorry… There is something else. I've wanted to tell you, but I didn't know what I was going to do and—'

'What?'

And finally she says it.

'Lucy, I'm pregnant.'

CHAPTER SIXTEEN

Lucy

After Amber confirmed her pregnancy, she said she thought Ben was the father, but couldn't be sure. 'There have been others,' she'd said intriguingly, but didn't elaborate – so much for our new-look 'honest and open' friendship. She did confess it had been a huge shock and she was still coming to terms with the news herself, which was why she hadn't told anyone.

'I didn't think it possible at my age. I came off the pill a couple of years ago,' she said.

'Will you try to find out who the father is for sure?' I asked, but she said she didn't plan to, not yet anyway.

'I don't want anyone, even Ben, forcing shared custody or visitation rights. I don't want him poking and prying into my life, the baby spending weekends with that slut he lives with. I want my baby to have a good father, and I don't care if he isn't the biological one,' was all she said.

The good news is, she's keeping the baby, and she's okay about it. She isn't delirious about being pregnant and she's worried about work – as she says, the timing is all wrong – but she's positive. Of course I feigned delighted surprise for her, told her how happy I was and how I'd be there for her for everything. She just had to tell me what was going on.

'No more secrets,' I said, and she shook her head, but her eyes didn't meet mine, which made me think there may still be things Amber isn't telling me.

I tell Matt later, when he comes home from work.

'It's… it's good and it's bad…' he's saying, as if to himself, clearly as upset as me. Like me, Matt knows about Amber's positive pregnancy test, but given our own history, we both need time to adjust, to get used to the idea now she's actually confirmed the pregnancy and that she's keeping the child.

'I know, it's bittersweet, love. That's what it is. I feel the same, so don't feel guilty for having mixed feelings… It's understandable that we can't jump up and down for joy – yet.'

Amber has hinted at her fears about being alone in the house now she's pregnant, and I want to offer her a permanent place at ours during the pregnancy, but have to ask Matt how he feels about it first.

'I was thinking though…' I start. 'Now it's been confirmed that she's pregnant, I think she should come back and stay with us. What do you think?' I half expect him to say no.

'It's up to you… if you feel, as her friend, you want her here, it's okay with me,' he says, resigned to what I know he feels will be an intrusion on our lives.

'Just until the baby's born?' I say, and he agrees, albeit reluctantly. He's such a lovely man, and I know he's doing this for me. I'd worried he'd show his disapproval of her being pregnant without a partner – something Matt and I feel strongly about as we both had absentee fathers, but I guess his kindness has won through all the doubts. 'Thanks, babe, she'll be so relieved. I'll pop over later and check on her, and suggest she comes back here,' I say.

'We can always look after the kid, if she needs us to.' He's sitting at the kitchen table, laptop open, and I stand up and walk behind him in the chair, putting my arms around him.

'You're a lovely man,' I breathe in his ear. I am so touched by his kindness but I also remember what Kirsty had said about him feeling our infertility as keenly as me, and as I hold him, I realise this is probably true.

So while Matt and I grieve for something we never had, Amber's baby is due in seven months. I am excited about a baby coming into all our lives, but the irony is painful for me. There's Amber, who's just 'okay' with the news, when for us it would be a dream come true. I know it's biologically impossible, and as much as we've both come to terms with our lot, it's times like these I wish for something that can't ever be. I made a fuss, telling Amber how happy I was, but there's part of me that can't help wishing it was us waiting for the patter of tiny feet, going for the scan, shopping for pushchairs, choosing baby names. Meanwhile, Amber's worried about how she's going to pay for everything, but I don't know why. She's loaded, she has that huge house and she must have made a fortune being on telly. But she's also worried about losing her job, or 'being sidelined', as she puts it.

'It's okay for you, you've got Matt,' she says, when I pop over to check on her.

'Be thankful for what *you've* got,' I say, trying to be positive, but making a point.

'Lucy, I've got no one… Nothing.'

'You have *everything*, Amber.' I'm trying to make her feel better, but she's determined to have her own pity party. *Where do I start? You've got a baby on the way and a fabulous home to live in, you ungrateful madam*, I think. But of course I don't voice my feelings, I just make sympathetic noises and tell her she'll be fine, which of course she will be, because I'm here for her and will be there every step of the way.

As much as I envy Amber's pregnancy, I do understand that this isn't what she planned for and it can't be much fun being single and pregnant. So I try to be there as much as I can, and do little things to cheer her up, try to make her see the upside of her situation and get excited about the baby. The other day I bought her some baby recipe books, along with the most gorgeous teddy bear with a cute little bow in its hair.

'Ooh, thank you,' she said and kissed me. But I noticed she left the teddy bear lying face down on the sideboard. I expect she probably just doesn't want to make a big fuss because she's minding my feelings – she's so sweet to me, saying how she wants me to be involved in the baby's life.

'We're like sisters… so you'll be its auntie,' she keeps saying.

'So come and stay at ours where "Auntie Lucy" can look after both of you,' I say. It's the day after I had the conversation with Matt about her moving in. 'You know it makes sense,' I say, waiting for her to jump at the chance, but she seems awkward and says she feels Matt doesn't want her to stay, and it isn't fair on our marriage to have a third person living there.

'That's absolute rubbish,' I insist. 'Matt loves having you to stay, and he worries about you as much as I do.' This, of course, is a lie, but I want her to feel welcome – for God's sake, the woman is pregnant and living in a big house with a bloody stalker at large.

Later that evening, I bring it up with Matt. 'I won't be responsible if anything happens to her,' I say. 'I don't know what you've said to her, but something has made her feel very unwelcome. And you agreed she could stay, so it's up to you to go and tell her you love having her here and that she has to come and stay with us for the baby's sake.'

So he goes over, and just in time by the sound of it because she confesses that earlier this week she had a heavy-breather call and she comes back to ours with Matt, grateful for the sanctuary.

'Why didn't you tell me, Amber?' I say.

'I didn't want to worry you. I know how upset you get.'

'It doesn't matter how I feel, this is about you and your safety. What did he say when he called?'

'He said "I can't live without you… I would rather die *with* you",' she said, clearly still scared.

We logged everything with the police this time, and they said they're going to put a trace on her line, but there hasn't been a call since, and they can't seem to locate where the call came from. Or they haven't bothered to.

Amber is in bits, so I suggest she goes and has a lie down in one of our spare rooms; in her condition she needs rest, especially after a shock like that. Later when Matt gets back from the gym he makes one of his quick pasta bakes, dripping in cheese, with a crispy topping and loads of what I call 'secret spinach'. He's made enough for two, and I don't think he's too chuffed when I invite Amber to join us, but she's sitting in our kitchen and clearly not going anywhere so what else can I do?

'It's so lovely to be here with you guys,' she sighs, as she finishes off the last of the garlic bread with no carb concerns (as Matt commented, she's definitely eating for two at the moment).

'You're going to stay, aren't you?' I ask. 'Matt explained, didn't he, that we're *both* happy to have you?'

'He did, and you're both so sweet, but you both have lives and careers and I hate being alone, but…' She looks like she is about to cry.

'What is it? Are you scared? Have you had any texts?'

'No.' She shakes her head. 'Nothing I can put my finger on, it's just sometimes… I feel like someone's watching me.'

'What do you mean?' Matt says, but I know just what she means. I've felt it too when I was in her house on my own.

'It's just… I think I've put something down, and when I go back to where I left it… it's moved.

'Oh God,' I say, clutching my chest. 'Are you sure?'

'Yeah. It happened with a scarf just this morning. I know I took it off in the hall and hung it on the bannister – I remember doing it – but it wasn't there when I came to find it. And it's that lovely blue one, Lucy, you know, with the tiny stars all over?'

'Yes, I love that scarf. I'm sure it'll turn up. I could come over tomorrow and help you look?' I say, not convinced that anyone would break into a house to hide a scarf.

'That's kind, thank you, but I've looked everywhere.'

'I'd offer to help, but wouldn't have a clue what I was looking for,' Matt adds, 'and isn't there something called "pregnancy brain", where the mother-to-be's memory is affected, or am I just being a sexist pig?'

'You're just being a sexist pig!' Amber and I chorus, which makes us all laugh, and it lightens the mood, lifts the tension, but only for a moment.

'I don't know, but I really don't think this has anything to do with me being pregnant… It's real, Matt,' she says. 'I came home from work the other evening, and when I walked in, I thought how lovely the fragrance was coming from my candles. But when I walked into the sitting room, I nearly died.'

We are both looking at her, waiting to find out what happened.

'One of the wicks was smoking. I hadn't been there all day, and neither had anyone else, but the candle had been lit. And it was smouldering… like it had only just been put out.'

I feel the prickle of goosebumps and make a lame joke about 'that ghost' to try and lighten the mood, but no one laughs, and Amber looks like she's about to cry.

'I need to reset the alarm,' she murmurs, as if to herself. 'I did it last time, when he'd been in my bedroom… messed with my stuff, smashed my photo frame… I think he's jealous; it was a photo of me and Ben.'

'Who… who knows how his twisted mind works?' I say, not wanting to have this conversation. If I tell her it was me that accidentally broke the frame, then it might be assumed I also wrote 'fucking slut' on her mirror. 'Please don't be scared,' I say, changing the subject. 'Think about moving here – but if you want time to think about it that's okay. In the meantime, just call us any time if you're scared, and one of us will come over, and you know there's a bed here.'

She nods. 'Thanks, Lucy, I really appreciate that.'

Later, Matt walks her home. She said she thought she'd heard someone in the garden the previous evening and she wanted Matt to check it out and he kindly went along.

I offered to go with them, but as Matt pointed out, 'What would *you* do if there was an intruder? Run like Usain Bolt like you did last time?' That made us all laugh. So I stayed home and did the washing up, relaxing with the rest of the wine and putting my feet up in front of the telly. They've been gone about an hour and I am just beginning to feel a little worried when they come in through the back door. They are both white as a sheet and Amber has been crying.

'What's the matter?' I say, rushing to them and going into what Amber calls 'Lucy's fussy mother mode'.

At first, neither of them speak, and Matt gives me an almost invisible shake of the head as he helps her to the sofa in the living room.

I follow them in, not knowing what to say or do, so just sit next to Amber on the sofa and hold her hand until someone is able to tell me what's happened.

'It's him…' she says. I can feel her shaking. 'Lucy, he's been to my house again. And this time he left a pair of baby booties with a "congratulations on your news" card on the back porch.'

I gasp, covering my mouth with my hand.

'We can't understand it,' Matt says, standing over her protectively. 'The only people who know about the pregnancy are us… the *three* of us.'

I shift slightly in my seat. 'You haven't mentioned it at work or anything?' I ask.

'No, have I hell. *You* haven't told anyone, have you, Lucy?' Amber says, looking alarmed. I am about to confess that I may have hinted in the staffroom to Kirsty, but the look on Amber's face tells me this isn't the time for honesty. 'Tell me you haven't blabbed this all over Treetops Estate.' She's turned her head and, as we're sitting close on the sofa, she's right in my face.

I feel quite intimidated, and don't want to upset her in her condition. So I say, 'No, of course not,' and attempt an indignant face. I feel like such a bad friend. I shouldn't have told anyone, but I'd been pleased for her – and it isn't like Kirsty or any of the teachers I work with are bloody stalkers. I'd simply wanted to share her good news. 'What about the doctors… the hospital?' I offer. 'Someone at the hospital might have seen your name – they might have talked…'

'I doubt it,' she snaps. 'And if they did I would sue them.'

'The father… fathers… one of *them* might have… guessed?' I admit I'm being a bit shady by alluding to the fact that there's more than one candidate for the role of Amber's baby-daddy. But it's just my way of fighting back a little. I seem to be on the receiving end of her anger these days. I put it down to her pregnancy and her being scared. We always lash out when we're scared – I know I do, and it's usually Matt on the receiving end of my grumpiness. Amber doesn't have a Matt though, so she has to make do with me.

Amber doesn't respond to my question about whether she's told the fathers, so I just smile and pat her hand while Matt goes and puts the kettle on. Once she's calmed down, she says she's sorry for being snappy with me.

'Don't worry about it, you're just scared,' I say reassuringly.

'Actually, I am. And after what's happened tonight, I'd like to take you both up on your offer of a bed, if that's okay?'

She asks this almost shyly, probably worried that Matt might still be funny about her staying, but before he can comment, I say, 'Of course.'

'I know I said I needed my space,' she says, reaching out for both our hands. 'But I'm beginning to realise I can't cope with this pregnancy alone – I need my friends.'

*

So it's been decided between us that Amber is moving in with us until the baby's born. Stalker aside, once she gets into the third trimester all kinds of complications and emergencies could occur, and this way she'll have us both and transport to get her to hospital in the event of anything happening before the due date.

I also feel it would be good for Amber to stay after the baby's born because I don't think she has a clue about babies. Sometimes, when we talk about looking after a newborn, she reminds me of a pregnant teenager, not an intelligent woman in her forties. Her lack of knowledge is shocking, nor does she want to learn either. The other day I suggested we try out some recipes for the baby and she looked at me like I was mad.

'Don't you just give them stuff out of jars?' she said, holding the baby cookbook at a distance like she might catch something. I just hope she can step up to the plate when this little one's born. As Matt says, thank God we're around just in case.

Now we've decided to make Amber more semi-permanent at ours, I've prepared two bedrooms: the smallest spare room (that we'd always said would make a perfect nursery for our own child) will be the baby's room – and the larger will be Amber's bedroom. Matt's been wonderful, and even gave Amber's room a quick lick of blush-coloured paint, and I've hung new pale grey curtains and bought a nice, glitzy lamp I know she'll love. And while Amber helped Matt make dinner last night, I pretended to go upstairs with a headache, but 'styled' the room, adding the lamp and new cushions and some fresh flowers – just for her.

After dinner we do 'the reveal'. I call her from upstairs, pretending I need her help with something. It's hilarious, because she's quite grumpy and at first just keeps saying 'What?' and refusing to come upstairs. But when Matt gives her a gentle push, she appears on the landing and I swing open her door and shout 'Voila!'

I can't believe her reaction; she just bursts into tears and hugs me again and again.

'Oh, Lucy, I'm sorry. You're so lovely and I'm such a grump. I'm a horrible friend,' she says through happy tears.

I assure her she isn't. 'You're tired and you're pregnant,' I say, sitting next to her on the new blush-pink duvet, 'and please don't keep apologising. I understand.'

'You're both so… kind…' she says, bursting into tears again.

She seems genuinely touched by what I've done, and I feel moved to tears by her gratitude. But now, in the cold light of day, we're dealing with the reality of what this move means. It isn't all about blush curtains and pretty lamps, it's about physically moving far more stuff than she needs but is insisting on bringing with her. Matt moved some of her stuff during the week, but we're moving the last of the things today as it's Saturday and I'm off and so is Amber. Unfortunately, Matt's at rehearsals, and I can see the car crash that's going to happen if someone doesn't help her, because she is so unrealistic, so impractical. I wanted to walk to and from her house to ours and I would have happily carried everything, but just now she got all stroppy and accused me of being controlling.

'Lucy! I don't want you parading all my stuff down Mulberry Avenue, it has to be packed away in the car,' she said, while I smiled sweetly, resisting a little reminder of who was helping whom.

I don't even want to think this, but if I'm honest, I'm beginning to wonder if we've done the right thing asking her to move in. I know she needed a safe place to stay, but since we gave her the lovely room and made her feel welcome on a more long-term basis, she's changed. She keeps telling me I'm bossy, while overruling me all the time, and it isn't just between the two of us. She's started to do it with Matt too. This morning, he asked us both what we wanted to eat for dinner tonight and I suggested we have roast chicken with vegetables because we have it in the fridge.

'Noo, let's have burritos,' she said, jumping up and down like a child.

I don't know why I overreacted, but I suddenly put my foot down. 'We've already got a chicken… and Matt's never made burritos,' I snapped. My next line was about to be 'and we're not a bloody Mexican restaurant'. Fortunately I managed to resist saying this. I'm not being mean about her idea of burritos – it's just that Matt and I are both working full-time while Amber lies on the sofa between shifts.

Meanwhile, Matt has taken my request to be nice to her almost too far and he smiled, all sweetness and light, and said, 'If that's what madam wants, that's what madam will have.' As if that wasn't annoying enough, he then announced theatrically that 'tonight is Burrito Night' and did an embarrassing little dance that made her giggle and me cringe. I didn't know who I was more cross with – her or him.

I try and put 'Burrito Night' from my head and concentrate on the task at hand: moving Amber and all her worldly goods a few hundred yards. She's keeping the house, just not living there for now, so there's no furniture to be moved, but here I am carrying the contents of a whole bloody wardrobe and every ornament she owns to the car.

She's just setting the security code on the house alarm now as I try to squeeze the last few things into her car. It's all classic Amber – chaotic and unnecessary – and it would have been far easier if we'd just carried everything across, and kept it to a minimum. I know she's pregnant and mustn't lift too much, but I would happily have done the lion's share.

I'm determined we're going to do it in one move, but we're at the stage where the boot of her car will only take a 5 lb bag, but I have a 10 lb bag to fit in. I'm now manoeuvring everything around the boot to try and force it and I'm exhausted. Amber is on her phone as I struggle, which has pretty much been the pattern of the move, and I'm trying not to become too irritated.

I drag a box along the bottom of the boot; it lifts up the carpet and I stop and look more closely. I put my head right into the trunk and in the dusk I see something glinting. With one hand, I use the torch on my phone, and slide the other hand under the lining. I can't see much but feel something cold, like metal, so I take out a couple of boxes. Then I carefully lift the carpet and I can't believe what I'm staring at. Lying in the boot of Amber's car is a knife. This is weird in itself, but what makes it even weirder is that it looks like the one I noticed was missing from the knife block the night of the intruder. It's the same brand, and the same size. It can't be a coincidence, can it? But if so, what's it doing in the boot of her car? Only she has the keys. So she must have put it there, but why? I'm now a little freaked out.

I hear her shoes clicking across the gravel and quickly shove the knife into a half-filled black bin liner. Maybe it's in here for her own protection given the stalker situation, but it's a strange place to put it, and not easily reachable if he attacks her in her car. Oh God, she might be planning to take revenge on Ben and the woman whose name seems to be 'the slut from accounts'. Or she might be planning to harm herself. Well, there's no way this knife is going from my sight until I know what's going on. I'll let her settle in, then ask her about it. I don't want to say anything now because I don't want a confrontation here on the drive; she's already told me off for being bossy, so to challenge her over the knife now might make her angry and she'll refuse to move in with us. I am keen she does this; it isn't just about Amber any more. I'm thinking about the safety and well-being of that baby.

I close her boot, wait another ten minutes for her to come off the phone, then sit in the passenger seat with the knife in the bin liner while she drives the few yards down Mulberry Avenue.

My mind is whirring. In the few minutes it takes to drive four doors down the round and park, a million different scenarios have crowded my head. All I know is I have to talk to Matt about it, see what he thinks, but if I do he might go off the deep end and refuse to let her stay. No, I'll wait, talk to him when I've thought this through and she's settled in.

When I get home, I unlock the house and shove the knife in the back of the kitchen cupboard until I decide what to do. I just hope by inviting Amber into our home I'm not inviting trouble…

SEVEN MONTHS LATER

CHAPTER SEVENTEEN

Lucy

Amber had a tough labour. I was with her for most of it, feeling every agony and contraction, and joy and relief at Mia's safe birth. It hasn't been an easy time for any of us. Amber seemed moody throughout the pregnancy, and I felt like I had to be the one jollying her along, even when, at times, I was hurting myself. I would never dream of telling her this, but watching my friend go through something I've always longed for is probably one of the hardest things I've ever had to do.

I'd always felt like an outsider growing up, and now I feel like an outsider regarding my childlessness. Pregnancy and motherhood feels like a secret club I haven't been allowed into, but I'm doing what I always do and making the best of it, smiling through tears while telling everyone – including myself – that everything's going to be fine. But in truth the irony of me comforting Amber through each stage of her birth wasn't lost on me.

It would have been so easy for me to resent everything about Amber's pregnancy but I'd tried not to and tried enjoy it with her instead. I was there for the first kick, the name choosing, the pink baby shower I threw for her, which was fun, but not easy. Amber didn't really know any of our neighbours and wasn't in touch with anyone at work either, so I didn't have a lot of options regarding guests. I thought a safe bet would be to invite the girls from book club and a couple of neighbours who live up the road who I thought

Amber would like. But on the day Amber was tired and didn't feel like socialising, and only made a brief appearance, charming everyone while offering her profuse apologies, and leaving after an hour to 'get some sleep'. I didn't mind. How could I begin to understand how a woman feels at eight months? Though the event itself wasn't easy, I enjoyed organising the baby shower. I loved all the pink balloons and cupcakes and felt like I was the hostess, especially when Mrs Shaw from next door asked if I was 'the mother-to-be'. I looked at Kirsty, rolling my eyes, and she smiled back, understanding, and despite our differences, I warmed slightly to my old friend.

When Mia was born, no one other than the book club girls sent Amber a new baby card. She doesn't have any family; it was always just her and her mum, and she hasn't seen her for years. 'She wasn't a good mother,' she told me. 'Always putting her latest boyfriend before her only child. I was lonely and neglected and I'll never forgive her.' Amber doesn't seem to have any friends other than me either – says her relationships with colleagues are always 'tricky' because though no one knows about the true nature of their relationship, they resent her being close to Ben, 'the boss'. I'm not convinced this is the only reason. I love Amber, but she isn't the easiest person to love; she blows hot and cold even with me.

I'd realised at the baby shower how much I missed Kirsty. We'd drifted apart and I wanted to offer the olive branch. So when Mia was a few days old, I invited her over to see the baby one Saturday afternoon. I wanted to see my old friend, and at the same time it might be useful for Amber to have an experienced mum around for advice. So Kirsty came over as arranged with a gift and cooed over Mia who was sleeping in her Moses basket downstairs while we waited for Amber to drag herself from her bed.

Eventually Amber wandered into the kitchen and sat down while Kirsty held Mia and I busied myself making cups of tea. 'I just feel like shit, Kirsty…' was her opening line.

Kirsty smiled. 'Well, you're a new mum, it's tiring.'

'Not *this* tiring. I feel terrible, all the time, no energy… You know?'

'Yes, I know,' Kirsty said sympathetically. I think she was warming to this more vulnerable Amber; she'd only ever seen the shiny, confident one until now. 'I understand how you feel. It's strange at first, this little life depending on you.' She was looking down at Mia in her arms. 'I remember the tiredness… like nothing I'd ever known. Add a sprinkling of messed-up hormones, and it's hell. Amber, you'll look back on this time and wonder how you got through it, and at the same time wish you could go through it all again. Trust me, when they get older and they're complaining because you can't afford to buy them £500 trainers and your singing embarrasses them, you'll wish you were back here.'

I nodded, feeling like an imposter – we were back in that secret club where mothers talked about stuff I would never really be able to share. I now knew how it felt to be woken in the middle of the night to tend to a crying baby – but didn't want to embarrass Amber by saying this. It might have seemed like she doesn't care and leaves me to do everything. There is an element of this, but I want to look after Mia, so I don't really mind.

I brought the tray of tea to the table, cut slices of cake and Kirsty asked Amber if she'd be staying with us now the baby was born. This felt a bit awkward for me; it was something none of us had actually discussed and I had mixed feelings. So I kept schtum and waited for Amber's response.

'Oh, we'll have to leave at some point,' she said. 'Lucy's been great, but we can't expect her to put her life on hold forever, can we Mia?'

I looked at Mia, asleep in Kirsty's arms, and felt a pang, like an elastic band being flicked at my heart. I'd cared for Mia since she was born. I love her, and helped her to grow. I'd rocked her in my arms in the middle of the night to soothe her to sleep, bathed her, read her bedtime stories that she may not have understood, but she loved the closeness, as did I. Being with Mia brightened my day, and I would sometimes drive too fast to get home, excited to see her when I finished work. And when I walked through the door her little face would light up along with my heart, and Amber would disappear to her room and I'd hold her, breathing in that heavenly baby scent. I'd feed her, the spoon a plane coming in to land in her mouth. I'd bathe her in bubbles and make her giggle when I put them on the end of her nose, or mine. And then the big, soft towel, warmed on the radiator, wrapped around her. Safe, warm and loved. Later, sleepy from warm milk, in her soft pink pyjamas, she'd fall into a snuffly baby sleep as I held her. I'd talk quietly, telling her how amazing she was and that she could be anything she wanted to be. I loved this little girl, and she loved me. And now Amber was going to take her away. I couldn't let her.

'You don't have to go anywhere,' I said. 'We love having you both here. Matt and I would miss you both so much. Anyway, you're only going back to yours when it's safe.' I stopped cutting cake and looked at her for emphasis.

'Oh yes, of course… You have to put yours and Mia's personal safety first,' Kirsty said, stroking the baby's head. 'Talking of which – how is everything with your stalker?' she asked. My heart sank. I hoped Kirsty wasn't about to turn this tea-and-cake session into something more combative. Referring to 'your' stalker was, to me, slightly passive-aggressive, implying he was someone Amber kept at home and brought to parties. Like she had made it all up. I know she never believed Amber, but it wasn't the time to start probing. Amber didn't answer, so Kirsty carried on. 'Have you heard from him?' she asked, like he might be a long-lost friend.

'*Heard* from him? I've had a couple of heavy-breathing calls. I think sometimes I'm being followed… if that's what you mean.'

I asked if anyone wanted more tea. Now wasn't the time to be dissecting the whole stalker thing, but neither responded, both locked in combat.

'Oh, that must be awful… and what have the police said?'

'The police do fuck all.'

I could feel the tension. I knew both my friends, and neither of them were afraid to confront an issue.

'I'm not being funny, Amber,' Kirsty said, pausing for effect. 'But it's not like anyone's ever seen this person. So how are the police actually expected to do anything?'

'What exactly are you trying to say?' Amber asked. Her face was like thunder, but Kirsty wasn't backing down. They were sitting opposite each other at either end of the table, and I was in the middle, just watching like I was at a bloody tennis match. I knew the subtext – I think we all did – and I'm not flattering myself when I say it wasn't a fight over a stalker, it was a fight over me. Kirsty was still smarting about mine and Amber's friendship; she was jealous and wanted to belittle Amber. I love Kirsty, but I couldn't get over how much she still disliked my friend, to the point that she'd cast doubt on the very existence of a stalker, and I had to step in.

'Look, there's no doubt that someone has been stalking Amber,' I said calmly, taking the baby from Kirsty so she could eat her cake – perhaps the lemon drizzle would soothe her? 'The thing we have to ask ourselves, as do the police,' I added, 'is who and why.'

'Exactly!' Kirsty said, putting down her fork and going in for another staring competition with Amber.

I sighed. I'd probably made it worse. Kirsty was using my comment as some kind of accusation and apart from sheer jealousy over our friendship, I couldn't understand why she was so hell-bent on making out this was all in Amber's mind. I was particularly irritated because I'd specifically asked Kirsty not to mention anything about the stalker, as the previous day there'd been a 'delivery' and I was feeling very uneasy. There hadn't been any texts for a while, and while Amber was pregnant she received nothing after the bootees, but within hours of Mia's birth, a huge bouquet of pink roses had arrived at the hospital. Amber had no idea who they were from, and what made it a little creepy was that virtually no one knew she'd had a girl at that point except me, Matt and Kirsty. Though Amber had also texted Ben's secretary and asked her to tell him, which I thought was a little stupid as he hadn't shown any interest or acknowledged any part of the pregnancy. 'She will have told everyone,' I said, 'including his wife.' But Amber insisted he wasn't with Geraldine any more and besides, his secretary was very discreet. Matt and I looked at each other over the cot and raised our eyebrows. I just hoped she hadn't brought trouble on herself again, because this time it involved a tiny, helpless little baby. Then the day before Kirsty came over to see Mia and I found a parcel by the door, just like the bird and the bootees, but this time it was on our doorstep. 'Have you told anyone you're staying here?' I asked Amber, a little concerned as we'd made the decision not to tell anyone but very close friends that she was staying at our house. 'If you've told someone in your wider circle of friends, the stalker may be in that circle and find out where you are,' I stressed.

'No, I haven't told anyone,' she said, watching as I put the gift on the kitchen table. It sat there for a few minutes, neither of us really wanting to open it, echoes of the dead bird coming back to haunt us both.

'Oh God, I thought this was over,' she said. She was sitting at the table, her head in her hands. It looked like it was up to me to open the package. Again.

'If it's something horrible I don't care what you say, we're getting the police straight over here,' I said, reaching tentatively for the parcel. 'This isn't just about your safety, it's Mia's too, and if he knows you're staying here we're *all* in danger.'

'Just open it Lucy. Let's get it over with.' She was almost in tears.

I slowly opened it up, and like the box containing the dead bird it was pretty, and when I opened the lid, more tissue paper blossomed out, just like last time. But *unlike* last time I didn't plunge my hands in. I carefully removed all the tissue paper layer by layer to reveal a perfume bottle. It was a Jo Malone perfume: black glass with a silver label and silver lid. 'It might be poison… a bomb?' I said, looking at Amber, who half smiled.

'No, it's nothing nasty – it's my favourite perfume. Dark Amber & Ginger Lily… I think it might be from Ben.' She picked up the bottle, almost cradling it.

'But if it is then it's wrapped similarly to the bird,' I said, 'and I really think we should call the—'

'Oh Lucy, it's fine, look,' she said, now all brave and cool as she took off the lid and sprayed it on her neck, the pulse points on her wrists.

'Don't put any of that near me or Mia,' I said. 'You might be happy to use something that just turned up on the doorstep, but I'm not.'

'It's gorgeous.' She smiled. 'It could be from a friend or a fan – my fans often send me nice things.'

'So why was it on my doorstep and why isn't there a gift card?' I asked. Not surprisingly she couldn't answer that.

'I just know this isn't anything to worry about,' she said, probably relieved it wasn't a dead animal. 'The things he sent were different, creepy, not like this, my favourite perfume, which smells like heaven and is named after me – Dark Amber.' And then she laughed.

A couple of days after she'd been round to see Mia, I called Kirsty to thank her for coming and told her about the perfume gift. I wanted to point out that mentioning 'your stalker' to Amber when I'd asked her not to was a little insensitive, especially as we'd received something on the doorstep only the day before.

'Oh, so Dark Amber likes Dark Amber does she?' she joked, still unable or unwilling to take anything seriously. I know she judges Amber, and the tea-and-cake afternoon had been very awkward, but I wished she'd see that this wasn't a figment of Amber's imagination. I suggested to Kirsty that we have a coffee together after work, and she agreed. I had to try and build some bridges. I'm aware that sometimes I try too hard to make people like me, to please them, but it's my way of making up for how I behaved when I was younger. I hurt people, didn't care about anyone but myself – and I have to live with that.

Despite my genuine attempt to build bridges with Kirsty, she just doesn't get it. Amber's my friend. Disrespect her, you disrespect me – I'd be the same if someone said something nasty about Kirsty. But the minute we walk into Starbucks, she starts. 'I suppose you come in here with Amber?' she says as we're ordering our drinks.

'Sometimes, yes. Why?'

'You just ordered something called "a cold brew latte with caramel cold foam". It's got Amber's name all over it.'

I resent the fact that she's implying that even my coffee choice is influenced by Amber. Yes, as it happens, Amber does happen to drink that, but she doesn't have caramel foam, she has vanilla. I don't bother to waste my time explaining this to Kirsty; the point of our coffee is to regroup, not tear each other down. I ignore her comment and as we walk to our tables with the drinks, I ask about her kids to stay on safe ground, and she tells me about her son Josh's twelfth birthday party, which is coming up.

'Two words… zombie crypt,' she says like I'm supposed to understand the apparently massive implications of this. I must look puzzled because she laughs. 'It's themed paintball parties, all the boys do it for their birthdays. I won't bore you with details – a teenage birthday party is something you'll never have to worry about...' As the words tumble out, she suddenly realises what she's said. 'God, I'm sorry, that was insensitive... I didn't mean...'

'Don't be daft. We've known each other long enough that you should be able to say anything without me being all hurt and sensitive,' I say, and I mean it. I would hate for anyone to feel uncomfortable about my childlessness. 'And yes, what a relief I'll never have to host a Quest Laser party,' I add with a giggle.

'It's Laser Quest.' She laughs. 'But it doesn't matter, you and Matt can spend your money on something far nicer than paying for a load of kids attacking each other and eating too much cake, fighting, vomiting... Shall I go on?'

'No, I get the message, thanks. I guess there are downsides to having kids.' I laugh and pull a 'horrified' face. This is nice, me and Kirsty having a coffee and just chatting about nothing, and everything, but then out of nowhere she pulls the dreaded rabbit out of the hat again.

'You know she's not the friend you think she is, don't you, Lucy?' Kirsty stirs her latte slowly, and I take a deep breath. Not this again.

'She's *my* friend. That's all I need to know. It's the same with you, Kirsty. I don't question my friends, I just enjoy their company, their support – and I'm there for them. I'm there for you too. Just because I'm her friend, it doesn't mean I'm not *yours*.'

She puts down her spoon and looks up at me. 'You don't get it, do you?' She's calm, not feisty and confrontational like she was with Amber. 'I understand that you have other friends, I do too. That isn't it. I just don't like her. I don't *trust* her – and I'm telling you this because I'm *your* friend.'

'Okay, okay. But look, I trust her. *You* don't have to, so let's leave it at that shall we?'

'I'm looking out for you, Lucy.'

'I know you are, but I don't *need* you to.'

'Okay, you don't want to hear me, but if you're going to continue to let her pull the wool over your eyes, I can't stand around and watch.'

'No.' I hold up my hand. 'I know what this is and you can't ask me to choose between you and Amber. It isn't fair – I can't and won't end my friendship with her just because *you* don't trust her.'

'Fine,' she says, standing up, leaving her drink untouched.

I'm shocked at her reaction. 'Are you going?'

'Yes. You're heading for a world of trouble with that one, and don't say I didn't warn you,' she says, pulling on her coat, throwing her scarf around her neck. She picks up her handbag and turns to leave, but fires a parting shot on her way. 'Call me when you need me – and you will.' And with that, she walks out, leaving me alone with my cold brew latte topped with caramel cold foam.

What can I do? I've tried to include her, stay in touch, but she just doesn't like Amber – and, let's face it, Amber doesn't like her. I don't blame Amber, because Kirsty seems so mean to her, then again I sometimes wonder if Amber likes anyone. I've also felt the tension between Amber and Matt during her stay with us; it wouldn't be obvious to anyone else, but I know them both so well, and honestly sometimes you could cut the air with a knife. I suppose they're both quite similar in a funny way: both passionate about their careers and what they are doing, both ambitious. But their similarities cause problems, because Amber likes to get her own way and so does Matt, which doesn't make for an easy time. And once again I find myself acting as mediator, jollying everyone along and bringing them together, the oil that lubricates the wheels. Now Mia's here I want to keep everything calm for her, because babies pick up on people's stress and tension.

If I'm honest, I've been a bit frustrated with Amber recently. She seems very down, and more edgy than usual. Some days I can't say anything to her without having my head bitten off, and when she's not finding things wrong with the way I change Mia, or the food I make her, she's just sleeping or has her head bent over her phone. She says she's worried about money, but a whole load of ASOS parcels arrived the other morning. Even Matt commented, 'Oh God, has Amber been shopping again?'

I just shrugged. 'It's none of my business, but what a new mum wants with fancy underwear and tight-fitting dresses is a mystery to me,' I said, rather bitchily.

Today, as it's Saturday and I'm off, I suggest we take Mia for a walk in the sunshine. 'It's a lovely day. Let's all get some fresh air,' I say brightly, trying to inject some life into Amber, as she's so lacklustre these days.

'I'm exhausted,' she sighs, without even looking at me. Perhaps she is – in fact she hasn't looked well recently; her skin is grey and there are dark circles under her eyes – but I suppose that's what having a baby does for you.

'Come on, we can take Mia to that lovely teashop,' I say, not really understanding why she's so 'exhausted', as it was me who was up with Mia in the night, and me who was up again at dawn feeding her. I don't mind – in fact it's usually me tending to her when I'm home so Amber can rest – but it seems to me she's 'resting' a lot these days. She's always been a bit moody, but she is just so offhand, quite rude.

'*You* take Mia to the teashop,' she says. 'I need a rest.' And with that she throws Mia's jacket onto the sofa and stomps upstairs. I feel like I've been shut down. I'm fed up of her complaining she's tired all the time – it's two thirty, and she didn't get out of bed until midday, and even then she just drank coffee and lounged around the living room. She even got Matt to make her some soup before he went to rehearsals. She does nothing around the house, has no interests other than online shopping, and I worry about her. You read all this stuff about postnatal depression, and women doing stupid things to themselves, and sometimes their babies, and I'm concerned. Am I the only one who's noticing this? Though Matt doesn't see that much of her, surely he's noticed how disinterested she is in everything? I wanted him to be aware and to look out for anything that might indicate she's unstable, so last night when we were alone I told him about finding the knife in her car months ago when I moved her in. He was, not surprisingly, shocked.

'Shit. Where is it now?'

'In our wardrobe, but that isn't really the point.' He could be so frustrating sometimes, picking up on stuff that wasn't relevant. 'What worries me, Matt, is why it was hidden in her car in the first place. She was really devastated at the time, she'd been let down by Ben and she'd just found out she was pregnant. Was she suicidal? Had she planned to drive somewhere and do something stupid? And if so, might she be that way again?'

He just looked at me. 'Who knows?' he said eventually.

'I'm concerned she might harm herself… or Mia.' I mentioned Mia in an attempt to engage him. It worked, kind of.

'No way,' he said, shutting me down quite firmly. 'Why would she do something like that? Only the other day she said she's never been happier.'

'Good,' I said. 'I'm glad about that, because she hasn't said anything like that to me. In fact she can't speak to me these days without snapping.'

I was surprised they'd even had a conversation about her happiness, but in truth I don't believe she *is* happy; I think, as usual, Matt is so obsessed with the school's production of *Annie* that he's missing what's right under his nose. I can see she's lost her spark. She seems listless, like she doesn't care about anything – even Mia.

'What she *says* and what she *feels* might be quite different, Matt,' I added, refusing to let the conversation die.

'I think you're worrying about nothing,' he said dismissively.

'So why did she have the knife hidden in the car?'

'Maybe she was using it for protection?'

'Perhaps. But hiding it under carpet in the back of the car is hardly easy access,' I said, but he wasn't really listening. Again. But I offered him more evidence. 'I told Amber the knife was missing from the block and she said she hadn't noticed… so why wouldn't she tell me it was in her car for protection?'

He looked at me and laughed.

'Are you laughing at me, Matt?'

'Yes. I think you're getting carried away. She probably just forgot about it. Life isn't like your TV crime dramas, Lucy – everything you find isn't a clue, things happen randomly and there isn't always a *reason*.'

He was really annoying me and I didn't want a row because I could hear Mia crying and Amber was having a nap. 'Well, I've put it safely away,' I said. 'We don't want any accidents…' And I went to fetch Mia, who was crying and needed feeding.

Holding Mia in my arms softened everything, and my mood regarding Matt dissipated instantly. Over the months, I'd meant to talk to Amber about the knife, but always held back. I didn't want to upset or embarrass her.

It was months ago. She has Mia now and life has changed – it probably isn't even relevant any more. So I've decided to take Matt's advice: stop trying to work out why a knife was hidden in the boot of her car, and forget about it.

CHAPTER EIGHTEEN

Lucy

When Mia is only a few weeks old Amber says she has to go back to work part-time and she arranges to work three evenings a week on the late bulletin. As I'll be looking after Mia and Amber is still a bit shaky about dark places late at night, I ask Matt if he'll collect her from work and he doesn't hesitate. He's so good about it, and never complains when she leaves him waiting for her outside the studio for ages while she hangs out with her colleagues after the show finishes. Sometimes they don't get back until way after midnight, and I know for a fact she's finished work by ten thirty. Poor Matt has to be up for work the next day and he comes home exhausted. It doesn't help that he can't relax when she's sitting around at home either, which is most of the time. Three's a crowd, but what can we do?

Matt and I aren't even alone in the bedroom – well, of course we are, but the walls are thin in these new houses and we might as well all be in the same room. Matt says we have to have sex quietly because it puts him off, knowing she's in the next room, but sometimes I can't help it. I try really hard not to push mine and Matt's relationship in Amber's face though. She's always saying how alone she feels and I don't want to make that worse, but she has Mia so I don't know how she can feel alone.

I know she loves her, you can see that, but I sometimes think Mia is a bit of an afterthought for Amber. I honestly don't think she'd actually thought much about who was going to look after the baby. Though she does know I love looking after Mia – she's the only thing that makes any sense in my world at the moment. Amber keeps saying she'll just put Mia in nursery when she goes back full-time, but selfishly I don't want this. I'd miss her too much. I'm seriously thinking about going part-time, so I can help out with Mia and she doesn't have to go to a nursery. There's nothing wrong with a nursery, but she's only a few months old and it's such a precious time, I think she should be with people who love her. She's the only one in the house who has a smile for me these days – Matt as usual is busy with work and the new play, and Amber's just, well, Amber.

We used to have such fun, but the longer she stays, the more I feel like I'm walking on eggshells with her. I never quite know what kind of mood she's going to be in. Sometimes she's affectionate though, like yesterday evening. She wasn't working, Matt was busy and it was just the two of us.

'I've made us a salad,' she said, when I arrived home from work. For Amber to do anything in the kitchen is a rare treat, and I opened the fridge, not expecting very much, but there it was, a huge bowl with exotic leaves and fruits and nuts. It looked delicious. 'I popped out to the shops with Mia,' she explained, and I was delighted that she'd actually done something rather than lie on the sofa in her dressing gown. 'I got you those.' She was pointing to a bunch of lovely pink roses which she'd arranged in a jug.

I was really touched. 'I've had a long day with Year 2 and this is just what I needed.'

'Well, you're always doing stuff for me, so I wanted to treat you,' she said. And later we ate our salad and watched TV together and had a few laughs.

Matt came home and joined us in the sitting room in front of the TV. I was feeding Mia with a bottle while Amber painted her nails and when Matt came in he made a huge fuss of Mia, whose little baby face lit up as soon as she saw him.

'Lucy, you're amazing with Mia. Isn't she, Matt?'

He nodded, looking at Mia with an indulgent smile.

'Ahh thanks, Amber, I love taking care of her,' I said. I sometimes felt Amber might be taking me and Matt for granted, but it was lovely of her to acknowledge what I'd achieved, working full-time and taking over with Mia every evening while Amber worked.

'Yeah, you really are embracing motherhood,' she said, prodding my stomach. 'You've even gained the baby weight! Hasn't she, Matt?'

Matt knows me well enough to know my weight is, like for many women, a difficult issue, especially as I've recently put on a few pounds. 'No comment,' he said, a smile playing on his lips.

I laughed along with Amber, but inside I felt so wounded. If it had just been me and her, I'd have taken it better, but Matt was there too, which made it worse. It felt like she was laughing at me and asking him to join in.

Tonight Amber's not working but has gone out for the evening. It's the second time this week and when I asked her where she was going, she just said, 'The Italian restaurant in town.' Her response seemed vague, rude even, because as the person who's looking after her baby tonight, surely she owes me a few more details?

Mia's asleep in my arms when Matt comes into the living room and sits next to me. He's touching her tiny hands and we both watch as her fingers furl around his, making his look like a giant's, and for a blissful few seconds I imagine how it might have been – how it could still be.

'Funny isn't it?' I sigh. 'This is the picture I'd imagined – you and me with a little one. I never expected it to be like this though.'

He's smiling at Mia. 'Yeah, funny the way things turn out.'

'I don't know what I'd do… if Amber left and took her,' I say. 'It would be like losing my own child.'

He turns away from Mia and looks at me, his face filled with concern. 'Lucy, don't get too close. One day Amber *will* leave and I'd hate to see you upset.'

'Don't worry, I'm a big girl. I'll cope. My heart will only break for a little while,' I lie.

He puts his arm around me and the look on his face is so tender. 'I'm sorry, Lucy.'

'Please don't apologise, Matt. It's no one's fault, just the way things are.'

'I just feel bad, especially now… with Mia,' he sighs.

'Do you think I should trust her?' I suddenly say into the silence.

'Who… Mia?'

'No.' I laugh. 'Amber.'

'Can you trust *Amber*? I don't know… Why do you ask?'

'Just the other day Kirsty said she doesn't trust her.'

'Oh, surprise, surprise. Kirsty's just jealous, you've said it yourself.'

'Yeah, I know. I just sometimes feel Amber isn't telling me everything. She's cagey about her love life, where she goes, who she's with. I don't know where she is tonight for example.'

'What love life? As far as I was aware, she doesn't have one,' he says, becoming all fatherly. He can be quite old-fashioned. He's always said Amber's promiscuous and he wouldn't approve of her going out on dates with a young baby at home.

'She's gone to the Italian with a girlfriend, hasn't she?' he says, picking up his iPad from the coffee table.

'A girlfriend? I thought it was a boyfriend?' I feel a sting of jealousy at the thought of Amber dining out with a girlfriend. Irrational I know, but surely she'd rather go out with me? 'No, it's a boyfriend. Judging by that tight, low-cut top she's wearing, I'm absolutely sure she's gone on a date,' I add bitchily. Perhaps Matt isn't the only old-fashioned one.

Matt doesn't answer, he's now abandoned our conversation for a script as usual, but it's still nice to have him here, next to me. I love having Mia here, but three adults makes it quite a full house, especially as I feel that one of those adults isn't really pulling her weight. Or perhaps I'm just feeling a bit prickly.

Matt and I are rarely alone these days, and even in bed we don't talk much, just fall asleep exhausted after work and caring for Mia. I wonder if we should have a holiday next half-term, just the two of us? I know he finds Amber irritating, and it would be good to get away, be a couple again.

I look down at Mia in my arms and wonder who Amber's with tonight. I assumed she was on a date because when I asked who she was going with, she tapped the side of her nose, indicating it was none of my business. This stung a little, but that's Amber – she's either love-bombing you with kisses or cutting you with her cruelty. I'd understand if she'd gone on a date, but to go out with a female friend has, irrationally, made me feel a little hurt, because I asked her if she'd like to go out the other evening. I said Matt would mind Mia, and perhaps we could go to the cinema and then try the new Italian on the corner. She said she didn't fancy the Italian, and besides, she was too busy.

'Have you noticed she hasn't got any of the weird texts since she came here?' I say to Matt. 'Just the flowers when Mia was born – and then the perfume. But I reckon she thinks that's her ex, not the stalker.'

'The stalker's probably given up because he knows she's living with us and doesn't want to get into a fight with *me*,' Matt says. He's puffing his chest out and flexing his arms pretending it's fun, but he really fancies himself since he started going to the gym.

'Yeah right, your big butch presence is *exactly* why Amber's psycho stalker stopped texting.' I roll my eyes and he laughs. At least he doesn't take himself too seriously.

Later that evening, Matt and I are alone together, Mia is sleeping upstairs and Amber's still out. I hate to say it, but I'm not missing her. I haven't suggested that Matt collect her, and I don't care what time she comes home, because it feels good just being here with

Matt. I'd almost forgotten what this was like, just the two of us. There's no drama, and I don't have to avoid sitting next to my husband in my own home just so Amber doesn't feel left out. She's constantly telling me how she wishes she could be married like me, and seeing us together reminds her of what she doesn't have. She even asked me recently if I'd mind not kissing Matt in front of her because it makes her feel lonely. I should have been angry with her, but what I actually felt was embarrassed, and since then I've felt like I'm being mean if I'm sitting near him, or touching him if she's around. But tonight, with her out of the house, I feel so much more relaxed – it's such a shame it can't be like this all the time. Just me, Matt and Mia.

'I think I'm going to ask Amber when she's moving back to her house,' I say.

'Why? What about the stalker?'

'I told you, she hasn't had any texts for ages. I don't think it's relevant any more.'

'What about Mia? You said you didn't trust Amber to look after her if you weren't around.'

'I think that might be the problem,' I say. 'I do too much for Amber, and it isn't helping her. I think it's time she took responsibility. I'll miss Mia, but as you said, she isn't mine and it's going to hurt me when she goes. But she has to go. Amber has to live her own life now. I could still have Mia for her when she's at work, two or three nights a week, but we need to get back to me and you. Three isn't a good number in a marriage – look what happened to Princess Diana,' I say, only half joking.

'That's silly,' he says. 'Until recently she was your best friend; you were always telling me how great she was.'

'I think we're still best friends, we just don't seem to be getting on like we used to. She's been so moody recently, and I feel like this isn't my home any more. She relies on us for everything – you and I do all the housework and a lot of the childcare and so she doesn't bother. The other day I asked her if she could help out by stacking the breakfast things in the dishwasher instead of leaving them on the side. She looked absolutely shocked and said she's too busy in the day with Mia and suggested we get a cleaner!'

I wait for his outrage, but there isn't any, so I keep talking.

'I mean… it's okay for her with all her money, but she didn't offer to *pay* for a cleaner,' I add. 'And she hasn't paid us anything to stay here – if you remember she told us she'd contribute to bills, but when I asked her she just said she'll pay us when she leaves.'

He gives a big sigh. 'And she will, Lucy. She probably doesn't see it as a big deal. Amber's rolling in it, so it means nothing to her.'

'It's not just the money. I don't know what she does all day, but I came home this afternoon and I don't think she'd changed Mia's nappy for hours.' I feel like such a bitch. I wasn't going to say anything but I'd been really angry when I saw how uncomfortable Mia was.

'Maybe Amber's way of doing things is different from yours. You're a bit of a perfectionist, Lucy…'

'Maybe, but not changing your baby's nappy, never putting a wash on, not clearing your own breakfast things, that's just lazy.'

He's probably just putting my grumbling down to pettiness, and trying to concentrate on his work, but I think he sometimes feels he's above trivial domestic problems, especially as he's working on a book, his latest thing. I offered to proofread it for him, but he said he didn't want anyone to read it. 'You can read the book when it's published and watch the film at the premier in Hollywood,' he joked. I feel a bit sad for him really. Matt sets very high goals for himself and, despite making a joke of it, really believes that one day he'll write that book, direct that film, star in that play. He has these huge expectations of himself and his life, and I can't help but worry that he'll crash and burn and life will disappoint him. At least I'll be around to hold his hand, mop his brow and help him back up when he falls.

'Anyway, another way of looking at the situation is – does Amber leaving mean Mia leaving?' I say, looking at him for a reaction.

'What do you mean, Lucy?' He's looking at me, puzzled.

'Well, Amber loves Mia but hates the responsibility, and she's never looked after her for twenty-four hours on her own. I reckon she might not want to take her with her anyway if she leaves here.'

'Of course she'll want to take her, Mia's her baby,' he says, horrified.

'Yes, but she's not exactly Mother Earth, is she? She'll still want to go out, still live her life. I doubt she'll look after Mia like we do. And if Amber does take her, she'll only be a few doors away. I'll keep an eye on things and if I see a sign of any neglect, I could go straight to social services.'

'You're scaring me, Lucy,' he says in all seriousness.

'I know. It is scary.'

'No, I mean *you're* scary. It's as if you're planning for this to happen… And what next? What would you do… try and get guardianship of Mia?'

'I wouldn't do that if Mia was well looked after, but yes, if needs be. I'm only thinking of what's best for Mia, and if that means being safe with *us* instead of being unsafe with a flaky mother, then for me it's a no-brainer.' I know I'm being hypercritical and disapproving of my friend, but I'm also being brutally honest. Amber has never shown that much interest in being a mother and wouldn't this be the best for both of us? I get the baby I love, who I've bonded with, who I always wanted, and Amber gets to live her life how she chooses.

Matt looks concerned, like he doesn't know me. I try to take his hand, but he pulls it away, which feels like a slap to me.

'Matt, I want Amber to go. It's time – but I don't want her to take this little one,' I say, looking down at the beautiful little bundle sleeping in my arms, finally feeling like a member of the mother's club.

*

Amber arrives home a little later, banging the front door noisily, which puts me on edge as Mia's now sleeping upstairs. And reinforcing my concerns earlier, judging by the state of Amber, she's in no condition to deal with a crying Mia if she wakes up. I'll be the one having to calm her down, due to the racket her selfish mother's making. She drops her keys on the phone table in the hall, creating a crashing sound, this is followed by the sound of her taking off her shoes and apparently hurling them against the wall.

Matt and I are still sitting in the living room watching TV; it's after midnight but Amber had told Matt she'd be home by ten.

'I can't do this much longer, Matt,' I murmur, as I hear her staggering into the kitchen and banging crockery around. This isn't the first time she's gone out at short notice, coming back late and drunk. I'm beginning to feel like Matt and I are the grown-ups living with a wayward teenager.

Eventually she staggers into the living room and, giggling loudly, plonks herself between me and Matt.

'Room for a little one?' she says, and Matt forces a smile, but I'm beyond that. She's really irritating me and I move onto the other sofa.

'What's up with you?' she slurs at me, then turns to Matt. 'What's up with her?'

He shrugs. He doesn't want any trouble, and Amber loves a bit of trouble. I wish he'd say something, tell her we're fed up and this isn't fair – but then again I spent the first few months of her stay asking him *not* to say anything to upset her, so I can't blame him for keeping schtum.

'Have a nice night?' I ask, trying not to sound like an embittered, ageing mother speaking to her carefree young daughter. And not pulling it off.

'Yeah, great… Kirsty's a fucking hoot, isn't she?'

I feel like a hot knife has just sliced into my flesh. 'Kirsty? Do you mean *my* Kirsty?'

She laughs. 'Ooh, I didn't realise she was *yours* – I just know her as Kirsty.'

'Did you bump into her while you were out?' I ask hopefully.

'No – a few of us went out. Some of the book club girls, you know?'

I feel the blood drain from my face. I haven't spoken much to Kirsty since the coffee shop, but I thought she might have let me know. 'I would have come too. You never said. No one told me.'

'*Someone* had to look after Mia,' she slurs again, looking at me unsteadily.

'Matt would have looked after her… I haven't seen them for ages…' I'm close to tears. I abandoned these friends for her and now she's going out with them and leaving me at home to look after her baby. She knew Matt was around, she knew I was free to go out, yet *still* she didn't invite me or even tell me.

'What is your problem, Lucy? You said you were happy to look after Mia.'

'I was… I am, but I didn't know what you were doing, that you were going out with my friends.' I just throw words into the air, unable to pin them down and process what happened tonight in my absence.

'For fuck's sake, they are not exclusively *your* friends, Lucy,' she says loudly.

Despite her intoxicated state I can see her eyes are wild and she wants to hurt me. I don't know where all this rage has come from, but it's pointing straight at me. Amber's hate is tangible. I can touch it, feel it wrapping itself around me tightly like a snake and I'm finding it hard to breathe.

'You say it every day: "I'll look after Mia, I love babysitting her, don't let anyone else have her, only me".' She says this in a whiny voice, apparently mine. 'But only on your terms, eh, Lucy? You'll only look after Mia if I'm doing something *you* approve of.' This last sentence is hurled at me, a nasty wrecking ball twirling towards my head. I can't bear it, I'm now in tears as Matt looks helplessly on. I feel like I'm drowning as I gulp for air. I don't know what's happened, but suddenly she's changed the rules. She's completely floored me and I don't know how to deal with it. All I know is that this can't go on. Amber's gone too far this time and I want her gone, but then there's Mia who's a different story altogether.

CHAPTER NINETEEN

Lucy

I'm still not sure what happened, why Amber was out with the book club girls and I was excluded. As Kirsty and I aren't really speaking, I'm not sure if I'll ever find out, but it's made me so cross on many levels. My own exclusion was bad enough, but Amber is the one who didn't like the book club and always suggested other things for us to do instead. I haven't seen the girls from the book club for ages, and wonder if perhaps they feel I abandoned them.

At the moment though, I don't have the time or headspace to work out what's going on. I was up all night with Mia last night; she has a temperature and woke up on the hour every hour. Amber might be able to lie there with her earplugs and eye mask and sleep through it, but I can't. How can she ignore the cries of her baby? Even though I've got much more on my plate than Amber with working all day, then coming home and doing the housework, caring for Mia, making supper for the three of us and squeezing everything else in between, there is no way I could just ignore Mia's cries.

After last night I'm worried about Mia and feel it would be wise to take her to the doctor. It's probably nothing, but you can never be too sure with young babies. So, after supper, I go upstairs to find Amber, who is sitting at the dressing table in her bedroom in just her bra and pants with the door wide open. We have to pass her door to go to our room and if Matt was up here, he couldn't miss her sitting there and he'd be so embarrassed. I wish she'd cover up more around the house; she's always wandering around with her robe half-open.

'Amber, you're outrageous. Your robe is wide open, I can see everything,' I said half-jokingly the other evening.

'Do you have any idea of the damage you've just caused by saying that?' she said, hand on hip, immediately on the attack. 'My mother made me ashamed of my body, and it's taken me years to accept myself, so please don't send me down that road again, Lucy.'

Of course I felt terrible, and next time she wandered around the kitchen like a bloody porn star between takes, I just ignored it. But I could see Matt's discomfort.

Anyway, I go into her room now, closing the door behind me as I do so, in case Matt comes home.

'I'm a bit worried about Mia,' I start. I don't want to scare her but I have to be clear this isn't just me being 'over the top', as she often accuses me of being.

'Oh? Is she okay?' She continues to apply eyeliner.

'Well, she's got a temperature and… It's just that a baby's temperature can indicate something else, an infection perhaps,' I offer, feeling like the bloody nanny talking to her employer.

'Ah, that explains why she was such a grump today,' she says, unperturbed, picking up her lipstick and slowly colouring in her lips.

'What do you think we should do?' I ask, trying desperately to engage her in this.

She purses her newly red lips in the mirror, and only when she's finished does she answer. 'I think,' she announces, standing up and walking across the room so I can see every inch of her perfect figure. 'I think we should see what she's like tomorrow.'

I'm surprised, though I don't know why. 'Oh. I was thinking we should really get her seen tonight, at the out-of-hours clinic…'

'Oh, Lucy, what are you like, you little worrier?' She throws me a patronising, faintly chastising look laced with a smile, and pulls a jersey dress over her head. 'Leave it until tomorrow. I'll see how she is and take her myself if absolutely necessary,' she says, now gazing at herself in the mirror. 'Ooh, be a love and pass me that necklace.' She wags her hand in the direction of the dressing table.

Somewhat taken aback, I go over and get the necklace, and hand it to her. She smiles too sweetly and puts it round her neck. I feel like her lady-in-waiting.

'Do you think this works?'

'Yes… I suppose so… So you're going *out*?'

'Yes, remember, it's the studio party tonight? Keith Hardy the newsreader's leaving. I did mention it.'

'Oh, I don't remember… So you need me to babysit Mia? Again,' I add, a little passive-aggressively I'll admit – she definitely hadn't mentioned it. I would have remembered.

'You don't mind, do you?'

'No, but with Mia not being well, I just thought…'

'Oh, she'll be fine, you worry too much. Mia will love being with you tonight. She adores her Auntie Lucy – almost as much as I do!' She gives me a peck on the cheek, and whereas once I would have been flattered by the show of affection, I just feel patronised.

'She's three months old, she doesn't even know who I am,' I snap.

'Three whole months.' Amber's now back at the dressing table dabbing perfume on her pulse points and pouting into the mirror. 'Doesn't time fly?' She glances over at me and smiles, but her eyes are hard and cold. 'Anyway.' She picks up her handbag from the bed, 'Keep an eye on Mia's temperature if you're worried, and call me if it gets very high and Matt can come early for me.'

She's become so presumptuous, like we're both here to serve her.

'Why don't you drive yourself?' I ask.

'*Because*, Lucy, I don't drink and drive!'

'You could *not* drink and then drive, just in case you're needed here,' I suggest, trying not to sound judgemental or bossy – two things she often says I am.

'And you could stop trying to run my life, Mrs Metcalf.' She says this in a 'jokey' way, but I know she means it, and if running her life means caring about her child, then yes I do. But there's no point in arguing about it.

Amber eventually leaves as Matt returns from the gym.

'I'm worried about Mia,' I tell him. 'It may be nothing, but she's got a temperature and…' She's in my arms, tired but unable to settle, her little nose running, and she has what I suspect is the beginning of a cough.

He immediately reacts and takes her from me, looking close into her face, like he might be able to tell what is wrong with her. He rocks her gently as he walks around the kitchen. 'What does Amber think?' He looks up at me.

'That we should leave it until tomorrow. But Amber doesn't have a clue… She was more bothered about what to wear tonight…' I stop, aware that recently I always seem to be making digs at her.

He sits down with Mia and I walk over to them, both of us looking into her face now. I put the back of my hand on her forehead. She is still hot. My heart is thudding.

'Let's check for any signs of a rash,' I say, gently lifting her from Matt's knee, causing her to grizzle slightly. I know I'm not her mum – God knows I'm reminded enough by Amber – but I just have this instinct she needs more than Calpol. I sit down and lift her little pyjama top, touching her tummy, then check her legs and arms, but, thank God, there's no rash. Yet.

'What if it's something serious? What if it's more than a cold, Matt?'

He looks as worried as me. 'How do we know?'

'We *don't* know, that's the point. She has to be seen by someone who *does*.'

I rub her back. She feels like a rag doll, and I panic, finding it hard to breathe. I just keep shaking my head. This tiny little thing is relying on me – on us. She has no one else to protect her, to look out for her, not even her mother, and I have to do something.

'Come on, let's take her to A & E,' I say, my mind made up. I grab her fleece and my jacket and Matt follows me down the hall.

'Can we justify taking her to A & E? I mean, are you overreacting? What if she's just got a cold?' Now he's starting to sound like Amber, and I'm not in the mood.

'And what if she hasn't?' I snap. '*Matt*! She's a baby with a temperature who's starting to feel slightly floppy. I'm *not* leaving this to chance – and I don't care if the hospital thinks I'm overreacting, or her mother's too busy to care. I'm taking her NOW! Are you coming with me?'

'Of course… Of course. I'll drive,' he says, grabbing the keys as we both run out of the front door, my heart thudding in my chest, the baby asleep now in my arms.

On the way, I call Amber several times, but she isn't picking up; probably too busy getting drunk to worry about her daughter. So I text and leave voice messages to tell her we are taking Mia to the hospital.

When we arrive, Matt drops me off at reception while he finds a parking space and I run in, clutching Mia to my chest. The receptionist looks up as I approach the desk; I am, by now, completely panicked.

'Can I have your name?' she says, like I'm applying for a bank loan.

'No… No… It isn't me. It's the baby, the baby… She's floppy, she's sleeping… high temperature… She's very warm,' I garble.

'I need your name…'

'Lucy,' I yell. 'My name's Lucy… Get a bloody doctor NOW!'

Even in the midst of all this, the receptionist shows no reaction, just shrugs her shoulders and picks up the phone to tell someone there is a baby with a high temperature in reception.

I stand, trying to breathe, and look around me for the first time. The waiting room is full and everyone is watching me, but I don't care, I just want Mia to be okay. Then Matt arrives having parked the car. His arms are open, palms upturned as if to say 'what now?' But I ignore this, and turn back to the receptionist who's staring at me with barely concealed hatred. 'Now, your name,' she says, defiant.

'I'm Lucy… Lucy…'

'You're the baby's mother?' she asks, and I look at Matt and back to her.

I know if I tell the truth they may not be able to treat Mia. They might need Amber's permission, and God knows if and when we'll be able to track her down to get that.

'Yes… I'm her… mother,' I say, not looking at Matt.

Eventually a nurse arrives who, when she sees Mia in my arms, dashes towards us, which scares me. She carefully takes Mia from my arms and tells me firmly and kindly to follow her to a small room. I set off with Matt by my side, running with me behind the nurse, and I grab his hand for support, both emotional and physical.

'I'm just going to do a quick check on your baby before the doctor gets here,' the nurse says as she ushers us into the little triage room.

She puts a stethoscope on Mia's tiny chest that, to my horror, seems to be moving up and down way too fast. I stop breathing myself, so it is quiet and the nurse can hear.

Mia wakes up as the nurse checks her, which is a relief; she'd been sleeping too soundly and that had worried me. But by the time the doctor arrives, she is screaming the place down.

'Your baby's going to be okay,' the doctor says reassuringly when he's finished examining her. 'But she has an ear infection which is giving her some trouble.'

'Oh no… I had no idea.'

'Well, Baby can't tell us what's wrong with her so we have to be aware of things like temperature, appetite…'

'She's been fine apart from the temperature… I've been checking it.'

'Good, but if this happens again, please don't leave it quite so long. Your baby's probably been in a lot of pain… I'm going to prescribe some ear drops, antibiotic. I'd like you to follow this up in three days with a visit to your GP.'

'Okay… I will,' I say, feeling like a bad mother – I want to explain it's not my fault, but no point getting into that now.

He looks at his screen. 'Name?'

'Mia… her name's Mia Young.'

'Before I can give you a prescription we need you to fill in this form, Mrs Young… just to confirm that you're Mia's parent, legal guardian, et cetera.'

He hands me the form and I shoot a look at Matt, who looks back helplessly. We have to get the treatment for Mia now, so I sign the paper as Amber Young.

Matt and I then rush to the hospital pharmacy for the precious ear drops. And only when we are home and we've given her the drops and she is finally sleeping peacefully do I allow myself to breathe again.

Later that evening, Matt goes to collect Amber from her party; apparently she'd texted him earlier to ask him, and he hadn't even mentioned it to me.

'I bet the selfish cow didn't even ask after Mia, did she?' I hiss into the darkness, when Matt returns home after picking Amber up.

'Yeah, to be fair, she asked about Mia. She felt bad she'd missed the calls. Her phone died. She didn't even realise what had happened. But she popped her head round the nursery door when she came in just then too and gave her a kiss.'

'Oh, big deal. She isn't actually going to lose her beauty sleep and have Mia in with her though?' Given Mia's infection and raised temperature she'd have been in my bedroom with me all night if she was mine.

'She didn't want to wake her.'

'I bet she didn't.'

'Don't get all worked up, love, everything's fine. Let's just get some sleep.'

And as Matt begins to snore, I lie in our bed feeling alone with no one to talk to. Again.

I lie in thick, dark silence hearing no sound from the rest of the house. Amber must have passed out almost as soon as she hit the pillow, clearly not too worried about her daughter being ill. So while the rest of the house sleeps, I get up, wander into the nursery and sit by Mia's cot in the darkness, the moon streaking through the curtains, giving me just enough light to watch her chest rise and fall.

'So many men, so little time' written on a fridge magnet she brought back from a trip to Blackpool with the girls. Kiss-me-quick hats and sugary rock shaped like men's penises... She disgusted me. A grown woman, a mother, behaving like that. 'I wish I had a different mother,' I said. 'And I wish you'd never been born,' she slurred. And later that night, as she lay in a drunken heap, I looked at her and wished she was dead. My own mother.

CHAPTER TWENTY

Lucy

The following night, things go downhill.

Amber had the cheek to complain because I'd 'forged' her signature to get Mia's prescription. 'How could you, Lucy? Pretending to be Mia's mum, really? Why would you do that?' she said when I told her.

I'd explained the situation, she knew exactly why I'd signed her name, but I couldn't help feeling that somehow this was all about creating trouble – that had it been anyone else, she'd have been thanking them for looking after her child. I made sure I told her in the kitchen in front of Matt, and was counting on him to back me up, but he just stood there, stirring pasta sauce like he was in a trance.

'Matt,' I snapped, 'will you please explain to Amber that I wasn't pretending to be Mia's mother?'

He slowly looked over at Amber. 'She wasn't,' he sighed, which wasn't quite the fierce support I'd hoped for, and I just left the kitchen in tears.

I'm now sitting upstairs on our bed while they both eat supper together downstairs. When did it happen that I became the one to feel isolated in my own house?

I sit here for a long time, feeling lost, hoping Matt might come upstairs and just be with me, hold me, so I didn't feel so alone. But he doesn't and when I hear giggling downstairs I can't bear to think my departure hasn't made a dent on their evening – it's like I don't exist here any more. It's my house and I'm the one hiding upstairs. It's madness – so I dry my eyes, wash my face and go downstairs. They're still in the kitchen and, unable to face them, I wander into the sitting room, again thinking *why do I feel like this in my own home?*

I sit down in the lamplight, in silence; it would be cosy if Matt were in here with me, and Amber was in her own home, but the room is filled with shadows. I cough, so they know I'm here, but no one pops their head round the door to say 'Hi Lucy' or offer me a cup of tea, or even some supper. I can hear them chatting now. I can't actually hear what they're saying, but I hear the tone; it's surprisingly easy, light, warm, flirty even, and the more I hear, the more distressed I become. No one has come to find me, not Amber to say she's sorry for accusing me of being a bloody baby kidnapper, or Matt to reassure me I did nothing wrong. They are carrying on their evening without me. I haven't been missed – and that hurts.

This is silly. I am in my own home and should be able to walk into each room without feeling like I'm being talked about, excluded. So I get up from the sofa, open the door and walk straight into the kitchen. Initially they aren't aware of my presence and are sitting close, heads together over the kitchen table. She's showing him something on her phone and I hear him say 'You're my everything.' I feel like I've been punched in the face. What's going on here, and when did these two ever sit so close? And, to confirm my worst suspicions, as they see me, they spring apart. The look on both their faces is identical. I'll never forget it. The only word that can describe it is guilt.

'Sorry to intrude,' I say sarcastically, swishing over to the kettle, turning it on, suddenly unsure, like I've walked into alien territory. I have just been dealt a blow, but I'm not even sure what it is. Should I be worried?

'We left you some pasta,' Amber says, and I can barely look at her. How dare she behave like it's her house, inviting me for the supper I paid for, and my husband prepared, in *our* house.

'So… she's your *everything* is she, Matt?' I say, unable to stop myself. I'm standing by the kettle, leaning on the kitchen counter, trying to look strong. But I'm not, I'm quite the opposite.

'What?' Matt says, attempting to look surprised.

'I heard you, just then, when I walked in and you didn't realise I was here. You said "you're my everything",' I hiss. 'Don't deny it, Matt…'

'Whoa, Lucy, hang on a minute.' Amber's arms are suddenly in the air like she's a referee trying to stop a fight. 'Matt didn't say "you're my everything". Why would he say that? He said "your things are everywhere"! I'm showing him photos of the place I lived in when I was in London. It was a bit of a mess, do you want to see?' She thrusts her phone at me, and sure enough there's a photo of a room in a house or flat or something and she's right, it looks a mess.

I don't know what to say. I'm not totally convinced he didn't say it, but perhaps I did mishear.

'You're hearing things, Lucy.' Amber's laughing now, and Matt joins in and I feel so stupid. I'm feeling fragile, misheard something and overreacted. 'Sorry, I'm just tired and… and, Amber, I'm still upset about before – you know I only signed that prescription so we could get the ear drops. I wasn't trying to be you.'

She stands up, puts out her arms and we both walk towards each other and into a hug. 'I'm sorry too,' she says. 'Matt explained everything, and I understand now… I feel bad. I'm sorry that you guys had to deal with all that on the night. Just put it down to my guilt… Forgive me?'

I nod, and smile, but I'm still pissed off with her deep down. I had explained to her, very clearly, why I'd signed her name, so why only when Matt explains it does she understand?

Later, when Matt and I are in bed together and Amber isn't there, listening in on our marriage, I tell him how I feel.

'Matt, this can't go on. I need some space, and I… I feel like you and Amber are ganging up on me.'

'That's ridiculous. I can't bloody please you – first you want me to be nice to her and when I am you're funny about it. I can't win.' And with that he rolls over and falls asleep and I feel the chasm between us widen, knowing that as long as she's here it will become wider and wider.

The following morning she's up, bright and breezy, pouring orange juice and being unusually pleasant, and I just come out with it.

'Amber, we never really talked about it – but when are you planning on going back home?'

She looks surprised, but, typical Amber, soon composes herself. 'So… you'd like us to go?' she says, making her face sad.

'I… No, I don't want you to go.' I backtrack, hearing the implied threat that she would be taking Mia with her. 'I mean, if you have things to do and want to spend time at yours, you could leave Mia with us a while?'

'Oh, thanks, so you want Mia but not me,' she says sarcastically. 'Sorry babe, we're a package.' She glares at me then adds a little giggle on the end to soften it.

Then Matt appears and she goes all girly.

'Orange juice, Matt?' she asks, like she squeezed it herself. It's bloody Sainsbury's.

He's putting toast in the toaster and she and I are now standing facing each other.

'Lucy thinks it's time I left here,' she says.

'I didn't say it's *time*, I just asked if you were planning to move back,' I say.

'Same thing really,' she snaps, then fakes a sweet smile. 'No, to be fair, Lucy, you've been fabulous, and you're right, it *is* time.

Mia and I will leave this weekend, if you don't mind us staying a couple more days so I can pack and arrange to move?'

'I didn't mean... You don't have to go *now*,' I say, knowing I've walked right into this. I look like such a cow. Perhaps I am. I'm virtually throwing out a friend and her baby when they are at their most vulnerable, and I'm scared for Mia – not because of the stalker, but with Amber as her carer. I can't let them go. I'd never sleep worrying about that little girl.

'Look, forget I ever said anything. You and Mia are fine to stay as long as you like,' I say, putting toast in next to Matt's. He's as helpful as usual. No support, not even a smoothing over, just deadpan, staring ahead like nothing's happening.

'No, Lucy, I've been thinking about going back for a few weeks now. We all need our space, and you need your life back. I'll start packing today—'

'You don't have to start today, it's—'

'No worries, no worries at all,' she says, and, picking up her glass of juice, she skips upstairs. I stand in the kitchen, helpless. I can't believe what I've just done.

'Well, looks like you got what you wanted,' Matt says, taking a huge bite of toast.

Have you ever had a secret that you couldn't tell a soul, even the person you love? I have. Mine's a secret about a murder. I was angry, resentful, and I wanted revenge for what had been done to my life. From when I was very young I always had to destroy what I loved, from teddy bears to teenage love, to marriage. I suppose you'd say I've never been able to make love work. I feel guilty, of course I do, but I pay for what I did every day when I look in the mirror and see a killer.

CHAPTER TWENTY-ONE

Lucy

Amber is preparing to leave. She's packed her stuff and is in the sitting room when I hear her screaming. I abandon the plates in the dishwasher and rush from the kitchen to see her thrashing around, absolutely distraught. My first thought is that something has happened to Mia, and I'm petrified.

I try to touch her but she recoils, now on her haunches, crouched in the middle of the room just clutching her phone and yelling for Matt.

'What is it? What's happened, Amber?' I'm now shouting so she can hear me over the noise she's making.

'Matt? Where's Matt?' she screams at me.

'Calm down, Amber, what is it?' I say, irritated that she's asking for him when I'm here.

'I can't go through this again… I can't!'

'What? What?'

'It's HIM,' she screams. 'He's been watching me…' She drops her phone like it's contaminated, and we both stare at it, lying there like a dormant reptile, dangerous to touch. Eventually, I pick it up; my hands shaking as I read the message.

You haven't been home in a while. I've been looking for you… have you left me Amber?

Then I scroll down to see the other one, sent seconds later.

You know what will happen if you leave me, don't you?

I don't move. I'm paralysed, not because of the text, but because Amber is screaming for my husband, and he is diving into the room, and throwing his arms around her. He's on the floor with her, his arms tightly round her, Amber's head in his neck – and I can see by the way their bodies lock together easily that this isn't the first time. As the tableau of the two of them takes shape, the truth unfolds before me, something that's been in my home, that I've lived with, but have refused to see.

'It's fine… I'm here.' Matt's face is buried in her hair. He's as shaken as she is, but not as much as I am. Matt, who's been so absent to me, is present for Amber.

Then he looks up, seems to remember I'm here, sees the phone in my hand and holds out his hand, gesturing for me to give it to him, which I do.

He looks at the text, frowning, wrinkles folding the skin across his forehead. 'Have you tried to press reply?' he asks.

'No. I have in the past when he's called or texted, but he must have blocked my number because you can't get through…'

He presses the callback button on the screen and then puts the phone to his ear with one hand, still holding her with his other arm. *He won't let* you *fall, Amber*, I think, standing there, the wallflower spectator.

'I'm getting through… I think…' he says.

'He's not going to answer though, is he?' I offer, angry at this scene in front of me and the way Matt's trying to be a hero for Amber.

Then suddenly, unexpectedly, there's a sound, a ringing sound.

'Is that coming from in here?' she asks, puzzled.

Matt shakes his head and, confused, he follows the ringing sound through the door and into the kitchen, quickly followed by both of us. I'm trying to put two and two together – but it isn't making any sense.

'It's coming from in there somewhere,' he's saying, marching towards the kitchen drawers, just as the ringing stops. 'Shit,' he murmurs, his forehead creasing, a look of dread on his face. I glance over at Amber, whose face is white. She seems rigid, rooted to the spot.

Matt presses the callback button again and opens a kitchen drawer, then the one next to it, desperately searching for the sound. He riffles through our memories – bottle tops, discarded gifts from Christmas crackers, champagne corks from happier times – and eventually he brings his hand out from the back of the drawer, holding a phone. It's still ringing.

Matt's looking at me and I think I'm about to collapse.

'It's your phone…' he's saying, holding it towards me, a look of sheer horror and confusion on his face.

It's my lost phone. 'What? I lost it almost a year ago. I haven't seen it since… I don't understand.'

They are both looking at me like they don't know who I am. I just keep shaking my head over and over again like I can shake all this away. 'It isn't me… Matt, I didn't send any texts… You have to believe me…'

'But it's *your* phone, Lucy,' he repeats as the ringing stops and we all stare at each other in horror. 'What's going on, Lucy?' he's saying, and now Amber's ranting about 'malicious calls' being illegal and accusing me of having been the stalker all along. But I don't even acknowledge her. I can't, I don't know what to say, how to defend myself. I don't know what is what any more, or who is who.

'Hang on… Hang on…' I say, raising my hands. 'The text to Amber's phone was from an anonymous number. Surely it would have said my name on your phone?' I say, turning to her.

'Yes, but this is the phone that sent the text,' Matt's saying.

'Matt, honestly... You *know* I lost it, you helped me look for it. I'm sure we even looked in that drawer.' I point feebly to the drawer like it's a witness and will prove my innocence. 'So why would it be there – who would put it there?' I try not to look at her, but the implication is clear.

'She's changed the SIM, that's what she's done,' Amber's saying, like I'm not even there.

'Why... why would I do that?' I look from one to the other and see nothing in their eyes. Is this really my husband and my best friend? Are Matt and I still us? Or is it them against me now?

'All this time, it was you, Lucy?' she's saying, and fresh tears are springing to her eyes. 'I know recently we've had our differences, but you're the best friend I ever had... I don't believe it... that you'd do such a ...'

'IT WASN'T ME!' I'm crying now, and the only way I can get my words out is to shout, to force them through my tears.

'Lucy, why would you do this... I thought we were friends?'

'This is fucked up,' Matt's saying, shaking his head. 'I don't *know* you, Lucy.'

'It's not ME!' I'm yelling.

Matt is caught in the middle of all this. He looks absolutely devastated; he's confused. Whatever's been going on with Amber, his life has been turned upside down by me, my friend and her baby – and now this. The way he's looking at me, holding the phone. I see a glimpse of my husband the teacher, and feel like I've just been caught smoking in the bike sheds. He's waiting for an explanation and just looking at his confusion, his hurt, is hurting me too. I wish I'd never met Amber, never brought her into our lives, our home. She's brought all this chaos and pain with her.

'Call the police, Matt,' she's saying, and I see how quickly the dynamic has changed. It's Amber and Matt against me. 'If you don't call the police, I will,' she says. I can see he's conflicted. He's torn between the two of us – perhaps he always has been? – but despite my tears and protestations of innocence I watch as she convinces him. 'It all makes sense now,' she says, glaring at me, but addressing Matt. 'She was the one making the harassing calls. She pretended to see the stalker at my house, she left the bootees when no one else knew I was pregnant. She must have left the bird too – God, it must even have been her that slashed my fucking tyres!'

Nothing is as it seems. This whole mess is about secrets we've kept, lies we've told. I wondered where it might end, but never expected this.

CHAPTER TWENTY-TWO

Amber

I wondered where it might end, but never expected this.

It was all so horrific. The police came, took Lucy to the station for questioning, then later that night Matt found the knife she was hiding in her wardrobe… *My* knife that I used to slash my own tyres, along with my missing scarf and – would you believe – my fucking pregnancy test. God alone knows what she was doing with those, and of course I've had to deny all knowledge of the knife.

Of course I know exactly why the knife was in my boot; as if I'd forget something like that. It was almost a year ago now. I'd heard Ben's wife had thrown him out, and assumed at the time it was because of his affair with me. He'd always said she knew about it, but apparently not – whatever. So I figured that the outcome would be the same whether she'd known or not – they'd get divorced and I'd get Ben. So I planned a stage-managed reunion with him. It would be easy. I'd have him eating out of my hand. I'd won him back easily before, but always had to be clever about it. I know him well and he doesn't like to be chased, it turns him off. I had to find a way to be alone with him, so he wouldn't be able to resist me and would think it was all his idea. I came up with this brilliant idea to go to work, park my car close to his at the TV studio and, avoiding all of the CCTV cameras, I would discreetly slash my tyre. I could use one of my Sabatier kitchen knives, then hide it in my boot and go and do my shift. Later,

Ben would leave around the same time as me, when I'd 'discover' the slashed tyre. He'd 'discover' the damsel in distress and think my stalker was up to his old tricks, and his ever-ready testosterone would start pumping. I'd shed a tear, he'd feel all manly and rescue me, and we'd fall into each other's arms – the fucking end.

So I was at my car, standing there, so ready, with an extra waft of perfume, a slick of lip gloss, looking shocked, abandoned – and fabulous. Everything had, so far, gone to plan: the tyre had been successfully slashed earlier, and now he was walking into the car park at the end of the evening bulletin. The timing couldn't have been any better, and I wanted to give myself a high five as I turned discreetly to see him weaving between the rows of cars towards me. As he came closer, I started the 'Oh my God, look what he's done now!' scenario, which involved me gasping in horror and looking forlorn. I did this with gusto, like a bloody method actor on speed, but when after several minutes he didn't appear at my side with a tyre-changing kit in hand, and lust in his eyes, I stopped my street performance.

It was so quiet. I couldn't see him, or hear his footsteps. Where the fuck was he? I surveyed the car park and, moving closer to where I'd last seen him, hid behind a Mazda to gaze through the lines of cars. It was pretty dark, with only a few lights here and there, and I tried to make out what was keeping him when my eyes finally focused on a figure in the distance. Yes! It was him, but why wasn't he walking to his car, which I'd parked close to so he would find me? I moved closer, and after a few minutes, closer again. When I eventually saw him in the semi-darkness, I had to hold on to the nearest car to stop myself from collapsing in shock – which set off the car's alarm… not part of my evil plan. Anyway, there he was, bold as brass, snogging the slut from accounts like they were starring in some sleazy porno. She was up against a car, with him all over her. So this was the affair Geraldine had found out about. I wasn't even on her bloody radar. I was so last year. As the car alarm screamed, I watched from a safe distance, unable to drag my eyes away from what was happening. It was disgusting, devastating and distressing all at once, and I just wanted to get in my car and drive home. But of course I couldn't because I'd slashed my own sodding tyre!

I was angry enough to do something terrible to his new car, like scratch it all the way down the side with the knife, but he was parked too close to a camera (I ran a key along his car a few days later when I'd confirmed the slut was my replacement and the reason for the breakdown of his marriage).

Meanwhile, the sodding car alarm was still screaming and the security guard was rushing towards me, like some out-of-shape action hero shouting 'I'm here, Miss Young.' So not part of my plan. To cut a long story short, everything turned to chaos and shit, and in the end I did the only thing I could do, and that was call Lucy. She was always great in an emergency, but, Sod's Law, the one time I really needed her she'd gone to bed and turned her bloody phone off. My back-up option was to call stroppy old Matt, her monosyllabic husband, who didn't really like me, but given my only other option was to stay the night with Felix the security guard in his hut until the garage opened, I decided to call Matt. I did this over the noise of Felix, who was now trying to stop the car alarm with one hand and waving his phone and threatening to call the police on my stalker with the other.

'I've already called the police, Felix,' I lied. 'They're coming to my home tomorrow to take a statement,' I said, willing Matt to answer quickly and chopper me out of there. I didn't want the police anywhere near my slashed tyre, for obvious reasons. Matt answered eventually and wasn't exactly delighted to hear from me, but he agreed to come along and fix my tyre and turned up half an hour later in his car.

'What happened?' he asked, bending down and looking at the tyre. Obviously I wasn't going to tell him what *really* happened, so said it looked like 'my stalker' had been around again. He rolled his eyes and just continued to scrutinize the tyre with the torch on his phone. I don't think he believed I had a stalker.

'Are you going to call the police?' he asked, looking up from the tyre.

I lied again that I already had and he accepted that. They'd been a few weeks before, when Lucy called them from JoJo's, but I told them she was hysterical and I didn't have a stalker, just an 'enthusiastic fan' who texted me a lot. That soon got rid of them. I didn't have the time or the patience to go through it all with them; I'd had lots of weird fans over the years.

I watched Matt change the tyre and marvelled at how easily he did it – this wasn't the scenario I'd had in mind, but it was a nice feeling to think someone cared enough to come out and save me. It was a warm night, and working on the tyre made him sweat. I could see his forehead was damp, so he took off his shirt to reveal a T-shirt underneath. I admired him in the glow of his phone torch, strong, muscular arms carefully taking the tyre off and throwing it around like it weighed nothing. Lucy had mentioned he was going to the gym now; and it was certainly paying off.

I'd never seen Matt in this way before, but he looked good. He was quite handsome, in a homely way, with his fair hair and strong, sturdy body. He wasn't my usual type, but I could see what Lucy saw in him.

When he'd finished, I thanked him profusely, and, facing me, he put both his hands gently around the tops of my arms, which felt intimate, but at the same time could be construed as just caring – like something a parent might do.

'The tyre's fine now…' he said, looking me in the eye, 'but are *you* okay?' This was said with such tenderness I had to resist the instinct to burst into tears and bury my head in his neck. I was overwhelmed. I'd had the most awful time, and was devastated at what had happened with Ben. I'd felt so alone, then out of nowhere he came and rescued me, and it felt like someone did care about me after all.

'I'm a little scared… I mean, he's done *this*. What next?' I heard myself say, looking back into his eyes, seeing something like kindness.

'Yeah, he won't do anything if I'm around. Now, you get in the car, start it and let's check everything's okay before you drive off, and I'll follow you back,' he said.

Okay, he was my best friend's husband, and it seemed like we had a connection, but at that point I was still in control. It didn't have to become anything more than another friendship. He was the male version of Lucy – and that's how I had to view him. And yet there was something tugging at my insides. I told myself it was probably a direct response to the stress, and the fact my heart had just been slashed along with my tyre. I couldn't help but compare Matt to Ben. Here was a man who didn't let women down – I'd never known that before.

Despite Matt suggesting I get in my car and drive off, I didn't, and we continued to stand facing each other in the darkness. The silence was thick and heavy and everything seemed to be standing still, until suddenly I reached up and kissed him, softly.

He seemed a little surprised, but allowed my kisses, his lips not moving. He was quite hesitant and unsure, but within seconds, his arms were around me, his kisses urgent. It all seemed inevitable. I tried not to think of Lucy as my hands glided up those strong, muscular arms, and the more Matt kissed me, the further Lucy and Ben receded. The agony began to pale; his kisses were slowly erasing the pain, taking away the sting that sat in my heart. I wanted to open myself up to him, consume him until I couldn't feel any more, his heart and my heart as one, our bodies tangled so tightly together nothing and no one could get in between us and hurt me again.

It's hard to explain, and I hated myself, but at the same time, with the swirling guilt and fear and hurt, a bud was growing, a thrilling spark of something new, something delicious – something forbidden.

I knew I shouldn't be doing it, but I felt a little earthquake inside as I pulled away, desperately conflicted, fighting with myself and my desires, my needs. I searched for Matt's eyes in the darkness and we both gasped.

Had that just happened, or had I imagined it? The kiss had come from nowhere. Never in a million years had I ever envisaged this scenario. Me and Matt Metcalf? Lucy's husband? Kissing?

I looked up and checked the stars were still in the sky because I felt such a meteoric shift. For almost half my life I'd thought my future lay with Ben. I thought he was love, and could provide everything I wanted, but here was someone who could maybe give me everything I *needed*. But that I couldn't have.

In silence, I climbed into my car, leaving Matt standing there, just knowing he had the same feelings as I did, that there was more to this, but I couldn't do anything about it. Here was another married man, another lover who belonged to another woman, only this time it wasn't someone I didn't know, had never met. I couldn't close my eyes and pretend she didn't exist – because she was my best friend. I couldn't allow this to ever become a reality, and I told myself it must never be given oxygen, never be allowed to breathe. But even then I felt like I was being swept out to sea on something I couldn't keep afloat – sooner or later I would lose control and it would pull me in.

Driving through the streets, I felt numb. I didn't know what was going to happen, just that it would. Lucy's husband was my fork in the road, and, right or wrong, whatever journey we were going on, from that night on I knew we'd be travelling together.

CHAPTER TWENTY-THREE

Amber

Matt followed me home in his car, and when I invited him in, he didn't hesitate, and we didn't even reach the sitting room before he gently pushed me against the wall in the hallway, and we kissed. I was lost, and, taking his hand, I guided him upstairs to my bed, where we made love, and I lay in his arms, wondering what I'd just done, what we'd just done. It was driven by lust and despair on my part, and if things had been different we'd have seen each other again, but we told each other we couldn't do it to Lucy. It wasn't easy. I tried to avoid him, but he was there in his and Lucy's kitchen cooking dinner, his strong, muscular arms stirring stews and pasta sauces. His secret smile just for me. I'd sit with her drinking Prosecco, and watch him when she wasn't looking. It was agony knowing he was so near and yet so far. I knew that in another time, another place, in another life, we'd have been lovers. Then I found out I was pregnant. I didn't know who the father was, but it could easily be Matt and after a while I moved in with them. I think I was probably a bit snappy with Lucy around this time, because in truth I was jealous. She got to sleep with Matt every night and I didn't. I remember one evening being particularly mean to her and feeling terrible because she asked me to go upstairs and when I got there, she'd turned one of their spare rooms into a lovely 'Amber room', as she called it. I cried, not just because I was so touched, but because I felt so guilty about the fact I'd slept with her husband. 'I'm a horrible friend,' I'd said, and she was kind and understanding and lovely. She assumed my tears were because I was hormonal, but they were tears of guilt made worse by her kindness.

In those first few months I felt more relaxed at theirs. Being with them made me feel safe and protected – the three of us were like a little family. I tried not to dwell on the fact that Matt and I had slept together and that there was an outside chance he might even be the father; I just wanted to be calm for my unborn baby.

When I was pregnant, I stayed around the house, all day. Lucy would come home about 4 p.m. and I'd look forward to spending time with her. She'd bustle in, chatting away, then she'd make mugs of tea and crumpets and we'd sip the hot tea and enjoy those buttery crumpets as we talked. She'd bring me little titbits from her day in the outside world – a funny thing one of the kids had said, a snippet of gossip, a rumoured affair between teachers. Like flowers, she'd lay the stories she'd collected before me on the kitchen table; they were her gifts to me, and I appreciated each one. Laughter, surprise, salaciousness, we shared it all. I'll never forget those moments. They were like our sleepovers and cinema trips – true female friendship. I remember Lucy telling me she used to envy a girl at school who once remarked in passing that her mother would be waiting with tea and crumpets when she got home from school. 'I always wanted that,' she sighed, biting into her crumpet.

I'd wanted that all my life too – and I think that's why we became friends. On the surface we're quite different, but underneath we're the same, both seeking safety and love, both recovering from our pasts. And sadly, now, both in love with the same man, and from the minute I fell for Matt, I knew our friendship couldn't survive.

Despite those initial early days, I began to find Lucy's mother-hen fussing more irritating than endearing. It seemed the more I pulled away and fought for a little autonomy, a patch of independence, the more she pulled the other way. It was like an emotional tug of war. We were both bound together by the same rope – but pulling in different directions.

At times, I wondered if she had an inkling about Matt and me; she began watching me closely, asking where I was going and who with. At first she made me feel like she was there for me and then before long I came to rely on her until I was in a situation where she'd provided me with a home and childcare and I felt this terrible sense of obligation to her. I was also obligated to Matt, but that was more complex. I'd told him all about my history with Ben, which he seemed to be vaguely aware of because Lucy had filled him in, but it turns out he's quite the manly jealous type where I'm concerned. I was surprised myself, but I liked that he didn't want to talk about Ben, didn't want to hear about my relationship with him because he was jealous. He said he'd like to punch Ben for the way he treated me for so long, and I found it touching because no one's ever cared enough to want to fight for me before. I subtly asked Lucy if Matt was a jealous husband. 'God no.' She laughed. 'I try and make him jealous sometimes by flirting with men in front of him, but he's never bothered.'

'He probably enjoyed it – fantasised about you being with someone else,' I said, enjoying the fact that Matt couldn't bear the thought of me with anyone else.

'Amber, you are outrageous,' she said.

I'm a terrible person. I hate myself sometimes, and know it would have been kinder to just walk away from both Matt and Lucy and let them be. But I couldn't, because to leave them would have broken both their hearts and mine. Lucy loves Mia and Matt loves me, and I need them both. I love Matt, but the truth is, he hasn't eclipsed Ben in my heart. I will always have feelings for Ben. He's been in my life for so long and I never really got closure when we parted. This doesn't diminish my feelings for Matt and the more I think about it, the more I feel like I could be in love with two people at once.

Matt's a less complicated man than Ben, and I assumed the relationship would be easier, more open too. But that's the problem. Matt and I realised we couldn't be apart; it was so hard under the same roof and we began sleeping together. It was so difficult, because this was the beginning of a love affair, and he naturally became more attentive to me, more openly affectionate, but we had to supress our feelings. Ostensibly this was so Lucy didn't see what was going on, but over the weeks and months I became uncomfortable with his shows of affection. Ben was cool, he wasn't demonstrative, and I'm not used to being loved the way Matt loves.

'If Lucy finds out, then that would solve our problem,' he said, when I asked him not to touch me as soon as she left the room. 'Lucy will divorce me and we can be together.' I find him attractive, I like sleeping with him and being loved but I'm not ready for a full-blown relationship and I realise now that part of Matt's appeal for me was probably that he was forbidden fruit.

It was like he lost his head after we started the affair, constantly trying to kiss me, embracing me at difficult moments when I was busy, or holding Mia, or just needing space. He told me he loved me all the time, and I remember one evening, when Lucy was still here, he was saying 'you're my everything' and Lucy walked in and heard him. I almost died, and managed to cover it up, saying she'd misheard, but I think Matt wanted to confess there and then.

Sometimes I could barely look at her, for the way she made me feel, through no fault of her own. When I was first pregnant, she gave me a beautiful little teddy for the baby and when she handed it to me I just cried. She thought I was crying because I loved the gift, but I was crying because I hated myself for what I was doing to her.

My mother always said I was bad. 'Rotten like your father,' she'd say. Perhaps I am.

More than once I'd told Matt it had to stop, and he agreed, but then we'd brush past each other on the stairs, or find each other's eyes across the room, and before we knew it we were making love. Sometimes, though, we'd just cuddle, and he'd tell me how much he loved me, how he'd loved me from the first moment he laid eyes on me. It was heady stuff for a woman who once turned heads and was now dealing with a different reality of being a mother, and being replaced for someone younger by her ex. I still needed to hear that I was attractive, sexy, and loved – and Matt did all that. And even when I told him the baby might not be his, he said it didn't matter to him.

'I hope I am the father,' he said, 'but what's yours is mine, and I'll love that baby like my own.'

I relished the rare evenings Lucy worked late or went out with her friend, dear old tight-lipped Kirsty who loves to judge everyone. And when Lucy stayed home we'd tell her there was a problem with the alarm at my house and we'd go back there and be together for a few delicious minutes. The sex was always rushed, secret, forbidden – and so exciting, especially when we thought she might come and find us.

Later I'd hate myself when we were all sitting round the table, Matt serving dinner from one of their Le Creuset wedding gifts meant to last a lifetime. I'd smile and nod, and sometimes cry and blame my hormones and Lucy would hug me and I would hug her back, knowing that, for me, a friend like Lucy was a once in a lifetime friend. And I was ruining her life.

Other times I'd hear them talking when I wasn't in the room. Their voices were warm, easy – flirty even. It surprised me the way Matt could go from all-consuming passion with me, his lover, to caring husband with Lucy, but I suppose he had to play the part or she might suspect. But just hearing their laughter in the house made me feel jealous, alone, like a child again, hearing the voices of my mother and another man… one of her many suitors who looked at her like she was a piece of meat. And Mum knew what she was doing; she knew the effect she had on men and used it to survive.

The first time I became aware of my sexuality was with one of my mother's boyfriends; he wanted me so badly, said I was teasing him. I let him do things to me, and afterwards he gave me ten pounds and told me not to tell my mother.

Those early experiences can set one on a course. It became far more refined as I grew older, but looking back it wasn't so different in the beginning with Ben. He wanted me and rewarded me for sex, just like the first man all those years ago – the disgusting beery breath was replaced by a fresh minty one, and the stench of unwashed armpits was now something French and expensive. Ben didn't give me money, it was far more subtle than that, but he used me just the same – paying for my services with lucrative presenting jobs and the promise of marriage one day. I like to think the transaction eventually turned into something like love. At least it did for me, but then he let me down, like all the other men I'd ever known, except Matt, who was different. Matt was more like Michael, my husband. He was genuine, good and pure – just like Lucy really – and I was like a nasty stain on their scrubbed-clean lives.

It was bad enough before, but after Mia was born the situation at the house became impossible. Matt and I had decided that we were going to move back to my house together and take Mia with us, but Lucy was under the impression it would just be Mia and me moving back. We kept putting off telling her, until one night when she virtually told me to get out. She said it was time I left, which I saw as the perfect opportunity for us to go, but still Matt was dragging his feet, so I told him I was going whether he came with me or not.

I knew he wanted to leave with me, but it wasn't my first rodeo, and after Ben I really didn't know if I could rely on Matt. And so there I was again, with another woman's husband, just hoping he'd come through for me. I don't know how much longer I could have taken it. I longed to be with him, for Lucy to be out of the picture so we could be together – but still the guilt. Always the fucking guilt, traipsing behind me like an unwanted dog with big sad eyes. The whole thing with Lucy's phone was awful, but it brought me and Matt closer and despite her being his wife, when he saw it was her phone and realised the implications, he said he wanted nothing more to do with her.

It didn't take us long to put two and two together after finding her phone hidden at the back of the drawer. Then, of course, there was the knife she'd hidden in their bedroom, and we found the pregnancy test there too. She'd ferreted that away in the back of the wardrobe, wrapped in the scarf I'd lost – the one she liked with stars all over it. Matt opened it up on the kitchen table and there it all was. I feigned surprise and said I knew the knife was missing but had no idea where it was or how Lucy had got her hands on it. I did feel bad about the knife; it was definitely the one I'd hidden in my car boot when I'd slashed the tyre. But then again, what the fuck was *she* doing with it?

'Mmm, we have to assume that the night she said she'd encountered an intruder in my home was the night she took my knife from the kitchen. She was the intruder, wasn't she?' I said, making sure Matt understood. 'She seemed like such a lovely woman, a kind friend. Who could have imagined the darkness inside her?' I added. 'I can't believe my best friend was my stalker.'

So the night we found her old phone and the incriminating text Lucy was interviewed y the police and kept in for twenty-four hours. I'd deleted all the previous stalker messages on my phone, so couldn't offer any evidence but it didn't matter because the single text found on her old phone was enough to charge her with sending malicious messages. I urged Matt to tell them about the knife and pregnancy test too, all wrapped in my starry scarf. I think he still found it hard to believe she could be so creepy and hated giving the bundle of evidence to the police, but as I said to him, 'Your marriage is over – you owe her nothing.' I knew he felt guilty because he cheated on her, but as I pointed out, 'She deceived us far more than we ever deceived her.' I finally convinced him to take the knife and the test to the police, pointing out that if he didn't I would. 'Matt, we are withholding evidence,' I said, 'and she needs to be convicted – she's a danger to herself and others.'

'That's funny, that's what she said about you – she said she'd found the knife in your car and that's why she hid it in the wardrobe, because you were a danger to yourself and others,' he said. The irony! And the cheek!

'That's rubbish, why would I be driving round with a bloody kitchen knife in my car?' I said. 'How dare she, of all people, say I'm a danger.'

After that I worried she might tell the police about finding the knife, so when I heard she'd been released awaiting trial, I told the police I was concerned for mine and my child's safety, that she was quite unhinged, and made it clear that if she was walking the streets we needed a restraining order. I told Matt as much, but he didn't seem overly concerned.

'Amber, she's not in our lives any more, it's over,' he said, but I wasn't so sure. I wouldn't be happy until she was in prison.

'She had a fucking knife hidden in the house,' I yelled at him, 'and wait until she finds out about you and me… God only knows what she'll do.'

I'd stayed on at their house, everything was there that we needed, and I couldn't afford to keep my house, so for now it was decided we'd stay put. But I told Matt she might even have kept her house key and could come in with another knife and murder us in our beds. I saw the fear in his face and knew I'd finally managed to convince him that she was very dangerous and capable of anything.

So, now she'd been charged and is awaiting trial and we have a restraining order and the crazy bitch can't come anywhere near me, my baby or her soon to be ex-husband.

Matt and I both feel that her affection for me bordered on obsession, but even *we* were shocked at the level of weirdness. My pregnancy test… What the fuck was that about? Maybe she was pretending to herself that she was Mia's biological mum? After all, she told the hospital she was when she took Mia there with a cold. 'God, she was always making a fuss over Mia, wanting to hold her and feed her,' I said to Matt. 'She was so highly strung about every little thing, running at every little cry or whimper, and the way she looked at Mia was so adoring, so… possessive.'

Matt was beside himself; everything he'd thought about his wife and their life together had shattered. 'I know, but she loved Mia, even if at times it felt a bit over the top. I just can't believe I was married to someone for ten years, and I didn't know her,' he said.

We were lying in bed together talking about her, about everything that had happened. 'I know. She was my best friend and I feel the same,' I said. 'I've never been scared of being alone before, but the texts, the creepy gifts, eventually it just got to me – I thought she wanted to help, but clearly she was the one doing it. I wasn't too concerned about the texts at first, and she kept trying to scare me, going on about how these things escalate, but I didn't rise to it… It must have been so frustrating for her.'

'Yeah… so she ramped it up, sent that dead bird, pretended the stalker was at your house. No one actually saw anyone, but she created real fear and panic until you gave in and came to stay with us.' He sighed.

I think Matt's quite a gentle person. He'd been manipulated and lied to and now it was like he was in shock, unable to believe anything.

'And when she thought I might leave and go back home she left the booties. I can't believe we didn't put two and two together. No one else knew I was even pregnant,' I added, putting the final pieces of the jigsaw in place.

'I guess it was her way of making you stay… She had you and Mia under her roof, so she could look after both of you,' he said.

'*Control* us, you mean.' I wished he was more on board with this; the language he used about her suggested a far more forgiving approach than mine. 'I just shudder to think what might have happened if you hadn't found that phone.'

'It was luck. I called the number and presumably she'd forgotten to switch it off. Amber, I should have seen this, should have realised what was going on… I feel responsible that this happened to you…'

'Matt, don't even think it – you rescued me. You always have and always will.'

'I let you down, babe.'

'You could never let me down, you're my everything.' I sighed and leaned into him as he kissed me on the top of my head.

And in that moment I felt like I'd finally found what I'd been looking for, sitting there together, entwined on Matt and Lucy's sofa – except now it was Matt and Amber's sofa.

A month after her arrest I hear Lucy has no job and is living in a crummy rented flat. Basically her life's gone tits up and it's all her fault. Serves her right for all the shit she's put me through. She appeared to be so sweet. I'd never have guessed. In spite of everything, I'd felt really close to her – but perhaps that was the problem. We became too close. There were times when I didn't know where she ended and I began. But I'm glad it's all over, and I'm glad we got the restraining order, because I sometimes think I hear her at night.

Along with all the other madness, it seems she's spread all kinds of gossip about me too. The irony of her telling Matt she took the knife away from me because I was dangerous is hilarious. I wasn't the one hoarding knives in the back of my wardrobe.

Her court case is coming up soon and I hope to God she's found guilty, because that will stop her blabbing to the papers. If she goes free she can deny everything and even implicate me – I can see the stories now, plastered across the tabloids: 'Amber Young "weathering" knife storm: best friend says she's a danger to herself and others. Today, Lucy Metcalf, 43, described how her former best friend, weather girl Amber Young, was a suicidal maniac hell-bent on killing herself and anyone who got in her way. With a big old kitchen knife she carried in her car.' Okay, I exaggerate, but I'm shuddering at the thought of the scorned woman/priapic press combo. Together they'll stop at nothing.

The worst, though, is Ben; I keep thinking about the newspapers having a field day with everything Lucy has to tell them and him reading about my potentially suicidal/murderous ways and want to die. But why am I still worrying about what Ben thinks? My own mother is still alive somewhere, but I don't care how she'd feel if she opened the paper and read about my penchant for the blade courtesy of Lucy. Mind you, she wouldn't be surprised; she always said I was evil. Like mother like daughter, I suppose.

Talking of Ben, I wish I could eradicate him from my head, from my life, but I can't because Mia looks so much like him – big dark eyes, dark hair, dimples when she smiles. Yes, I think we know which tree that little fruit fell from. Sometimes I want to call him up and tell him he has a daughter, but given my history with men, why would I want to saddle her with an absent father? Ben might pay money if the courts forced him, but he wouldn't take any responsibility – a baby with his former mistress wouldn't fit into his shiny new life with the slut. (I heard they'd moved in together. She got what I didn't. Slut.)

As for Matt, while he thinks Mia might be his he'll be more invested in us as a couple, and right now I need the emotional security Matt brings. I love living with him in his cosy little home, and Mia's happy here too. We are a little family, and that's what I've always wanted. I stay at home in the day looking after Mia, cooking dinner and waiting for Matt to come home; he often brings me flowers and always makes Mia laugh. I love our life, it's simple, and for me it's so different to anything I've ever had before. I've always been single, snatching nights and weekends with Ben, but this is real.

Sometimes, though, I wake in the night, and a shadow comes over me, worrying what Lucy might do when she finds out about me and Matt. I just keep thinking about a conversation we had once when she talked about what she'd do if she caught Matt cheating. 'I don't know what I'd do, and I don't want to be tested,' she'd said, 'but I'd probably kill them both.'

CHAPTER TWENTY-FOUR

Amber

The trial didn't last long; Lucy was found guilty of trespassing and making a malicious call and got a six-month suspended sentence. I wept at the injustice.

'It's nothing for the year of agony I went through,' I said to Matt. 'All the torment, the fear, the texts, the stashed weapons, the "gifts" and constantly feeling like I was being watched.' But I'm glad it's over now. I feel I can get on with my life and am even considering moving to London, or finding TV work in Cornwall or Devon, so I can forget all the horrible things that have happened here, behind the floaty curtains on Mulberry Avenue.

I think Matt senses my slight withdrawal, and though I don't want to hurt him, I don't want to make promises to him that I can't keep. And now the court case is over, he wants to talk about finding out if Mia's biologically his, settling down and starting a new life. 'We could even have more kids,' he said to me this morning before he went to work.

Sometimes I feel a bit trapped with Matt and I don't think I want to commit to a family/settling down/a wedding with him. Before the court case, I was feeling very insecure. I was struggling to look after Mia without Lucy and I welcomed Matt's big, strong arms around me. But now, despite it being a terrible outcome for us, I feel like I've moved on. I'm stronger, I want to go back to work full-time, I'm ready to go out there and fight again. And when

Matt embraces me with those big strong arms now, I feel like I'm being pinned down and I feel this rising panic and want to shout at him to get off me. The problem is that Matt wants forever. He wants to divorce Lucy and head straight down the aisle with me, but I don't know any more.

He's changed since Lucy left, isn't as laid-back – he wants to know what I'm doing, where I'm going, just like she did, and I find it a bit of a turn-off. I think I must be like Ben. I want to do a bit of the chasing; I don't like it when it's too easy. For twenty years I was 'the other woman', and then I went and did it again, but this time I got him – and now I don't know if I really want him. I'm beginning to wonder if me and Matt only worked when Lucy was around and I wanted her gone. Be careful what you wish for.

'You don't love me any more, do you?' he said the other day, just as I was going out to work.

My heart sank – *not again.* The pained look on his face, the repulsive spectre of a grown man being needy.

'I'm not sure how I feel,' I said, in all honesty. 'I need to work out what happens next.'

So the following evening Matt cooked a meal, set the table, lit candles and bought good wine. It was lovely, and I was delighted, until I saw a box on the kitchen counter that looked suspiciously like it might contain a ring.

'Babe,' he said, 'we've had a difficult few months, but now the court case is over and the divorce is going through, I was thinking…' His eyes were all gooey in the candlelight. His hand reached for mine across the table, and I immediately moved my hand away.

'What were you thinking, Matt?' I asked, trying not to show the panic in my face.

He reached over to the counter to pick the box up. My heart was on the floor. I didn't want to hurt him, but I didn't want to marry him either. So before the circus began, I put my hand over his to make my point, and hopefully prevent him opening the bloody box.

'I may be going way too fast here, cowboy,' I said brightly, to make my rejection seem softer, 'but if you're going to ask me to be your wife, I'm delighted and flattered… but not ready… yet.'

In an instant, he went from pert and hopeful to absolutely crushed.

'Don't take it the wrong way, darling. I'm not saying no, I'm saying let's wait. You know I love you to bits… but we've both been married before, and we have a few things to get through before we even think of marriage.'

'But we can get engaged…' he said, a flare of hope in his eyes.

'No, babe… not yet. You have to get divorced first and we both need to be sure we're doing the right thing for us… and for Mia.'

'We are, I know we are. I've never been more sure of anything…'

I gently kissed him. Long, promising kisses that soothed and placated him and led us to the bedroom, where I managed to magic away his marriage angst and make a rejection feel sweeter than it should.

Of course I tell him I love him. I say he's the love of my life and all the other clichés – but who knows? I didn't have love as a child. Mum had her own problems and I was lonely. I didn't feel anything like love until I met Michael. For years he was my first protector, my lover, my rescuer, but loving me weakened him, and it seems to have done the same to Matt. Ironically, this has made him less attractive to me – I want the manly rescuer, not some guy sitting at home complaining I'm never there, trying to kiss me every five seconds and asking where I'm going if I so much as leave the room. He seems to do less and less outside the house, doesn't work late, isn't as involved in the plays like he used to be and he's even given up on the gym.

'I only went so I could get your attention with my new body,' he said the other night. 'I've got you now.' And the way he's acting, he's determined to keep me.

The only 'me' time I have now is when I go to work. I present the evening weather permanently, so it works well because he can look after Mia in the evenings. Sometimes I go for a sneaky drink after work and tell him I had to do the 'tech clear-up' – there's no such thing, but he doesn't know that.

Yes, Matt's become far too clingy and it's made me realise the reason I found Ben so irresistible for so long was because I was never sure of him. And that was part of the excitement.

I met Ben when I was still married to Michael. We were happy – Michael and I – we had a nice flat, both had decent jobs and a good life. We'd met in a bar in London; I'd left home, I was very young, he was ten years older and he knew about life. Within weeks of meeting him, I'd moved into his flat and within a year we were married. His family didn't approve. I was some working-class girl from the wrong side of the tracks; they said it would never last, but he said we'd prove them wrong. And we did… for a couple of years. Michael gave me the home, the security and, most importantly, the consistency I'd craved growing up. I always knew he'd be there, he never let me down and for a while I was in heaven. But it wasn't what I was used to, and it wasn't long before I craved uncertainty, the not knowing, the fear that had filled my childhood. It was what I knew. So I had to go and spoil things and sleep with Ben Bradshaw, the enfant terrible of television, the talented maverick… and married with children.

I never stopped loving Michael, but Ben was my exciting dirty secret, and after a while I wanted more than just the odd night – I wanted Ben full-time. It was a horrible mess, but after months of rented afternoon hotel rooms and snatched kisses in the lift at work, we agreed to leave our marriages and run away together.

I didn't waste any time. I didn't want to continue living a lie and hurt Michael any more than I had to, so I told him straight away. I was very honest, said I loved someone else, and packed an overnight bag and left immediately, while he begged me to stay.

I was young and selfish and Michael wasn't my future, Ben was, and I wasted no time in going straight to the hotel, where Ben and I had arranged to meet once we'd told our respective partners. I checked in and waited in the room where we'd plan our new lives together. I waited, and waited, and when it got dark outside, I had this horrible feeling that he might not be coming, which was confirmed when the hotel reception rang. At first I thought they were calling to tell me he'd had an accident, so sure was I of our future together – only an horrific accident could stop him from being with me. But they were calling to tell me Ben had 'a family emergency', which of course was his way of backing out.

Ben had allowed me to ruin my own life, my own marriage, but hadn't kept his part of the bargain. So I went back home, to the only real home I'd ever had – with Michael. But things were never the same and I'll never forgive myself for what happened.

I'm thinking about Michael when my phone rings this morning. I panic slightly; it's not a number I'm familiar with. But I pick up anyway, and hear Ben's sexy voice.

'Amber… It's Ben… Ben from work?' As if there was any other Ben in the world. I've seen him around the studio in the last few weeks, but as I don't work for him directly and have a different line manager, our paths rarely cross. I'm amazed that his voice still has the ability to turn me to mush.

'You've changed your number,' I say.

'Er… Yes, I… A different contract.'

And I suddenly realise with deep embarrassment that I'd made rather a lot of calls to his old number when we'd parted last. He'd changed it so I couldn't contact him.

'Do you have five minutes… quick chat?' He's straight to the point, no messing about, but that's Ben.

My heart misses a beat. Is he calling to ask that we get back together or is he ringing me about work?

'Yes… I just have to listen out for Mia,' I say, sounding like the perfect new mum, which I'm not (though since Lucy left I've been forced to learn fast).

'I was just wondering how you are.'

I relax at this; it's music to my ears. 'I'm good.' I'm smiling from ear to ear but don't want to give anything away. He wants me back, he can't live without me. But this time even if we do get back together, I won't make it quite so easy for him. 'Look, Ben, it's good of you to call, but is this about work?'

'Yeah… kind of … It's about the case you were involved in. The stalker? I watched it closely.'

I don't say anything. My heart drops. Where the hell is this leading? Is he going to use the stalker drama as a way to get rid of me at work? Not good for the brand, the advertisers don't like it et cetera. I'm clutching the phone to my face while pacing the living room. What if I lose my job? My career? Apart from Mia, who I adore, whose sweet little face is what gets me up each morning, work is the only thing that's keeping me sane.

'I love the late shifts and the audience figures are good, I think.' I try to hide the question in my voice.

'Yes, they are. You've always been a popular on-screen talent.'

Thank God! So he isn't calling to sack me.

'I'm calling because… I'd like to chat. Perhaps we could have coffee, talk about the court case?'

I have to sit down – how intriguing.

I realise in this moment that the answer is YESSS! I know I'd also sleep with him in a heartbeat, but I continue to play it cool. 'I'd love… to have coffee with you,' I say. Whatever happened between me and Matt, I know that it's over. There's only one man I want, one man I've ever wanted – Ben.

So while other teenagers kissed and drank cider in the park, I sat on the sofa dreaming of stormy oceans and endless continents. I watched in awe as those weather girls purred over warm fronts and tingled as they talked of Arctic winds. Those women had time for me, they were perfect in their designer suits and shiny hair – they didn't piss their pants and fall down the stairs drunk. They were real women.

CHAPTER TWENTY-FIVE

Lucy

I received a letter in the post from Matt this morning, informing me that he would never come to terms with what I'd done. He said that Amber was happy now I wasn't around, that her mental health had suffered because of me. He said he didn't know how I could sleep at night after what I'd done to her, the trauma I inflicted on all their lives.

These days, my life is so different. I live in a small, rented flat, I have no job and Matt's letter felt like something from the past, another life, another time. I can barely say her name, I'm filled with such resentment and hatred – she's taken everything, and she did it right under my nose. She pretended to be my friend. I gave her so much and still she took more.

I can't comprehend what's happened to me. In just a few hours my life changed, and nothing will ever be the same again. I lost my home, my job, my marriage and my future – there's nothing left to live for – and it's all Amber Young's fault. The police only found one message on my lost phone, but still I have a suspended sentence and a criminal record. And my crime? My crime is that I cared too much about my friend. As it is, I can't go near her, Mia, my husband or my home, and if I do anything that is considered to be against the law, I'll be sent straight to prison.

I thought I'd done the impossible and transformed myself, changed my life, fought nature and nurture and come out the other end as Lucy – kind, sweet Lucy, the teacher married to Matt. I thought I'd changed, but perhaps it's my destiny. People who knew me as a kid had me down as someone who would end up in prison. Even my own mother said I was trouble, so she wouldn't be surprised at the way things turned out for me. But I tried so hard, I really did, and for a while I thought I was winning.

From an early age I had problems at school; my family was considered dysfunctional, and I was emotionally unstable. Now I can see that like many children from 'difficult' homes I was simply unsupported and misunderstood. I'd fight, scream in class, swear at teachers and didn't attend school; I was angry and antisocial.

Then, in my final year, Miss Brownley became my year tutor. As a new, young teacher, she was an idealist, believed anything was possible and, where other teachers hadn't bothered, she tried to reach me. She'd ask my opinion, seemed to care what I thought and most of all wasn't scared of me. Until then, teachers had behaved defensively towards me, as if I might stab someone every time I walked into the classroom. I was staggered when Miss Brownley asked me to stay after class and, instead of reprimanding me for something, invited me to join the English reading group with all the swotty kids. My instinct was to say fuck off, but I said a grudging 'okay' because even that torture would be better than going home, and the fact she'd even bothered to speak to me like I was human made me feel special. The other teachers treated me like an animal, probably because I behaved like one. So I started her reading group and discovered how books could help me escape my horrible life.

I loved being around Miss Brownley; she smelled of fresh, cut flowers and sunshine, unlike my mother, who reeked of nicotine and alcohol. She glided to the blackboard, putting pencils through her long auburn hair to keep it there; she was effortless, graceful, beautiful – a goddess to me. In the following weeks, I stayed on after school tidying the classroom, reading the books she'd given to me, and sometimes she'd stay behind too and mark her papers.

'You not going home tonight, Lucy Lou?' she'd say. The nickname she always used for me made me feel like I belonged. As a teacher myself I now realise she must have guessed I didn't want to go home, and was probably concerned about me. I see the warning signs with troubled children in my class – they are only small, but the imprint is already there for life. I always hope that I've got there in time before the damage is done – but when is too late?

Then one day, Miss Brownley invited me to her house for tea. I couldn't believe it, I'd never even been invited to tea by classmates and so-called friends. No one's mother wanted me near their kid, so to be invited by my favourite teacher was amazing. I could barely concentrate on my lessons all day, and after school I went home, where I told my mum, who didn't care because she had more pressing business with a vodka bottle and twenty ciggies. So with Miss Brownley's address written on a bit of paper, I ran all the way there, unable to contain my excitement. I was sixteen years old and I'd never been in a house like hers: a lovely little cottage with groaning bookshelves, a squashy sofa and a kitchen heady with the strange and exotic aromas of garlic and basil. We talked books, books, books, my blissful escape into other worlds, kinder, cleaner, more tranquil lives. I remember pointing out that she shared the same first name as Daisy Buchanan from *The Great Gatsby* and she recoiled in horror.

'I do hope I'm not *like* Daisy Buchanan,' she said.

'Yes, she's beautiful, like you.' I was confused, I'd meant it as a compliment.

'It's not about how people *look*, Lucy, it's who they are that matters,' she said, hunting for the book on her crammed bookshelves and flicking through until she found what she was looking for and then reading out loud: '"They were careless people, Tom and Daisy – they smashed up things and creatures and then retreated back into their money or their vast carelessness…"' She looked up from the dog-eared Penguin copy, with its orange spine and yellowing pages. 'Daisy was rich and beautiful, but she isn't someone to aspire to.'

'No, I take it all back, you're *not* like Daisy,' I said, and she laughed.

Miss Brownley seemed to me to be the opposite of Daisy Buchanan; she was far deeper, more thoughtful, more loyal even. My Daisy would never hurt anyone. But later that summer, I realised how much like Gatsby's Daisy she was – she smashed up my life... She'd given me hope where there was none, then retreated back into her safe little life. My Daisy's carelessness had been as vast as Daisy Buchanan's.

But during that first perfect evening in her home, how could I possibly envisage what would happen as we chatted and she cooked glamorous Italian food? I'd never had Bolognese before – it tasted strange and exotic and quite delicious. We ate outside at a little wooden table on rickety seats in her tiny garden and afterwards we watched the sun disappear behind the trees. My personal heaven on earth.

'Miss, I feel like we're in Italy,' I said, and she smiled affectionately.

'*Ciao bella*!' she said, lifting her water glass to meet mine, and we clinked them together.

After we'd eaten, she showed me the roses in her garden, making me close my eyes to smell their sweetness. I can feel it now, the velvet rose tickling my nose as she held it to me, the rich, heady fragrance of summer. As we stood amid the blooms, her hand accidentally brushed mine – it was nothing, yet at sixteen, for me it was everything, and the frisson went through me like an orgasm. Dusk was enveloping us in warm pink and I dragged my eyes from the sea of pink roses to look at her. She was already waiting for me, her eyes on mine, and I wasn't surprised when she reached out her hand, the softness touching my face. It felt surreal when her middle finger began stroking my lips. I was dizzy with desire, the roses like pot in my nostrils, my head filled with the moment, everything crowding in.

I closed my eyes, waiting for the kiss. But it never came, and after a while I opened them, and could see from her face, the glitter in her eyes, that she felt the same way. It would be our secret.

Before I could say anything, she'd moved to the table, collecting our empty plates, chattering about how she had lots of marking to do and she'd drive me home now. I was confused, but at the same time I was so happy, because I knew she felt the same as me. We had all the summer ahead of us and it was a matter of time before we kissed in her beautiful garden.

The next day in class, I held our secret close, just watching her, mesmerised. I let my imagination run away with me, daydreaming about us living together in that lovely little cottage. It was innocent, naive – but for a damaged child looking for love it was also intense, a fire that couldn't be extinguished without someone being hurt.

When she invited me again for tea, I was beyond excited, taking along a bunch of giant daisies bought with money I'd taken from mum's purse. I considered asking her that evening if I could go and live with her; she'd told me once she was lonely and I was lonely too. I proudly presented my bunch of daisies to her at the door as she swept me up in a warm hug. Then she grabbed me by the hand, pulling me into her home, me tripping behind her, giddy with expectation, my face flushed with the promise of what was to come.

We walked into her warm, cosy kitchen. I remember a row of mismatched glass jars filled with deep amber chutney lined the windowsill; they each had red-and-white checked covers that looked like hats. All neatly labelled, the whole picture epitomised a clean and tidy life, one with labels and lids all neatly planned and laid out in a row. How beautiful they looked. How clever she was. How I wanted to live this life.

'There's someone I want you to meet,' she suddenly said in a grown-up voice as we entered the kitchen. 'Tony, he's my fiancé…'

I couldn't quite take this in. She had someone else? She'd betrayed me with someone called Tony. Everything I was hoping for – my escape, our new life together – was gone in a moment. And here he was, a smug smile on his face, a patronising hand reaching out to shake mine. My rival, my nemesis, was standing in *our* kitchen. I wanted to take the kitchen knife and stab him right there and then.

I don't know what came over me, but I remember silently heading straight for that perfect row of amber chutney. Wiping my arm across the windowsill, I toppled them all, and they came crashing down, a mess of glass and fruit. The sweet, tangy fragrance hit me even in my traumatised state. I screamed obscenities at both of them as they stood in shock, Daisy with tears streaming down her face, him standing in front of her protectively. And then he bundled me out of the house and locked the door. I'll never forget the clicking of that lock; it was a metaphor for my life. As if I would ever have done anything to hurt Daisy Brownley.

It was all so horrific, I still sometimes cringe now at my reaction, my lack of control, my animal rage and hurt. In that moment, I proved all the teachers and social workers right, and proved Daisy Brownley wrong. All the words that had been used to describe me were accurate – I was antisocial, out of control, violent and unpredictable. But in reality I was little more than a child who thought she'd found love. And lost it.

I never saw Daisy Brownley again after that summer, which made me sad – but there was so much worse to come.

CHAPTER TWENTY-SIX

Amber

I'd implied to Lucy and Matt – and everyone else – that number 13 was mine, that I'd bought it when I moved here to be the weather girl, but in reality it was just rented. I couldn't afford to buy it on my own, so arranged to rent until Ben joined me and then we'd buy it together, but when he dumped me that all collapsed. But I couldn't bring myself to leave, so just paid ridiculous rent and got myself into debt because I had an image to keep up. Everyone on Treetops Estate seemed so impressed by my rather minor celebrity. I didn't want to disappoint them, so kept up the pretence. I used to tell everyone I was going away for weekends in Cannes on millionaires' yachts. I've never been to bloody Cannes – I just wanted to give the girls at the book club a thrill and let everyone think I lived this amazing fucking life of parties and champagne. What I was really doing on my 'fabulous weekends' was staying in the house with the shutters closed getting some bloody peace and quiet and trying to fight the demons that come to me when I'm alone in the dark. Sometimes I am overwhelmed by what I did, by what I had and lost and by my empty, pointless life with no future. I've always been tormented by my failure to succeed and, though I have my beautiful baby, I still feel regret about the past and fear for the future. And now there's no place to hide. I've really gone and fucked everything up. I'm stuck in a bloody three-bedroomed rabbit hutch with someone else's husband. It's a huge mistake and it's all my fault. And guess what? The grass wasn't greener and this isn't what I wanted, and what makes it even worse is that I am the antithesis of everything I ever wanted to be. I am living my worst nightmare – I take care of Mia, I clean and I wait for Matt to come home at night. There's no Lucy to babysit, so when I'm not at work I'm tied to the house – and Matt's become so needy I don't even fancy him anymore.

And now, I'm sitting in a local coffee bar with Ben, who called me up to say he wanted to talk to me, and I can't help but compare him to Matt. I gaze at my sophisticated ex in his designer suit, with a sprinkle of cultivated stubble and those eyes that mean business, and I know I'm already in trouble. I watch his fingers toying with a small packet of sugar. He glances up at me every so often, and each time our eyes meet, I feel a flash of heat in my chest.

I look down at the pushchair with my child (our child?) asleep inside. I had to bring Mia along because there was no one to look after her, as Matt's at work, and I'm now wearing my Mother Teresa face, hoping Ben will see the wife-and-mother potential rather than just the bedroom potential. I wonder about the slut from accounts, but don't feel it appropriate at this stage to ask anything personal.

I wondered if I'd feel anything, and I'm slightly unsettled to realise I find him as beautiful and charismatic as ever. I see other women sipping their coffee and glancing over at him, and I reach out, touching his arm proprietorially. I couch this as a way of emphasising my words, but it's a 'hands off' gesture to anyone watching who fancies their chances.

'So it was your best friend all the time?' he asks.

'What?' I panic, think he's talking about my affair with Matt. My guilty conscience strikes again.

'The stalker?'

'Oh yes, I'm devastated. I went through hell, and never imagined in my wildest dreams it was the person closest to me…' I touch my eye with my napkin. The tears aren't flowing quite enough today; trouble is I'm too damned elated at being with him. All I can think about is the last time we did it – against an exposed brick wall behind JoJo's.

'It must have been dreadful, but I wanted to see you because… Well, I thought it would make a good interview.'

My heart tips a little. Ah, so this is why he's meeting me for coffee, having changed his number and ignored me for months. Work. 'Oh… I don't know…'

Then again, if I have something he wants, he might try a little harder.

'Always the journalist.' I smile. 'Chasing a story…' *When he isn't chasing women*, I think, a residue of bitterness still sitting in my chest.

He looks at me beaming, his eyes moving slowly down to my décolletage. He always loved my breasts. I move slightly so he can get a better look. I might as well remind him what he's missing, and I like the way this gives me some control. I know I can have him if I want him, and I do – but I've learned my lesson, and this time I won't make it quite so easy for him.

'It's an amazing story… It has all the ingredients. It'll really resound with our viewers. I was thinking a short interview in the studio on the live news programme. If that goes well, who knows? We could give it to the documentary department, see if they fancy doing an hour-long?'

'I'm not sure,' I say, calm, considered, wanting to say 'where do I sign?' but wanting him to work for it. 'It would be very traumatic.' I bat my eyelashes and put my coffee stirrer to my lips. Okay, I know a wooden coffee stirrer isn't exactly the most seductive prop, but I have to work with what I've got, and I've always been resourceful. This is a very interesting conversation. I was so close to it I hadn't even considered mine and Lucy's story might be of interest. But seeing the glint in Ben's eye, the answer to everything could be right under my nose – so I pick this up and run with it like a true professional. I may be a weather girl, but I've worked in newsrooms all my life and I know how it works. This could be my ticket to a new life, a great story, lots of sympathy, plenty of exposure, leading to big headlines, and dare I even hope for the offer of presenting roles? And with Ben's support, we might be able to pick up professionally (and personally?) where we left off years ago, when Michael died and my career turned to shit. When he asked for this chat, I knew I had something Ben wanted. Well it seems I do, and in spite of me wanting this too, I'm not just handing it to him on a plate. After the way he treated me I won't just roll over - he's damn well going to beg for it.

'I've had a few calls… from the tabloids,' I lie. 'Oh, and Piers Morgan wants to do something with me,' I add vaguely. 'But I don't know, I've been through such a lot… Do I really want to join that circus, Ben?' I give him big eyes, pouting lips and even manage a little tremble of the chin, which seems to have the desired effect.

He sits forward and I see it again, the glimmer of excitement, the glint in his eye – sex and a good story, that's all Ben has ever needed.

'Obviously it's up to you who you choose to go with,' he says, trying not to sound desperate, too pushy, 'and if indeed you do decide to tell your story at all.' And then he gives me that look, that secret smile that says so much, and my knees go weak. 'But I can assure you, Amber, that if you go with us then I will be there to support you 24/7.'

I take a few seconds to regroup, then come back at him. '24/7 you say? Funny… Piers said the same,' I lie. God, I'm enjoying this!

'Yes, but I mean it. We're good together, you and me, don't try and deny it. Let's do this, Amber – who knows where it could lead? I can see the headline: "TV weather girl in stalking storm". We can do a big, exclusive interview, I could talk to a few papers, see if we can get the tabloids to play, give us plenty of press, build those audience figures. You could make a lot of money – and you know they'd lap it up.' Then he pulls back slightly, not wanting to scare me off I suppose, but he had me at 'we're good together' and I am so up for it. But I continue to play it cool.

I raise my eyebrows. 'I might,' I say, concealing my excitement and deep joy. 'Perhaps we'll need another meeting to discuss this in more depth,' I suggest. After all, I'm in the driving seat now. Funny how the tables have turned.

I go home from the meeting with Ben, my head full of sparkles, only to be greeted by Matt wanting to know why I'm so late.

'For fuck's sake Matt, I told you, I had a business meeting,' I say, irritated, trying to microwave some food for Mia and check my phone for messages from Ben at the same time.

I look over at him sitting at the kitchen table, poring over some hopeless 'screenplay' that will never see light of day, and want to scream. Apparently he's writing his autobiography and I wonder who would be interested in the life of a drama teacher in the Manchester suburbs. Thank God I have Mia. She's the only spark of light in this darkness and I adore her. She's almost a year old now, and nearly walking; she took a few faltering steps this morning, and I clapped as she tumbled to the floor, giggling. It made me laugh, and seeing me laugh made her laugh and we were both rolling around the floor laughing at each other. She's a happy little girl, and that's all I wanted for my daughter – happiness – but sometimes I wonder if I'm good enough for her.

I often wonder if Mia remembers Lucy, or at least has some vague recollection of another mother figure in her life who's now absent. Lucy was, I have to admit, brilliant with Mia. She was good at all the practical stuff, like bathing and feeding and changing, but she also engaged her. Even at a few months old, Lucy was giving her cloth books and bright toys that made noises when you pushed buttons, talking to her all the time, and soon Mia was making baby noises back to her. I remember Lucy saying, 'She's such a chatterbox.'

'She takes after you.' I'd laughed. And sometimes, when my little girl's playing or sleeping, I stop and think what it would be like to never see her again. And I feel so sorry for Lucy, because in spite of everything, she loved Mia like her own.

Now, without Lucy's guidance, I doubt myself even more as a mother. I worry I'm not worthy of this brown-eyed angel with soft curls and a perfect rosebud mouth.

I find it hard to believe now, but I never wanted children, and thought the nearest I would ever get would be an eccentric aunt to a child of a friend. I would have been someone who'd sweep into their lives, bringing gifts and fun and irreverence, before sweeping out again. But this mothering thing is for the long haul and sometimes, when I think about the mountain I have to climb to make sure this little girl is safe, educated, confident, happy, financially solvent, I'm overwhelmed. That may sound selfish and I adore Mia so much, but I just can't help feeling that with my genes, and my mother as a role model, I won't be able to give Mia what she needs.

Matt isn't as much help as I'd hoped he'd be. He soon got bored of looking after Mia in the evenings while I worked (or went for 'meetings' with Ben) and said he needed to be at rehearsals for the new production at the amateur dramatics group. He stopped for a while to spend time with me, but it seems he'd rather spend his evenings with a bunch of wannabes than looking after my daughter, who, as I pointed out, he says he loves as much as his own, even if she isn't.

The other night, I was on my way out, all dressed up, and he said, 'Where are you going?'

'I have a meeting about work,' I lied. I was meeting Ben for dinner to discuss the live interview, among other things.

'You can't go out tonight,' he said.

'Er, yes I can,' I responded, walking to the front door to leave.

'And leave Mia on her own?'

'What?' I walked back down the hall. 'This is what we agreed, that while I'm at work you'll look after her. It's not like I'm out socialising.'

'Who knows what you're doing, and who with? I don't. And I'm going out myself, I have rehearsals.' With that, he picked up his jacket, pushed past me in the hall and slammed the front door. That woke Mia up and she started screaming.

I was incandescent. How could he do that? Having been stuck in all day, I would now be stuck in all night – and I was beginning to realise maybe that's exactly what Matt wanted. He wanted me locked away like a battery hen. Unable to leave, to live my life, do anything on my own. He'd felt the chill and was scared of losing me, but he wasn't going to keep me on lockdown. I wasn't going to be tied down by him or any other man.

I called Ben and said I had to cancel our dinner. He seemed as disappointed as me, but I told myself that being unavailable that night would make him want me more, in every way. Then I remembered Stella of the beige sofa. Stella had two little ones of her own and was also starting a business from home as a childminder – perfect. So the following day I contacted her and invited myself and Mia round there for a play date to see if Mia liked her and the other children. Mia's walking now and 'chatting', and within minutes was playing happily – she took to Stella and her children straight away. But I think Mia's favourite resident at Stella's is the cat, Molly, who she tries to ride like a horse.

I stayed at Stella's for a quick coffee and was surprised when she chatted quite openly about Lucy. Apparently, Kirsty is back in touch with Lucy, and she told Stella that Lucy's still saying she didn't make any calls or send any texts, that it was her phone with a different SIM card so her number didn't come up on my phone.

'I hardly think that's a defence,' I said. 'She was the one who changed the SIM. I can't believe she's still in denial after being convicted of the crime and given a suspended sentence,' I said. But Stella just shrugged, happy, sitting on her safe little fence. Whatever. As long as she's available to look after Mia whenever I need it, I don't really care what she thinks or who she believes.

Thank God I had the foresight to organise reliable childcare because I've certainly needed it since Ben started the 'my best friend the stalker' ball rolling. Our meetings have been regular and intense: long talks, discussions about my future – and an unspoken knowledge that we both still have feelings for one another. I've agreed to everything as far as the exclusive interview and the promise of presenting work that he dangled in front of me. But I didn't give in to his rather obvious propositions involving the two of us sleeping together again and resuming where we'd left off. 'Not while you're living with someone else,' I said, referring to the slut from accounts. I want him, desperately, but this time I won't share him, and realise that I'll have to play the long game to get what I want. If I keep him waiting, he will want me more and when we finally do get together it will be for good. But in the meantime, there are a few other things to consider, not least of which is Matt, who is turning into a rather large obstacle to my future happiness. It isn't like I'm in the same position I was with Michael. Matt isn't the type to do anything stupid, but I have to be careful because I don't want him running to the bloody papers and branding me an adulteress and an unfeeling bitch, just as my star is about to rise again. And to date, things on the career front are definitely looking promising – the exclusive interview I did for Ben's news programme really struck a chord. During the programme it began trending on Twitter as #StalkerStorm and within days everything started to change for me, for the better.

Weather Woman in Stalking Storm – Transcript of TV Interview with Amber Young, interviewed by Maddie Watkins

MADDIE: Welcome, Amber, it's good to have you on this side of the studio for a change, but under rather unfortunate circumstances. Some months ago you were involved in a court case where someone who stalked you for many months was on trial. But this wasn't just a stalker, was it, Amber? It was someone you knew.

AMBER: Yes, Maddie, it was… The stalker turned out to be someone I loved and trusted… My best friend.

VOICE-OVER; TV FOOTAGE OF AMBER: She was the glittering celebrity who'd captured Lucy Metcalf's heart and mind when she read the weather late at night. Lucy was single and lonely and it would be many years before the two women met, but when the glamorous weather woman came into her orbit as a neighbour, it didn't take long for Lucy to become obsessed. As Amber explains: 'When we were first friends she went to my beauty therapist and had all the same treatments as me, then she went to my hairdressers and had her hair coloured exactly the same. I think she wanted to *be* me.' But soon Lucy's obsession became dangerous and it all came to a head when Amber discovered that Lucy was the stalker behind a series of threatening and violent actions that left Amber terrified for the safety of herself and her newborn baby.

MADDIE: Scary stuff, Amber.

AMBER: Absolutely. She seemed like the loveliest person… you know? Very caring, very sweet – and when I was frightened, after the heavy-breathing calls and obscene texts, the vile gifts left on my doorstep, she invited me to stay with her and her husband. She was a good neighbour.

MADDIE: Not only was she your neighbour, Lucy Metcalf was a respected teacher, your best friend. She was there for you when you were scared and desperate – or so it seemed.

AMBER: Absolutely, Maddie. Lucy was the one person I would always go to if ever I needed a friend… and she was wonderful – well, at the time. I realise now it was all part of her act.

MADDIE: Is it true that she was never actually present when you received these calls and texts?

AMBER: No, she wasn't, but of course I didn't realise that until after she was caught. She even walked me home one morning and screamed when she opened what I thought was a gift left on my doorstep. It was a dead bird.

MADDIE: A 'gift' she must have left?

AMBER: Yes, and that's what scares me the most, Maddie, that she could be there and cry with me, be scared with me – she was even the one to call the police – and yet all the time—

MADDIE: It was her, she was your tormentor. And the knife… Tell me about the knife she stole from your kitchen that was found hidden in her wardrobe with her prints on.

AMBER: Yes. It was a really sharp kitchen knife – it could easily… hurt someone badly, and to think all the time I lived there she was keeping it in her room. No one knows why. She also stole my pregnancy test…

MADDIE: Your what? I'm sorry, could you just repeat that?

AMBER: I know, I know – we still don't understand why she did that. She went into my bedroom when I wasn't there, went through all my drawers, smashed a photo frame, tore my silk dressing gown off its hanger, then wrote something… vile in my lipstick on the mirror. [Dabs her eyes with a tissue] I was forced to take out a restraining order as soon as I discovered it was her, Maddie. She must have been hiding so much rage. If she could do such… such damage to my things, what else could she do? I had my daughter to consider.

MADDIE: Of course, little Mia… Here's a photo of lovely Mia, Amber's daughter, who's now twelve months old.

STILL SHOT OF MIA.

MADDIE: She's gorgeous, Amber…

AMBER: Thank you, she's everything to me.

MADDIE: So you were a new mum at the time it all unravelled; it must have been dreadful for you. Do you think Lucy Metcalf's obsession with you extended to your little daughter Mia?

AMBER: I do, Maddie. It was all very sad; on the surface, she seemed happy. She was married, a teacher, had a lovely home…

MADDIE: But it turns out she wasn't as perfect as she seemed.

AMBER: No, Maddie. Unfortunately, Lucy hadn't been able to conceive a 'longed for' baby, which was a source of great pain. Also, her marriage was on the rocks. She was very unhappy… It was very sad, tragic really. I think the problem was that she hated herself, Maddie, and she wanted to be me.

MADDIE: Really?

AMBER: Oh, yes. She once passed herself off as Mia's mother at the local hospital – she actually signed my name on an official document. I just shudder to think what might… have happened if she'd not been caught… [Sniffles] Can I… can I have a tissue please?

MADDIE: Do you feel like you can go on, Amber? I know this is very distressing for you.

AMBER: Yes… yes it is, but I'm fine. I have to do this to help others. I don't want any other woman to have to go through what I did.

MADDIE: This is so brave of you, Amber. I realise it's very difficult for you but you're doing the right thing. The court case was stressful too, wasn't it? This was your best friend. How did it feel to face her and realise what she'd done?

AMBER: It was devastating. In court, I had to steel myself and tell everyone things that she'd told me in strict confidence. It was agony. I was betraying my best friend – but I had no choice. When we first started to be friends, we'd have lovely 'girls' nights in' when we'd dress up in cute onesies, put on face masks and share our deepest secrets… like girlfriends do.

MADDIE: [Nods]

AMBER: Then one evening she told me how, when she was much younger, she'd been in a sexual relationship with an older woman, her teacher. It sounded to me like

> she was obsessed, but I didn't think anything of it. She was just sixteen. I didn't see the significance then, but this was clearly a pattern: she finds a friend, becomes obsessed and it takes over her life. I've had time to think about it all and her behaviour probably all stems from having a difficult childhood. Her mother never really gave her any attention, any love, and so she latched on to other women in her life. But throughout the court case, I clung on to the vain hope that it was all some horrible mistake. Sadly it was true. My best friend, my neighbour, the woman with whom I'd shared everything, was also my stalker.
>
> MADDIE: Thank you, Amber, I know that was tough. [MADDIE turns to camera.] That was just a taste of the horrific ordeal that Amber Young went through with the person who stalked her – her best friend. Coming soon, an hour-long documentary special telling the full and frank story in Amber's words – *Amber Young: My Friend, My Stalker.*

That interview was only the beginning. Maddie played it just right. Sympathetic but not too soft that she stopped the interview when I wept, and she asked all the right questions – she would, she'd been well briefed. Apparently, the viewing figures went through the roof, and the documentary was shown a week later on network TV throughout the UK and has been tipped for several awards already. It's since been syndicated and been shown on TV news stations all over the world, something I never expected in my wildest dreams. Along with instant fame, the documentary gave me the opportunity to announce that I would be campaigning to make stalking laws more rigid. And it was all part of the new package – Amber Young, former victim turned mother, role model and now campaigner.

I went on as per script about how the whole 'traumatic experience' had affected my life and the lives of those around me and eventually went in for the money shot. Holding Mia for the cameras, I cried and said, 'This isn't about me. It's about her… She's who I'm doing it for, and with your support, we *can* make this a better, safer country for all our children.' It was better than any weather report I'd ever done, and there wasn't a dry eye in the house as they say.

So now, *everyone* wants my story and 'TV's Amber Young, stalked by her best friend' is suddenly worth a lot of money. I'm receiving offers every day, from network interviews on prime time and a slot on *Loose Women* to advertising deodorant and HRT, which my new agent said to give a wide birth – I have to think about my brand now. And trust me, it's so much better than thinking about washing Matt's dirty socks and thinking I had no future.

Yesterday I had a call asking if I'd be interested in flying to the US to do talk shows there and this morning my agent said several publishers have expressed an interest in the rights to my story. I actually cried – real tears too. Life is mad, isn't it? Just a few weeks ago the very the notion of writing my life story (not to mention the advance, which my agent reckons could be in the six-figure region) was unthinkable. Yet here I am, Amber Young, back in the game, only this time sharper, more tuned in and ready for anything.

I'm thinking I might call the landlord and see if he's rented out number 13 yet. I haven't seen anyone move in, so I'm hopeful it's still empty and if it is I can now afford to buy it and move back in, leaving Matt to sulk in the shed he calls a home. Although perhaps it's a little too close for comfort, especially with the other development that happened in the last few days.

Yes, breaking news – I finally gave in to Ben. It's all over with the slut from accounts, and I heard this from several reliable sources so I knew it was a matter of time, and when he arranged dinner at a fabulous hotel, plied me with champagne and told me he'd booked the penthouse suite for the night, I'm only human – how could I resist? Mia was safe with Stella, and I rang Matt and told him I was working so late I would be staying with my female colleague at her nearby flat. I wasn't ready for the conversation with Matt, but I was so ready for a night with Ben, especially when I saw the suite. The space was wall-to-wall glass and chrome, high-count bed linen in fifty shades of grey, champagne in the ice bucket and rose petals on the bed. It would have been rude not to.

It was the most amazing night. We made love until dawn and after breakfast we did it again. It's early days, but we have the great excuse of lots of lovely late-night 'meetings' to discuss my career and I've asked for his 'guidance' on what to do next. Matt isn't too chuffed about it, but what can he do? The truth is I've outgrown him and I think he knows it. I feel a bit sorry for him really. He keeps asking when we're getting married, but as I told him, I never actually said yes. I placate him by saying I won't leave him, but that's only because I have to – until the advance from the publisher comes in. As number 13 is still empty, the landlord will sell to me and I can pay outright and move in immediately once the advance is through. Obviously Matt knows nothing about this and I do feel terribly guilty – but it's for the best. I know he thinks he loves me, but even he isn't happy – we just make each other miserable. It's a shame really, how much Matt wants a family, and I do feel guilty because he has no family himself. His father died when he was a baby, then his mother died when he was quite young in some tragic accident. He's been through the mill and just wants the white picket fence and someone to love him, but sadly that isn't me. I now see it for what it was: a fling. I'd thought it was love, but it was just lust. For me anyway.

'I'll never love anyone else,' he says. 'Even if you leave me, I'll just sit here and wait for you.' He probably thinks it's what I want to hear, but it's actually the opposite of what I want.

Last night he'd cooked a special meal as it was my night off, but I had to break it to him that I was going to a meeting and it involved my publishers and dinner, so I wouldn't be eating or staying home.

'Can I come along?' he asked in all seriousness.

'No, because someone needs to be here for Mia, and besides, it's just boring stuff about my book.'

'Yeah, but I could talk to your publisher about my autobiography,' he said, and I almost laughed.

'Sorry babe, another time, eh?'

'I don't believe you're even meeting your publisher.' He started again with all the paranoid shit about me being 'unfaithful'. 'You're seeing *him*, aren't you?' he said, and he seemed really angry, which isn't like him. I think he's feeling insecure because we're coming to the end of our rainbow, as someone famous once said about their divorce. Can't recall who it was – in fact at the time I thought it was quite pretentious – but I think it says it all and has inspired the title of my autobiography, *The End of My Rainbow*. There's a vague link to weather, and it hints at sunshine and rain, which one would expect from a weather girl – it's perfect. And my agent bloody loves it.

Anyway, the end of mine and Matt's rainbow is definitely on the horizon. He had a mood on him last night and refused to look after Mia while I went out. 'I'm not sitting here alone caring for your baby while you go sleeping around,' he said.

I was furious, it wasn't like him to say things like that, but it hadn't taken him long to change his tune. 'What happened to "I don't care whose baby she is – she's part of you, so I'll always love her"?' I yelled as I packed all her baby stuff to ship her over to Stella's.

He was so pissed off when I stormed out, but there was nothing he could do because I'm clever enough not to be dependent on him, which is quite delicious. No man is ever going to tell me what I can do and where I can go – I'm not my mother. She was a mess, completely manipulated and ruled by men all her life. She lost her mind and in the end she couldn't even parent me. She had to get the local council to do it. I may be a lot of things – not all of them good – but I will *never* be my mother.

Stella was delighted to see me. 'Ooh, I've been watching you on the telly, and in all the papers,' she gushed.

I pretended it was all nothing and promised I'd take her out next week as a treat for looking after Mia. 'We'll have cocktails at JoJo's. It's so swanky in there. It will blow your mind,' I said. She was so excited, I honestly thought she might wet herself – after all, she's got three kids. That pelvic floor's got to have taken some pounding.

That said, I won't need Stella for much longer. I'll soon have enough money for a nanny, but I don't want to be one of those celebrity mothers who dumps their kid on some teenage nanny. I want to be a good mum too, and be involved in her life and her upbringing. I want to show Mia how to be just like me, self-sufficient and independent. If I teach her one thing, it will be to know that in the end no one's looking out for you, not even your lover or your best friend – the only person you can rely on is yourself.

CHAPTER TWENTY-SEVEN

Lucy

I tried to be a good wife, a good friend. I didn't do anything wrong, yet here I am, on my own. Since the day I was arrested, no one has been in touch: friends don't answer my calls and texts, and old neighbours cross the street or look the other way so they don't have to speak to me. I'm 'the stalker', and thanks to the court reports and all the interviews and publicity she's created, I'm as famous as she is – and not in a good way. I still feel shocked by everything: Matt's complete abandonment and the way Amber's spoken about me publicly. I know she's upset, but I honestly thought she might have reached out to me, yet instead she's vilified me, said such terrible things, and I can't believe she's repeatedly told the nation the secret I shared with her all those months ago. She revealed it in court which was devastating enough, but to be discussing this and elaborating during TV interviews is so hurtful. This was my friend, someone I trusted more than anyone, except perhaps my husband, and she seems to have no remorse, no shame. And each time I hear an interview or read an article it's as if she's taking the knife out and plunging it back in again and again. I know I should just wait for the storm to pass, for people will move on and forget. But I can't forget – and now the local kids have discovered where I live I'll never be allowed to forget. I often wake up to blood-red graffitied windows declaring my new status as 'stalker' and 'psycho'. Yesterday they rang the changes with 'fucking lesbo', yet another reminder that she's shared my deepest secret with a million strangers.'

When a middle-aged woman is accused of stalking she's judged far more harshly than if it were a man accused of the same thing. And despite my protestations of innocence, no one wants to listen because it's a macabre fascination, a great story. I'm also convinced the vile criticism constantly levelled at me is made worse by the fact that I'm not young or beautiful, or a mother – it's like I'm not even a 'real woman'. As someone who didn't know me pointed out loudly in Tesco Express the other day, I must be 'fucking sick'. I've never thought about it before, but it's easier to publicly abuse a woman. For a start I probably won't thump my abuser, and more is expected of me, because of my age and gender. A woman of a certain age. Old enough to know better. So when total strangers call me up and shout 'you sick fucking bitch, I hope you die' down my phone, I apparently am the one with a problem. No one has yet even taken the trouble to ask, 'Lucy – did you really do it… and if so, why?' That's the slash-and-burn world we live in, I suppose, but ironically, I'm scared to walk down the street at night in case someone recognises me and decides to take revenge on behalf of 'lovely' and 'brave' Amber Young.

Amber's story is all over the tabloids: moody reflective photos of her staring out over my garden telling of her 'shock' and 'horror' when she discovered the stalker was her 'best friend'. Apparently I've ruined her life, turned her into 'an anxious mess', but she seems to be doing okay, sitting on *Loose Women* in her designer blouse, her hair all curled, her lips glossy, a tissue never far away on set. Of course, she's telling her own narrative, not mine, and though the truth lies somewhere, it isn't in her tear-jerking tales of best-friend betrayal. *She's* the betrayer, and it's her who ruined *my* life.

I can only imagine the conversations around the dinner party tables of Treetops Estate over coffee and mints. 'She seemed so normal' and 'She taught my Jack. If I'd known she was so dangerous I'd have taken him out of that school.'

But among the estranged colleagues from work and old friends who don't pick up their phones and keep their distance in case what I have might be contagious – there has been one light in the darkness.

Just after the trial, Kirsty texted, asking if I'd like to meet somewhere to chat.

> *I told you I'd be here for you when you needed me, and I won't say I told you so. I'll just say do you fancy a Chinese? I reckon a nice meal will cheer you up.*

I almost wept, I was so touched. Poor old Kirsty, who had worked out what Amber was like right from the off, who I'd unceremoniously dumped for my exciting new friend, was throwing me a lifeline. I immediately texted back to say yes.

I can see it all so clearly now. Amber stopped me from living my life. I gave up my friends because she offered more exciting alternatives. She dangled a new and different life in front of me like a sparkler in the darkness, and I grasped it and got burned. My marriage was stale, I was childless and jealous of my friends with children. I had nothing – and she saw that weakness and seduced me. She filled me up with her needs until I couldn't fit anyone else in. I made her feel valued and valuable when she was at her lowest. And then Mia came along and I was useful to her, on a practical as well as an emotional level. She knew I loved that little girl and would do anything for her – I still would – but Amber's so bitter I sometimes think I'll never see Mia again, and that's what hurts most of all.

Amber told the court that once she'd moved into my home, I'd isolated her, manipulated the situation, and wanted her life, her baby. She said that I sent the texts and the gifts so she'd move from her house and stay with me, describing me as her jailer, but

I wasn't. Amber was *my* jailer, and in a very subtle way, she took over my life until I was the isolated one, left with nothing.

The very prospect of meeting up with Kirsty restored my faith in friendship – though after what I'd been through I was perhaps a bit more cautious than I would have been before. But Kirsty and I had been friends for years (as she pointed out during one of our last rather heated discussions) and when no one else wanted anything to do with me, she was offering to go out with me in public.

Kirsty and I met outside the Chinese restaurant and when I saw her teetering down the road in heels, I wanted to cry with happiness – and regret.

With tears in my eyes, I reached out to her. 'Kirsty, I'm sorry. What can I say?'

She smiled kindly. 'Nothing, you daft cow. Now let's get inside or we'll both catch our deaths.'

We sat down and ordered the Royal Peacock Banquet for two, and it felt like old times. Before Amber.

'Thanks so much for getting in touch, Kirsty,' I said, tears of gratitude springing to my eyes again. 'This has been the worst year of my life…'

She discreetly handed me a tissue under the table. 'I know, love, I know. And I wasn't going to say I told you so – but I saw what she was like from the beginning… You just wouldn't listen.'

'I honestly didn't see it. I just really liked her. She was so funny, and so *fun*. Then there was the pregnancy, and what with all the calls and creepy gifts, she was alone and I just felt like she needed a friend. And I was worried for the baby. God, I still worry about Mia. I miss her.'

She smiled affectionately and put her hand on mine. 'I know. I can see only too clearly how it happened. You've always been a bit too kind, Lucy. People take advantage of you. Amber used you, anyone could see that.'

'I know that now,' I said, feeling rather foolish. 'And the minute she didn't need me any more she got rid of me… I'm so sorry I didn't listen to you, Kirsty.'

'Don't keep apologising. I'm just glad you came to your senses… eventually.' She sighed, putting down her wine glass and starting on the spring rolls.

'I think she liked the attention,' I said. 'She said it didn't matter, told me she'd had loads of weird texts and calls in her career. It came with the territory apparently… yet she seemed to make more of a fuss in front of other people. Then the night she got the text at our house – the one they were able to pin onto me because it came from my old phone – she went bonkers. So dramatic, throwing the phone to the ground and sobbing. It just doesn't add up.'

'What are you saying? Do you think it was her all the time? Pretending she was being stalked?'

'It's crossed my mind – but why would she blame me? She's lost her babysitter, she's lost her best friend… It doesn't make sense.'

She pushed the plate of spring rolls towards me. 'Eat up, you've lost weight… It makes sense to me.'

'How?'

She held a crispy roll aloft and looked at me in exaggerated surprise. 'Lucy, you handed *everything* to her – you even moved her into your home with you and Matt!'

'It was just to keep her safe.' I sighed, knowing the three-in-a-bed story was probably another one being peddled around Treetops Estate. 'I thought she might do herself harm. She was pregnant, someone was stalking her and there was a baby involved… I just wanted to keep her and Mia safe.'

'*You* keep *her* safe? Trust me, Amber Young can look after herself, my love. It was *you* who needed looking after. I should have done more,' she added. Then, taking a glug of wine, she dabbed her napkin, leaving a bright pink lipstick stain on the white linen.

'Can't you see? Of course it makes sense for her to blame you for the stalking. She could get rid of you, get you out of the house.'

'I know things weren't great between us in the end, but I resented her being at the house, not the other way round. She had no reason to want me to go. She was planning to go back to her house that week.'

'I wasn't going to say anything…' she continued, then stopped eating, put down her chopsticks and turned to face me. *Oh God, what now?* 'I … I feel bad telling you this if you don't know already, but are you aware that Matt and Amber are… together?'

'Together… in what way? As far as I know she's still staying at our house with Mia, isn't she?'

'Oh yes, she is. God, Lucy. I'm sorry. You don't know, do you? I mean they're *together*. As a couple.'

The shock raced through me. 'No… I didn't know that. But I find it hard to believe. Kirsty, they don't even *like* each other! She always said I could do a lot better than Matt, and I had to beg him not to be rude to her when she first moved in.'

'They say the wife's always the last to know.' Kirsty sighed, reaching for a prawn cracker. I'd suddenly lost my appetite. 'There have been rumours, but I only felt I should tell you when I saw it for myself,' she said, and I could see it was upsetting her to tell me this. 'They are blatant, Lucy, walking around the estate pushing the baby, holding hands, his arm around her… I'm sorry. She even told Stella he wanted to marry her.'

That would explain his letter soon after the court case telling me he never wanted anything to do with me ever again. I thought about the way the three of us lived together, and wondered if something had been going on back then and Amber really did want me off the scene. I think back to times when I'd walked in on them chatting, heads down, giggling, and felt relieved that they were getting along. Then there was the time when I was sure Matt had said 'you're my everything' but Amber had laughed it off, said I was hearing things.

Perhaps I was hearing things I didn't want to hear and it was easier to put my hands over my ears and pretend everything was fine.

'It's okay... They're welcome to each other,' I said, but it wasn't okay, and she must have heard the crack in my voice. This happened in my own home under my nose, and yes there were times I might have been surprised at their closeness, but I was so busy working and looking after Mia, I refused to see it. I was *causing* the problem for them, not solving it. Amber wasn't the third wheel. I was. 'I don't want to even think about it...' I said eventually.

'No. Fair enough, I wouldn't either, but after telling you not to bother with book club, she soon came back without you. Did you know she'd rejoined?'

'No.'

'She wanted to come back to the book club, wanted us all to be friends... asked us over dinner.'

'Yes, I remember. Everyone went for an Italian and I wasn't invited. I was at home minding Mia.'

'She messaged us all and invited us to meet up there. I assumed you were going too. I was still feeling a bit pissed off with you so didn't get in touch, but I went along hoping you'd be there. When I arrived, she was lording it over everyone, paying for everything and just being... Amber. I knew she was up to something. She kept hinting that you were being 'possessive' and didn't like her going anywhere without you.'

I felt another stab of the knife. 'What else did she say?'

'I don't know. Once I realised you weren't with her, and it was the Amber show, I left. I wasn't letting her pay for my meal so she could bitch about you all night. God, I hate her! And she's suddenly best friends with Stella,' she added, before taking a sip of wine.

Stella of the boring beige sofa? 'But Stella's not exactly Amber's type...' I said, trying not to be rude or unkind about Stella – even though Amber had definitely said before that she thought Stella had to be the most boring person on the estate. 'I can't see Stella drinking champagne in fancy wine bars. That's what *we* used to do.' I couldn't help it, even then, after everything. I felt a little stung that Amber had a new friend, and the strange thing was, *her* betrayal hurt even more than Matt's. Perhaps it was because this burgeoning new friendship with Stella was proof that I wasn't special after all – just more vulnerable.

'Well,' Kirsty said, 'Stella and Amber are besties now. But, mind you, Stella does look after Mia every now and then.'

'Ahh, childcare – that'll be it.' I sighed.

'Oh yes. I think Amber finds out what you are useful for and then she uses you for what she needs… It's why I wanted to reach out again. I just always knew your friendship was by *her* design, not yours.'

I could see it so clearly now; Kirsty was right, she'd always been right. Amber made me *want* to be her friend, and once we were close and I revealed things to her, she used it to manipulate me. She'd stored up my secrets for a later date when she might need them and then she spat them all out – first in that courtroom, then later on TV to make her story stronger, more titivating. To get what she wanted. It was her testimony that damned me. My husband wasn't her only betrayal – and she'd gone on to betray me over and over again.

'Amber's like a chameleon. She adapts to her surroundings; a glam celebrity one minute, housewife and new mum the next,' Kirsty was saying, while shaking her head in wonderment. 'I have to give it to her, Lucy, she gets to know her victims. I just wish Stella could see it, but I couldn't convince you, so I'm not wasting my energy. Maybe she'll only see it when Amber's shagging *her* husband.' She looked at me.

And I felt stupid. Again.

'I never imagined she'd want Matt, not in a million years,' I said, still trying to assimilate the information. I couldn't believe Matt would want Amber either, but perhaps he was just another one of Amber's victims, falling for her act.

'Oh, I doubt she wants Matt, she's just playing games. She wanted to prove to herself that she could get him if she wanted to. And she did. I read an article in the hairdresser's about manipulative behaviour the other day,' she said, spooning Cantonese chicken onto her plate, 'and it was like it was written about Amber. She's essentially a con woman. Like a parasite. She mirrors people until she has them and then she uses them for whatever she can get. It might be money, a husband, a home… even childcare! It's how she survives – she's charming and charismatic, but actually very dangerous.'

'Yes, I'm beginning to see it. Having said that, Amber may have wanted my husband, but I doubt she ever wanted anything material from me – I had nothing and she has so much. She wouldn't want my home. She has a beautiful home of her own and loads of money.'

'The house was rented. Apparently she has nothing.'

'No.' I was shocked.

The revelations kept coming. I couldn't believe it, I just sat there at a table with my congealed Chinese food, open-mouthed. 'But her beautiful furniture, the lovely garden…'

'I know someone who works at the estate agent who looks after it. She rented that place fully furnished. And when she met you, she'd just realised she couldn't afford to pay the rent because her boyfriend had just dumped her and wouldn't be moving in. She knew she wouldn't be able to stay there much longer. You thought you asked her to stay with you, but she made it so you couldn't do otherwise.'

I'm shocked again. But of course she did. I should have seen it but was too impressed, too beguiled by her.

'She could tell you wanted a bit of excitement, that you and Matt weren't exactly love's young dream any more, but she knew you lived nearby and I guess she needed somewhere convenient to stay until she could work out what to do next.'

Spending that evening with Kirsty was bittersweet, and full of nasty surprises, but it cleared my head and I started to see things differently. Perhaps in a weird way Amber did me a favour by stealing Matt. And Kirsty was right, we weren't happy, and if he cheated on me with her, then he isn't who I thought he was – and she's welcome to him.

Regardless, Amber stole from me. She took what was closest to my heart – my home, my husband and Mia – and she also stole my secret and told it to the world. So it's now time she paid for what she took from me.

CHAPTER TWENTY-EIGHT

Lucy

'I woke up this morning and when the doorbell rang, I rushed to answer it,' she's telling the reporter. 'I've recently been the recipient of beautiful bouquets, bottles of champagne and wonderful cards from newspapers, TV companies and the general public. I'm so lucky to have such wonderful support. I've been carried through this dreadful ordeal by sheer human kindness,' she gushes, a tear almost escaping from her eye. 'After the court case I'd stopped worrying about being alone, who might be watching me or when the next text or horrible gift might arrive. So when I opened the door to find another bunch of dead flowers, I almost collapsed on the doorstep.'

I turn up the volume on my TV. Amber's done yet another 'tell-all'. I was hoping the circus might have died down by now, but she won't let it.

'Do you think it's the same person? Lucy Metcalf?'

'Who knows? The police are dealing with it. I'm just focused on working on improving the anti-stalking laws. For everyone.' She holds a tissue to her dry eye; mustn't ruin her make-up.

The TV reporter is lapping it up. She's nodding slowly, her head to one side, desperately trying to look like she cares. She wants to be sad and scared for Amber, she wants to empathise, but she's as fake as her interviewee – so excited by the story she's practically wetting herself. Meanwhile, the cameraman's clearly pretty excited too – positively making love to the dried-up bunch of brown roses Amber is saying were left for her this morning.

I was going to contact her anyway. I need to make her pay for what she's done to me, and there's no time like the present. I'm furious. Once again my name is being dragged through the mud, so after a morning of pacing around my flat, I decide to face her head-on and warn her I'll take legal action if she implicates me in any more of her TV drama. I dial her old number, surprised she hasn't changed it. So she wasn't scared of the stalker getting in touch again.

'I hear you're going to be the poster girl for anti-stalking laws,' is my opening gambit.

'Lucy, I don't know why you're calling me but it's harassment. And as for my campaign, I'm not going to back down on this. You committed a crime, and in my view you haven't paid for it.'

'I haven't *paid* for it… Have you any *ide*a what I've been through, what I'm still going through?' I start, but Amber is talking over me. Her story, her issue – always more important than anyone else's.

'I have set up a petition to increase sentencing for stalking and already have 50,000 signatures. After all, a six-month suspended sentence is hardly an adequate punishment for what you put me through,' she adds. 'And why are you calling me on this number? It's harassment.'

'Amber, you have no idea about legislation. You don't know the first thing about changing laws, it's just talk.'

'How dare you—' she starts.

'How dare *you*!' I say, and there's steel in my voice I've never heard before. 'Thanks to you I have *nothing*. I live alone in a bedsit, and I don't have a job, and no chance of getting one either with this hanging over me. I see it in their eyes when I go for interviews – *here comes the stalker* – and they're scared… People are scared of me, Amber.'

'And quite right too,' she snaps, still playing the victim. 'You don't deserve it after what you put me through.'

'I didn't put you through anything. But around the time we met, you'd been dumped by your *married* boyfriend. Your first married boyfriend, that is. So you lied about someone stalking you to get his attention… to get me and Matt to put a roof over your head.'

'Lucy… Why are you telling these… lies? You're just jealous because out of this horrible experience I've made something positive. I'm changing laws. I'm on the front pages. TV shows want me as their guest.'

'How lovely that you've finally got what you wanted – you worked hard for it, Amber, but thanks to your so-called "celebrity",' I continue, 'I don't even have my anonymity. I can't walk down the street without being abused. I've had to close my Facebook account because of the filth total strangers were posting about me. It works both ways, you see,' I say. 'Your fame has made you the talking point. You're finally a water-cooler moment, Amber, but so am I. And while you're winning, it's destroying me.'

'This is boring. I'm going to put down the phone and—'

'DON'T you *dare* put the phone down. If you do, I will tell the press everything. All your dirty little secrets… Your childhood, your married lover, what really happened to your husband… Not to mention the knife.'

'What *about* the knife?' Suddenly I hear something like fear in her voice, and it gives me a delicious thrill.

'That it was hidden in your car.'

'Oh, you really are sad, Lucy,' she says, brazening it out. 'Do you really think the papers will be remotely interested in a *stalker*'s lies? *You're* the weirdo, *you're* obsessed with me and no one wants to know what *you* think,' she hisses.

'Oh, I think *my* story's just as interesting,' I reply, knowing all her name-calling is just bravado. I have caught her unawares. She wasn't expecting quiet, accommodating little Lucy to fight back, but I will make her pay for what she's done to me. 'At first I couldn't understand why that knife was in the boot of your car. I was actually worried – I genuinely thought you were going to use it on yourself.'

'Don't be ridiculous…'

'Do you want to know what I think, Amber?'

'Not really.'

'I think you slashed your own tyres,' I continue regardless. 'I think that's why the knife was in your car. Like everyone else, I assumed the stalker did your tyres, but recently I've been giving it a lot of thought – and when Matt came back from rescuing you that night, I remembered he'd said he couldn't get into the car park without a staff pass. He said the security was so tight, he had to fill in a form at the gate and still someone escorted him to you and your car – so whoever slashed your tyres had to be someone who worked there. I'm sure you had your enemies, but we know the slashing was done with a big, sharp knife – just like the one hid under the carpet in your boot. Coincidence? I don't think so… And if you slashed your own tyres, what about the texts, the dead bird… Can you see where I'm going with this, Amber?'

'Yes – the fucking loony bin! I had nothing to do with the texts, or the dead bird! They were you.'

'Oh, stop it, Amber, you stalked *yourself*, didn't you? One of the things you said in court was that I was never there when you received a call or a text… That's because NO ONE was there. You're the sicko, the psycho, the *sad* one. You texted *yourself*!'

'Thank you, Miss fucking Marple, but you know damn well you were the stalker, and whatever I did or didn't do with the knife, it doesn't change the fact you hid it in your bloody wardrobe! Along with my pregnancy test! Do you know how *fucking* weird that is?'

'No. I'm not the weird one, Amber,' I say. 'Not only were you your own stalker, just so you could get my house and my husband—'

'Don't make me laugh. I don't want anything of yours.'

'No, you never did – but you took it. You took it just because you could. You ruined my marriage, my life and you betrayed a friend, and just like my home and my marriage, our friendship might not have meant much to you, but it was everything to me. We shared our biggest secrets and promised each other we'd never tell a soul. I trusted you, and you broke your promise.'

'Look, give me a break. I'd had too much cheap Prosecco and was dressed as a fucking unicorn. You seduced me into telling you things I've never told anyone.'

I flash back to that night, when she told me how she'd walked out on Michael, her husband, even after he begged her to stay.

'He'd threatened to kill himself if I left,' she said, 'and do you know what I did, Lucy? I laughed. I laughed in his face and went off to meet Ben in our hotel, never thinking for a minute that Michael would do himself harm. But when Ben didn't turn up and I went back to Michael, it was too late.' I remember her crying as she told me she'd found him in bed. 'I thought he was asleep. I climbed into bed next to him. I wanted to make it right, to say I was sorry… Ben had hurt me, but Michael was there waiting, and I reached out, touched his bare chest, and it was cold. It was a coldness I've never felt before or since, and yet when I put my ear to his face, I think he was still breathing… It was very shallow, but there was something.' I asked her if she called for help – it was the first thing I would have done. 'No, I'm ashamed to say I didn't call for an ambulance right away.' I asked her why, and she looked at me for a long time. 'Because I told myself this was what *he* wanted. I told myself that even if he was alive, he was desperately unhappy and therefore I was being kind to him. But since then I've realised, it's what *I* wanted. I was besotted with Ben and I didn't love Michael any more, could never give him what he wanted, because he wanted me. It felt like the kindest thing to just lie there and hold him. Later I called for an ambulance.'

I was shocked at this revelation. She might have been able to save him – and she chose to not even try. It wasn't something I could have lived with, and the fact she'd told me suggested that she couldn't keep it inside any longer. She'd carried the secret around with her for years and it was hurting. I told myself she was very young, confused, and she'd had her head turned by Ben, who seemed to me like a manipulator, even more of a user than she turned out to be – and that's saying something.

She went on to tell me that Michael had left a note saying he couldn't live without her. 'He wrote that when I left him to be with Ben, I'd taken away his heart and his future. I only found it later. It broke me – but I never told anyone, how could I? If anyone found out, I could have been accused of murder, or manslaughter at least. I told everyone Michael had been depressed, and that seemed to be accepted and I almost believed it myself, that I played no part in Michael's death, that there was some kind of chemical imbalance in his brain, which was depression and had nothing to do with me. But what I didn't know was that only the day before he killed himself he told his sister about me leaving him for Ben and how he didn't want to live without me. She openly blamed me for Michael's death, tormented me for years by telling the press I was leaving him, that I had a lover and that was the reason he took his own life. I just kept denying it, and after a while she gave up, but she was right to blame me. I still blame myself.' I remember her tears; she still felt such guilt and grief all these years later. And now she's on the phone, scared to death it's come back to haunt her and I'm going to reveal her secret. Just like she revealed mine.

'You have nothing to gain from telling the story,' she's saying now.

'Nothing to lose either, Amber. Thanks to you I have *nothing.*'

But she isn't listening, she's thinking about how this will affect her. 'You have no idea what this would do to me. Think of his poor family too,' she says, clearly desperately grasping at straws. 'Just imagine the fallout. No one would believe you anyway. Besides, you wouldn't betray my confidence like that.'

'*You* did.'

'I told the court about your teacher because I had to prove you were… obsessive, that you liked women – that you'd been abused, whatever. It's hardly the same thing – it's not like you virtually killed someone and hid the fucking note.'

'My secret was just as important and precious to me. Yet you think your secret is more important than mine,' I say. 'Which doesn't surprise me, because you think the world revolves around Amber Young and it's only her that matters. But a secret is a secret.'

'You… you can't take this away from me,' she's saying, her tone moving from anger to anxiousness. 'Not now, not when I've worked so hard.'

'Worked so hard at what? Destroying people, their marriages, their lives, their careers, for your own selfish happiness? Sharing my secret helped to make up the jury's minds and every other right-thinking person in the country was with them, because you made it seem like I'm… damaged. Unstable, obsessive… but it wasn't like that.'

'We're all fucking damaged, Lucy.'

'Yes… some more than others. But the fact is I can't forgive you for what you did to me. And watching you waving dead flowers on screen this morning helped make up my mind.'

'I didn't *say* you'd left the dead flowers.'

'But you put them there, didn't you? If you went to the police there'd be no CCTV of me leaving my house because I didn't. I was there all morning. I didn't leave any dead flowers on your doorstep. There is no stalker, is there, Amber?'

'I'm not a total bitch. There's nothing to tie you to the flowers. Yes, okay, you got me, I put them there, but I didn't do it to drop you in it.'

'But you sent them to yourself to keep the story alive, to keep yourself relevant regardless of the damage to me.'

'I told you, I didn't say it was you who left them.'

'You *implied* it might be me, and that's all your adoring public needed to send out a lynch mob. But I'm glad it's given you another headline. You won't be forgotten like last time,' I add sarcastically. 'Anyway, I've been in touch with the press and now my suspended sentence is up, I can tell my story,' I say. 'So someone's coming to interview me in the morning.'

'NO! Lucy, no!'

Then I add a final caveat. 'Along with the potential murder of your own husband, there's also the matter of the disappearing husbands that you've stolen. You seem to have taken mine *and* Geraldine's, and I'm sure the press will love thinking up a weather-relevant headline for that. In fact, I think I'll suggest one when I chat with them: "Weather Girl in Husband Stealing Hurricane".'

'You wouldn't.'

'Of course I would. As I said, I've got nothing to lose any more. Thanks to you.'

Silence.

'But then again, what would that achieve? I might get a few quid for the story, a nice warm taste of revenge, but that wouldn't last long.'

'No, it wouldn't achieve anything,' she agrees.

'It wouldn't be enough to take me round the world, would it?' I ask, offering her a lifeline.

'So what is it you want, Lucy?'

'I think you know me well enough to know I'm a fair person and I believe in justice. Not the kind of justice I was on the receiving end of in that court, where your lies and lawyers ran rings around me, and not the kind of lies you were peddling on TV this morning. I want something far more honest and civilised.'

'How much?'

'Oh, Amber, now you're being vulgar…'

'Just tell me!'

'I want the painting.'

'No.'

'I think it's only fair.'

'It's not *fair*... It's worth thousands. It's all I have... of him. Besides, I want to leave it to Mia when I die.'

'Don't bring Mia into this.' I pause but she doesn't capitulate, so I continue. 'I can see we aren't getting anywhere and you obviously don't want to give me the painting, so I'll just have to take my pleasure from letting the world know the truth about Amber Young. But where to begin? The *stolen* husbands? The *dead* husband? The TV star who slashed her own tyres, pretended to have a stalker and took her innocent best friend to court and ruined her life? An embarrassment of riches, wouldn't you say? I might even get that criminal record overturned... get compensation for a wrongful conviction. Mmm, on second thoughts, forget the painting...'

'No... No... Let me think. I can get you some money. It would just kill me to lose that painting. I love it. I don't care what it's worth, I just want to keep it. It's mine. It's my past...'

'You should have thought of that before you began your wrecking spree.'

'Look, I'll have it valued, and instead of giving you the painting, I'll give you the money.'

'You don't get it, do you?' I say. 'I want you to give me something that's precious to you – because other than Mia, I don't think there's anything or anyone else you care about. You stole my life, you took everything precious from me, so now you have to pay me back – with the painting.'

'Take the money, it'll save you the trouble of selling it...' she tries.

'No. The painting or nothing. I'm going to put the phone down and talk to my friends at the press.'

'No, don't, don't. Okay, it looks like the only way I can come out of this with my career and reputation intact is to give you the fucking painting, you sad cow. It's yours,' she says. 'I hope you'll both be very happy.' And she slams down the phone.

I must have seemed so malleable, so easy to manipulate, and Amber must find it hard to realise boring, safe old Lucy has a backbone after all – and quite a sting in her tail.

Mum was so busy making up for lost time she never had any left for me. But he did – he watched me, and from the vile, disgusting words he murmured under his breath at me I knew what he was thinking. I also knew that when he tried to touch me, she wouldn't stop him. She didn't care enough to protect her only child, and that thought alone hurt me to the core.

CHAPTER TWENTY-NINE

Lucy

Amber's painting arrived early this week and I've already found a private buyer – it was a quick sale, which is what I wanted. It isn't life-changing, but it's enough for me leave the UK and travel around for a couple of years. Next week I'm off. Starting in Nepal (I like the irony of starting there), I'll spend a few months there and then move on. I hope in the next couple of years to see America, Australia and the Far East – all those places you see on the TV and on world maps that live in your head but you never think you'll visit.

I wasn't comfortable taking from someone else, but Amber owes me, and she needed to be taught a lesson. She's spent so many years trampling over other people, without a thought for the consequences. I think it was time she paid up. People like Amber will do anything to get what they want. And at the moment I'm struggling with something that I want from her. She was so angry about the painting, I doubted she'd agree to my request. But yesterday I called her, and told her I'd be off on my travels very soon. I also asked her for a huge favour.

'Before I go away, there's something very important I want to ask you,' I said.

'Oh, what?'

'I would love to come and say goodbye to Mia. I miss her so much, Amber. I know it's been horrible between us, but I love her and surely you wouldn't deny me – or her – a final goodbye.' I could hear my voice cracking with emotion. 'Throughout all this I've thought of Mia so much, and to be honest I find life hard without her, and just to see her, to give her a last cuddle, hold her a while, play with her, is all I ask.'

I was amazed when, after only a few seconds, she didn't keep me waiting or even try to torture me. She said, 'Okay.'

'Really?'

'Yes. Come over tomorrow.'

At first I was elated. I rushed out and bought some toys and a little dress for Mia and was so excited about seeing her, my heart ached with happiness. But now I keep thinking about what Kirsty said, about Amber being dangerous – and she's making it so easy for me to see Mia, I'm suspicious. I think I might just be walking into trouble. She's so competitive, and I won the last round. She hasn't had her pound of flesh and she might be looking to pay me back. As I pointed out to her, if I go over there I'll be contravening my restraining order. I could be sent to prison.

'That's okay. It's all in the past. I've forgiven you,' she said.

'That's very kind of you,' I replied, sarcasm dripping down the phone. 'But I'm not sure I've forgiven you… and I'm not sure I trust you either.'

'But you want to see Mia.'

'Yes I do, very much.'

'Then you'll just have to risk it, won't you?'

I agreed to go over there and before I got off the phone, she asked if I'd sold the painting. She seemed pleased when I told her I'd only got half the expected amount for it.

'Serves you right, you thief,' she said, laughing victoriously.

'You've never taken anything seriously,' I remarked, 'especially other people's marriage vows.'

'Oh, Lucy, chill out – you're such a prude. I can see why Matt was so quick to move on. He needed a bit of fun, someone who wasn't so serious.' And she laughed again. More to herself this time.

'You can keep him. I'd rather have the money from the painting any day,' I said, 'even if it wasn't as much as I thought. I can get to the places I've always wanted to go.'

'Good for you,' she said, and put down the phone. She wasn't interested in where I was going, but that was typical Amber; if it didn't involve her, it wasn't relevant.

As desperate as I am to see Mia, I'm not that keen on coming face to face with Amber after all this time. Kirsty says she's told Stella she's going to America to do a talk show; apparently she's going to be 'the English Oprah'. I imagine she's pretty unbearable, showing off and being really full of herself. Funny really, Matt always said she was full of herself; who'd ever have thought things would've turned out like they have? Kirsty says Amber brought champagne to the book club last time but was a bit rude about Marjorie's vegan quiche, which caused an upset. I hate to say it, but I think I would have enjoyed that and back when we were friends Amber and I would have giggled all the way home about 'quiche-gate'. Meanwhile, apparently Stella's annoyed because Amber's interviewing for nannies now she's in the money, and Stella feels used and dumped. Welcome to the club, Stella. Kirsty also says Amber's writing her autobiography, and apparently she received a six-figure advance.

'We'll be able to buy it next Christmas and read all about her life,' Kirsty said sarcastically.

'I might give it a miss.' I laughed. 'She tells such lies, it'll all be fiction anyway.'

It just shows you it doesn't matter what kind of a person you are, if you're famous people will pay to hear your story, and you can't turn the TV on these days without her popping up. She was all over the daytime talk shows last week – looked like she'd had botox, and had long, voluminous extensions in her now caramel-and-copper hair. She looked like an airbrushed version of her old self.

I have to confess, I too am guilty of presenting a rather airbrushed version of myself. And it comes from years of suppressing who I really am – the angry, fighting teen, the about-to-be-expelled schoolgirl is never far from the surface. It was, in effect, what happened to Miss Brownley, my lovely teacher who caused me to make the change, to be someone else.

The day after my terrible visit, I was still hurt and angry and had a particularly nasty argument with a boy in my class, who accused me of being 'a lezzer in love with Miss Brownley'. I lashed out and ended up in the headmistress's office.

'I thought you were finally managing your anger issues appropriately, but this… this reaction to someone making a mean remark this morning was wholly inappropriate, Lucy. I'm recommending you be moved elsewhere,' Miss Craddock said sternly. 'St Cuthbert's has a special scheme for students like you. They can help you with your problems and…'

I didn't hear anything else. I knew kids who'd gone to Cuthbert's 'special scheme', kids on the edge, who sniffed glue or cut themselves. There was much teen 'folklore' about the place from my contemporaries. Colourful and lurid tales were told about the angry place behind locked doors, where plastic cutlery was a necessity; a spoon could take out an eye.

'I'm not going there, Miss, no way – I'm not bloody mental!' I yelled in the headmistress's face.

She went on to dress it all up as some wonderful educational establishment where I could 'find help and support', but I knew different.

'I fail to see what your defence could possibly be with regard to attacking James Mackie and I'm afraid I will have to suspend you with a view to moving you to the St Cuthbert's—'

I didn't wait until she'd finished her sentence. It wasn't just about me fighting James Mackie. I reckoned that Miss Brownley had said something after I trashed her home the previous day. She must have been straight on the phone to old Craddock and got me expelled and, worse, committed to what everyone knew was the school equivalent of a mental health careclinic.

'Has Miss Brownley said something?' I asked, furious that the woman I'd worshipped had dropped me in it.

'No, in fact Miss Brownley has been one of the few teachers singing your praises of late…' she started, but I didn't believe her. Daisy had done this; she'd done exactly what Daisy Buchanan did to Gatsby and abandoned me.

'So unless you have anything further to say, I shall be making the recommendation,' she said, pen poised over paperwork to sign away my future.

'Miss Brownley kissed me,' I heard myself say. I was sixteen but hadn't a clue what I was doing, the implications of what I was saying. I wanted to get Daisy into trouble with Miss Craddock because I thought she'd done the same to me. I found out a long time later that Miss Brownley hadn't told on me; it was the maths teacher Mr Jackson who'd said I was being difficult in class and I'd just flipped. What I told Miss Craddock was a lie, a total lie, but the minute I'd said it and I saw her face I knew this was *big*. And when she asked me to repeat what I'd just told her, I did – and elaborated even more. I knew I couldn't take it back.

'Did she… touch you?'

I nodded. At this, she called the deputy Mr Darlston to come in, and my mother was called (who arrived an hour later, wearing a stained top and reeking of alcohol, much to my shame). It was all such a mess, this circus I'd started, and it went too fast too soon, so by the time I realised the significance of what I'd said it was too late to change my story. Miss Brownley was suspended later that day. I never expected that and cried because I felt so guilty about the impact my words had had on the life of someone I cared about. I was horrified. I cried so much everyone assumed it was because of the way Miss Brownley had 'abused' me and Miss Craddock kept apologising for what I'd 'been through'. All I could think about was how lovely Miss Brownley had been to me in her cosy little home that smelled of warm garlic, and knowing I'd never go there again made me cry even more.

I heard she'd given up teaching and gone to live in Ireland. Julie Baker's mother told her that Miss Brownley had 'a breakdown' after what had happened. And Julie, who knew something had gone on involving me, but wasn't sure what, took great delight in telling the class that Miss Brownley's 'breakdown' was all my fault. But I already knew.

I often think of Daisy Brownley even now. I try not to think about what happened afterwards, but I go back to my sixteenth summer and that evening in her garden, the happiest time in my life. I've spent all these years since trying to find that happiness again, and all my life it's eluded me. I hoped by loving Matt I could erase the past, cover it with new, more wonderful happy things, but even my wedding day didn't come close to that almost kiss, the soft touch of her fingers on my mouth, the potent scent of roses and my first awakening to something like love.

CHAPTER THIRTY

Lucy

Pulling up outside my old house to see Mia feels so weird. I'm really nervous, which is silly – or is it? I'm visiting my former best friend, who's now in a relationship with my husband. She accused me of being her stalker, took out a restraining order against me and made sure I was convicted of this in court. *What could* possibly *go wrong?* I think as I walk up the drive and notice how it's become rampant with weeds. It's not like Matt to let the garden go to seed. Then as I knock on the door I notice it's been a while since anyone scrubbed the doorstep, or cleaned the windows, but then again if Matt's working Amber won't do anything – it'll all just be left.

Amber eventually opens the door and I have to say I'm taken aback. It's been six months since I last saw her in court. I was expecting total gloss and glamour to greet me – but now she looks terrible. She's positively emaciated, and older, so much older. I was ready to have my breath taken away by the glamorous TV star, but without the make-up and the hair extensions I can't believe it's her.

'Wow, have you been on a diet? Are you eating enough?' I say, unable to stop myself.

'What's it to you?' she says, a smile in her eyes. 'I've lost a few pounds. Got to be thin and gorgeous for NYC.'

'You didn't look this thin last week on breakfast TV.'

'Because it was pre-recorded. We filmed it weeks ago,' she says, clearly put out that I'm not impressed with her weight loss. She walks ahead down my hall, and what I see is this frail woman who looks at least ten years older than she is. I genuinely wonder if she's developed an eating disorder.

She ushers me in, which is weird, because this is still my house, and the weirdness of this momentarily distracts me from her shocking appearance. We walk into the sitting room and it's strange yet familiar; the wallpaper Matt and I chose together from Homebase one wet Saturday afternoon is still on the walls and my velvet cushions still adorn our old sofa. Nothing's changed, yet everything's changed. The place looks as neglected inside as it did on the outside. Looking at pale, haggard Amber, I'm not surprised the skirting boards need a good clean; she doesn't look like she has the strength to do anything. She has to move a load of glossy magazines off the sofa before I can sit down and that alone seems to leave her breathless.

'Are you all right?' I ask, as I sit down.

She smiles. 'I'm fine, absolutely fine.'

She's sitting on the edge of the soft easy chair. It looks huge in contrast to her now tiny frame. Her voice is smaller too – this wasn't what I expected at all.

'So you're off to New York soon,' I say, taking control of the conversation and wondering why the dynamic between us has changed so dramatically.

'I was… I am. I've postponed it, just for a couple of weeks. I haven't been feeling too good. It's great to be wanted, but it's taking its toll and – did you hear – I'm going to be the English Oprah?'

'Yeah, Kirsty told me.'

She's wanted this kind of attention for so long. I imagined she'd thrive on it, and yet it seems to have weakened her. It's ironic, because in spite of everything, suddenly *I'm* the one who's doing exactly what I want, while Amber's still waiting. My round-the-world flights are booked, the new chapter in my life sorted, yet I'm the criminal who only a matter of weeks ago was on my knees with nothing. Who's winning now, Amber? Winners and losers, that's how she always saw us – and I was the loser until now.

We sit in silence. I reject her offer of a cup of tea. I don't want this to go on for any longer than it needs to and I'm not sure she'd actually make it to the kitchen without collapsing.

'Amber, I'm off to the passport office later. I have to pack up my flat, put everything in storage. I can't stay long. Can I see Mia?' I worry she's going to take her revenge on me for the painting by suddenly changing her mind about me seeing Mia – that would be torture for me, and she knows it.

She raises her head and looks at me; her eyes are glassy, grey and leaden as storm clouds. She doesn't say anything. Then she seems to gather herself together, like she suddenly remembers why I'm here.

'I've never really been big on girlfriends, but I want you to know that in spite of what's happened, I did value what we had… you and I. And I know you had your issues, but the way you've always cared about Mia is so special. I do appreciate everything you did, for both of us, when she first came along.'

I shift in my seat. I wonder if she's playing games with me. Even in her physically weakened state I don't trust her.

'I've told you before my mother and I never had a good relationship,' she continues. 'She was only interested in her boyfriends. I always came second, and she never showed me any real love. Consequently I feel no love for her. I don't know where she is, and I don't really care. My biggest fear is that Mia will feel the same about me.'

'Then don't let that happen.'

'How can I stop her from hating me though? I'm basically living my mother's life!'

'Break the cycle. You said your mother never showed you any real love – so make sure you love your little girl, and that she knows she's loved. Learn from the past. Don't allow the past to colour the future, it's gone. That's what I'd do if I was a mother.'

'I'm sorry that didn't happen for you, Lucy. I honestly hope you find what you're looking for one day.' She sighs, looking into my eyes, and it feels so genuine, I'm touched by what she says.

We'll both soon head off for new horizons, yet even now it feels like there's an invisible, unbreakable tie between us forged through love and hate and friendship. And however angry we both feel about what we've done to each other, we've touched each other's lives, and we're both changed from the experience. For a while, we sit in a strange, comfortable silence, both thinking our own thoughts, until I realise that time's running out.

'Can I see Mia now?'

She nods, but she sits looking at me, like she still wants more from me before she allows me access to her child. I stand up and still she's staring at me, and I feel claustrophobic, like I can't breathe and have to get out of here or it will kill me. I can't fathom Amber, never could, and her last words to me are as bewildering as ever, but make me feel uneasy.

'Lucy – if when she's older, Mia ever asks you what I'm like, I won't blame you for telling her I'm the worst friend, the worst person, the worst wife. But will you do me a favour? Will you just make sure she knows that in spite of all my faults I love her more than anything or anyone in my life? Because I really, really do.'

CHAPTER THIRTY-ONE

Lucy

Suddenly I hear the front door and Matt walks in.

'Hey, I… didn't expect you…' Amber says, looking up at him.

'I'm early,' he answers her, but he's looking at me like he's seen a ghost.

'Amber said it was okay for me to come and see Mia,' I say defensively. I don't know if Matt is aware I was coming. I wait for his reaction; the last time I saw him was in court.

'Hi Lucy… This is awkward,' he says light-heartedly.

'Yes, it is, isn't it?' I agree, but he isn't interested in me. Amber's in the room.

He walks over to her, puts his hand on her shoulder gently, and I can see love in his eyes. He never looked at me like that.

'Oh… Well as long as Amber's okay with you being here – that's… okay,' he says, rubbing his hands together. 'Cup of tea?' he asks brightly, and I shake my head. That would be weird. Me drinking tea with my ex-husband and my ex-best friend in my former marital home? No thanks.

But, classic Matt, he rushes off into the kitchen to make tea for Amber. He was always the host, happiest in the kitchen with the kettle on or making meals and feeding people. And for the millionth time in my life I think what a shame it was that we couldn't have children. Would our lives have turned out differently if we had? Would they have been the glue we needed to weather the storm of Amber? I don't ponder this for long. It's too painful and I have to be positive; things have a way of working out, don't they? Matt has Mia now and finally the opportunity to be a dad. I suppose he'll adopt her, and as soon as our divorce comes through they'll get married. Life goes on.

Eventually Matt returns with her tea and as he hands it to her I can feel the tension between them that I once mistook for hatred. But now I know it's love or lust, whatever you want to call it – it's whatever brings people together, even the unlikeliest couples. I'm relieved to discover their union doesn't hurt me any more – but still I shouldn't be here. I have lots to do, and I must see Mia. She's the only reason I came here and put myself through this.

'I have to get off,' I say, moving to stand up. 'Could I perhaps see Mia before I go?'

'Yes, she's upstairs, probably asleep,' Amber says.

'I'll go and get her.' Matt walks towards the door.

'No. Don't disturb her if she's asleep. I can just see her in her cot.'

'Okay,' he says, so I follow him out of the room, leaving Amber alone. Ironic really; in the house where we always planned a baby, a nursery, here we are, husband and wife going upstairs to see the baby in her cot. Except Mia's not my baby – and Matt's not really my husband any more.

The door is half-open when we walk in and, expecting Mia to be fast asleep, I'm overjoyed to see she's wide awake and smiling.

'I can't believe how she's grown,' I say, instinctively taking her out of her cot and holding her close. She's smiling and saying words that only she understands as I hold her tight and kiss her little nose, which tickles her and makes her laugh. 'She always liked that,' I say, giggling. 'Yes you did, didn't you, Mia?'

Meanwhile, Matt pulls a face at her and she giggles more, going into hysterics the crazier he looks.

'Uncle Matt's got a funny face, hasn't he?' I joke.

'Actually, she calls me Daddy now,' he says, a little awkwardly.

'Oh… oh, of course, that makes sense.' I try not to show my surprise, my little sting of jealousy. Amber got everything, the husband and the child, and despite being excited about my travels, I wonder if I would actually swap places with her in a heartbeat.

'Lucy… about you and me…' Matt starts, and I can feel another awkward moment coming on.

'You think we should hurry through with the divorce?' I try to pre-empt him.

'Yeah. I mean, absolutely we should. Amber and I would love to get married – for Mia.'

'Yes, of course. Let's get things moving on that. No point in delaying anything.'

'Great, yeah… Amber'll be pleased, not because… just… you know?'

I nod vigorously, too vigorously.

'Sorry… about everything, Lucy… I didn't want to hurt you. I just can't help how I feel.'

'Look, it happened. We're all a little wiser, and I genuinely hope you'll be happy. Just don't let Amber break your heart.'

'Like she did yours?'

'I guess so,' I say, feeling stupid. I was duped by both of them, a cuckoo in my own nest. 'But I'm okay.' I paint on a smile and add another lie to my long list. I'll never be okay again after Amber. Most people come into our lives, we know them for a while and then move on, but a few stay in our hearts and minds. And Amber's lodged in mine.

'I was really cut up for a while,' I say. 'I never expected – I had no idea that you and Amber…' The air is thick and I don't want to open up old wounds but there's a huge part of me that still hasn't had closure. Perhaps I just need to bury everything, and start my new journey? 'I wish you both well,' I say.

'Yeah, thanks.' He doesn't look at me, just nods a little, then holds out his arms for Mia and we go downstairs to Amber, and we say our strange goodbyes, my once best friend, once husband and me. And I climb into my car, leaving them, a little family on the doorstep of my once home. I start the engine, on my own voyage now, alone, and I'm filled with excitement, and fear. But as I pull away, waving and driving towards my future, I wonder if she'll break Matt's heart like she breaks everyone else's, and can't shake the sense of foreboding filling my chest.

I can't bear to be apart from her – with one of us in another country. How will I survive? I keep thinking about the fun we had, how cute she was in that little unicorn suit, the way she looked at me… the way we used to be. I want it back, but I think it might be too late.

CHAPTER THIRTY-TWO

Amber

Saying goodbye to Lucy is surprisingly tough. I feel like I'm saying goodbye to a part of myself. After all that's happened, you'd think I'd be glad to wave her off. But it's only now that I realise how much we once meant to each other. I will admit I made friends with her because I knew she lived nearby. I'd seen her neat little house from the outside, could tell she was a fusspot, a busybody who might just look after me a bit. Subconsciously, that's what I've always been looking for, someone who'll care about me, someone to come home to.

Matt was there for me too, he understands me, knows how it feels not to have a family. We've clung to each other during these difficult months, and that's the problem. We were clinging – not loving. I think my hormones, my fucked-up childhood and his lovely, caring nature were a potent cocktail to a woman like me. And between us we created something unreal, a love that doesn't really exist – just a desperate need and a sprinkle of lust.

I've come through it. I'm starting my own journey, just like Lucy. I want new adventures with Ben, but Matt wants me, and I don't know how to tell him it's over.

It's madness, but I miss Lucy's advice at times like this. She'd know what to do, what to say. But I've never been very good at goodbyes, not since Michael anyway.

Matt can sense something's not right though; he's edgy and argumentative. I never promised him forever, but I just don't think he wants to face what's happening to us. Despite his lovely ways, Matt does have a mean streak. I remember Lucy saying he occasionally said really hurtful things to her, but she put it down to him being a Scorpio – 'they have a sting in their tail,' she'd said. I smile, thinking of weird little Lucy with her theories about everything.

Seeing her again has inspired me – she could have so easily given up after losing everything, but she hasn't. If anything she's become stronger, more independent. I envy her and want that for me too. No more waiting until I feel well enough, strong enough – I have to get moving and book on that flight to NYC. Trouble is, I'm still suffering from nausea and loss of appetite so after Lucy left I made an appointment with the doctor for later in the week. The new nanny starts tomorrow, so I'll have all the freedom in the world, and can set off for New York without Matt trying to stop me by refusing to do childcare.

Also, now the money's coming in, I've paid back the rent I owe on my house and, I haven't told Matt yet, but Mia and I are going back to live there after I've been to New York. I like it here at Treetops, and though some might think I'm mad moving three doors down from my ex, I've done crazier things – and if he's uncomfortable, then he's the one who should move. One day, I'd like to buy Greenacres, make it Mia's forever home. I never had one of those and for her I want everything that I didn't.

So with plans to move and all the offers coming in I've taken a lot on recently, and my health's suffered. I'm exhausted, and everyone's telling me to slow down, but this is my time. I've been receiving offers I just can't refuse, and the world of TV and celebrity is so fickle I have to make hay while the sun shines.

She'll never know how much I loved her. Oh, I'd been married, thought I'd been in love before – but never like this, not with her. She's mine and she always will be. She knows it too, but she thinks she has a different story to mine – she doesn't, we're all tangled up in each other forever. She can't leave; she can't go so far away. I can't live without her, and I know what to do to keep her with me, because I've done it before.

CHAPTER THIRTY-THREE

Amber

I've been feeling a little better these past couple of days. I went to see my doctor, who checked me over and said I needed to rest and eat properly. She said if I felt the same in a couple of weeks she'd refer me for blood tests. This is what the NHS has come to, with all the government cuts. Unless you're terminal, doctors barely have the time or resources to do anything. The good news is, though, that from his perfunctory look it seems like I don't have anything horrific or obviously wrong with me. So I took the bull by the horns and booked my flight times, then I called Richard, the TV exec in New York, and he promised me a limo would be waiting at JFK.

'I hope you're ready for success, Miss Amber,' he said, in that lovely American drawl.

'I sure am ready for *anything*,' I said, in my fake American accent. I know how to play the game. Along with the pilot episode for the talk show, there are offers from a couple of panel shows, and the one-hour special, 'Amber Young: My Friend, My Stalker', is about to air. It's all very exciting but I do feel a bit guilty about dragging Lucy through the mud again. Having said that she'll be halfway round the world in Nepal, and hopefully won't even know about it – or care.

Matt is another story though. After Lucy's visit, he said they'd talked about divorce and she was as keen as him to finalise everything. 'We can get married then!' he said excitedly, seemingly still unable to grasp that I don't want to marry him.

'Matt, you asked me before… and I said no.' I tried to say this gently, but he was devastated.

'No, you said "not yet", you didn't say no,' he mumbled, and I was sure he was going to burst into tears, making everything so much worse – I hate men who cry.

So then I told him it was over, and I was moving out after New York and the floodgates opened. He just stood there in the kitchen sobbing – and I just kept hoping he'd pull himself together because I wasn't changing my mind. As fond as I am of Matt, and as grateful as I am for him being there when I needed him the most, it was never wave-crashing love on my part. I fancied him, even may have loved him a little at the beginning, but I wouldn't give up this new opportunity for anyone, and to be honest, he'd just get in the way. Of course I didn't tell him that when he suggested we could get married. I just said I needed space and my work commitments were so huge I didn't have time for a relationship… the usual PR shit we often use in our personal relationships.

Finally, he seemed to accept what I was saying, and he made us both a cup of tea, like old times. After more talking, he even admitted he'd half-expected me to leave him, so it wasn't a surprise, which made me feel a bit better about everything.

'I've been in denial,' he said. 'I love you and all I ever wanted was a life here with you and Mia, but—'

'I know, darling…' I said, wishing he'd stop talking and go and work on his writing or something. Apart from anything else, I'd booked my hairdresser to come over that night and I couldn't cancel her – you have to book her months in advance – so I was bloody relieved he pulled himself together before she arrived. I doubted she'd pick up on his mood, or any tension between us, but it was better if he was out of the way. These days I have to be so careful. As soon as your star rises, your price goes up, and a snippet about my home life with my stalker's ex is worth a fortune to some people. Anyway, as I said to him, it's been coming for a while (I've been bashing him over the head with hints that I'm moving on for weeks) and now it's time for a fresh start for both of us. Hallelujah!

So things are finally working out for me. Matt has been told, the new nanny's settling in and I've suggested that she and Mia move back to Greenacres while I'm away in New York. After all the excitement and glamour of the Big Apple, I didn't want to have to come back to Matt and his sad eyes. I'd hate myself.

Maybe when Lucy returns from her world travels, they'll get back together. Who knows? In fact, the more I think about it… That would be very convenient. I could leave them as I found them, a little shaken by my intrusion in their lives, but it could make their marriage stronger and leave me free to exit stage left with Mia.

He went upstairs to work on his autobiography while I waited for Teresa, my hairdresser, to arrive. She was early, and did something fabulous with a set of profanely priced extensions that I have to say took years off me. But even my new hairstyle didn't take away the guilt I felt about Matt. He gave me everything I thought I wanted, only for me to realise that when I had it, I didn't want it after all. He genuinely cares, and for him it's true love. But true love's for other people. I don't really deserve it, and anyway I'll be gone in a couple of days and without me around Matt can begin to move on.

I woke up this morning and my hair was still gorgeous even after a night's sleep, and Matt said how nice I looked when we had breakfast together. He seems okay considering, and the only time I noticed a little anger was when I gave Mia my scrambled eggs – I only gave her a mouthful but he was really nasty.

'I made them for you… not her,' he snapped, snatching the plate away.

'What's wrong with you?' I said, angry at his childishness.

'Nothing, but I made them specially – for you.' He sighed, tipping up the plate and emptying the lot into the bin.

Later, as I was going through some photos on my phone that my new agent had sent to me, he wandered into the sitting room.

'I'm sorry, Amber, about before… I was angry. It wasn't about the eggs. I just need to get used to the idea that you're going away tomorrow, and you aren't coming back.'

'I know, but we can still get together, go for coffee and – I'm sorry, Matt, I didn't mean to turn your world upside down.'

'Well, you did that all right,' he said, shaking his head. He sat down next to me and helped choose the best photos. 'You look beautiful in them all,' he said.

'You mean that, don't you?' I smiled.

He nodded, and I wondered idly if I'd ever meet another man who would love me like Matt did.

'Do you have an early flight?' he asked, getting up from the sofa.

'God no. I hate those God awful dawn flights, I have a late afternoon one. You know I look shit before noon, and it takes me two hours to stagger out of bed and try and rev myself up these days. I'm permanently tired.'

He laughed at this. 'You never look like shit.'

I rolled my eyes in a 'you're kidding' way.

'Amber – I want to ask you a favour.'

'Okay, what?'

'Would you – would you stay with me tonight?'

'You mean sleep together?' I asked. We hadn't had sex for weeks. I didn't want to be with him; my head was too full of Ben.

'Yes… spend the night together, you and me. I'll cook dinner, we can talk, and… I know when you get on that plane tomorrow that we're over. I still love you… but I think a final night together would help me come to terms with what's about to happen. If we can just say a proper goodbye.'

What could I say? In spite of feeling tired and wanting to preserve my energy for my new career, I felt like I owed him one last night of passion. So we move Mia and the nanny over to number 13 and I agreed that Matt and I would swing from the chandeliers (well, Lucy's Ikea light fittings) one last time.

'I'm making my boeuf bourguignon,' he calls from the kitchen, and I feel an unexpected twinge of sadness. The last time he made that the three of us sat around the table. Lucy was telling us about one of the boys in her class who was particularly cheeky but funny, and I remember almost choking, I laughed so much. God, I do miss her. I wish things could have turned out differently; well at least for me and Lucy.

'And maybe some red wine?' I say, remembering the lovely Merlot we drank that night.

'Yes, I have your favourite Merlot– already opened and breathing.'

'You think of everything.'

'You'll never find another like me,' he says, and I don't answer. It's probably true. 'Why don't you pour us both a glass?' he says. The kitchen is steamy, pans bubbling, the air warm and fragrant with herbs as he makes a rich and probably delicious gravy.

'I'll miss this,' I say, pouring the wine into two glasses.

'You don't have to, because you're always welcome here. I'll be waiting,' he says. And we clink glasses and I think how lucky I am that we can be so grown up about all this. And how things have all worked out, and for the first time in my life, I'm saying goodbye with my heart intact.

TWO WEEKS LATER

CHAPTER THIRTY-FOUR

Lucy

I'll never forget the phone call. I'd been in Nepal about a week; the signal was weak in the village I was staying in, so they'd left a message on my phone. I'd been to a local orphanage, hoping to secure some voluntary teaching work. I took my time going back to my room, enjoying the warm sunset, remembering her painting and feeling a pang of guilt that I took it from her. I remember the sounds of children playing outside, just under my window, and how the curtains in my room floated at the open window, just like my curtains on Mulberry Avenue. Then I listened to the voice message and everything changed.

It took me a couple of days to get a flight back to the UK and I cried all the way. I didn't know what exactly had happened or what I could possibly do, but I had to be there. The details had been sketchy, the police didn't want to say too much, but they called me because she'd left a letter addressed to me, with her solicitor, only to be opened in the event of her death. Even now the idea seemed farcical. Amber Young, Weather Girl from Manchester Tonight – dead. When I arrived back in the UK, the first thing I did was head straight to Dolby and Partners, where I was ushered into a room and handed an envelope with my name on.

Hi Lucy,

Remember me? It's your best friend, Amber. I wanted to let you know that whatever happened between us, you were the best friend I ever had.

I don't really know what went wrong for us – I know you became obsessed with me – but whatever was going on in that crazy old head of yours, I know, in your own way, you loved me like a sister. And I loved you the same.

I know I always made out like I was the best, that I could do anything. But I had no real confidence, hated myself, always have – but you'd tell me I was amazing, and say you were proud of me – and no one in my life has ever told me they're proud of me. I wanted to tell you that.

I also wanted to tell you that I hated your taste in films – candy floss for the brain. I didn't want to hurt your feelings, but Jennifer Aniston in a 'hilarious' romantic sodding romp is not my idea of fun. I'll tell you now, I hated every single minute of that shit, but you'd sit there like a nutter in your unicorn onesie, laughing and swooning. And I couldn't help it, you made me smile, and you'd turn and look at me while handing me popcorn, cake or advice and despite your dubious film choice, I felt like someone actually cared. And in those moments I was happier than I've ever been, before or since.

You gave me so much, and you asked nothing of me except my friendship. We hurt each other badly. It was all a mess and I do take some responsibility for the car crash that ensued and hope you consider us to still be besties.

Anyway, I'm writing to ask you the biggest favour I've ever asked of anyone. I'm flying out to New York in a couple of days and being a mum has made me realise that I have to finally grow up. So I've decided to do the kind of fussy thing you always did and in the unlikely event that the plane falls from the sky and I die, I wanted to ask if you will look after Mia?

You'll probably never see this letter. When I die at the ripe old age of ninety-five having had a great time, my fifty-two-year-old daughter won't need a guardian, and you'll be in a care home barking at the moon. But just in case you're reading this and your answer is 'yes', which I hope it will be, I'd like to make some stipulations; I want my little girl to have what I never had. I want her to have a mother who loves her, who puts plasters on sore knees and kisses them better. I want her to have a mother who cuddles her, plaits her hair and tells her she's beautiful. A mother who waits up to ask her about her first date and who dries her tears when her heart's been broken. I want her to have a mother who guides her, listens to her, asks her about her feelings, her friends, her life, and who fills a bucket with popcorn and watches trashy films with her. I don't know anyone else but you who could do this.

So, Lucy, if I'm not here to love my little girl, please would you do this for me? Make her feel loved and secure, and make her laugh and inspire her to be an amazing woman, and a good friend.

One more, final request – please don't overfeed her on cheesy romcoms and too much bloody cake, OK?

Your best friend always,

Amber xxx

According to the police, Matt and Amber were in bed, they died in their sleep. The detective looking into the deaths described it as 'a tragic accident'.

'There were the remains of a couple of empty wine bottles, which would suggest they'd had a lot to drink that night and just didn't wake up,' the solicitor explained when I pushed for more information. 'The nanny says they wanted some time alone,' she said. 'Seems they were planning to move into her old house. Her career was on the up… apparently she was going to New York to talk about a chat show. And all that ruined because they lit a couple of candles in the bedroom and fell asleep – will people ever learn?'

Thank God Mia wasn't in the house when the fire started; she was with the nanny in Amber's old house ahead of Matt and Amber moving back there. I asked lots of questions, but like anything that's difficult to accept, it was also hard to understand.

Have you ever had a secret that you couldn't tell a soul, even the person you love? I have…

I'd begged her not to go out that night. I told her I loved her, but all I saw was her sluttish face laughing at me, mocking me. So I crushed her sleeping pills and put them in her cup of tea. As always the pills made her sleepy and weak. She needed me, and I liked to be needed. That night she didn't go to meet him, she stayed home with me, and never woke up. I was 15, and I've carried my secret with me ever since, never telling anyone how my mother died.

EPILOGUE

Twelve Months Later

I stand barefoot in the beautiful whitewashed room of number 13 Mulberry Avenue and wonder what kind of fate this is. From the first moment I saw Amber Young, I was drawn to her beauty, her sparkle, her lust for life. She was impossible to resist, and she'd had me in her thrall.

Then she stole my husband, my home and my friends – then she had me arrested and convicted, and told the world how unhinged I was. But I'm trying not to be bitter, because it eats you up, so what I try to remember of Amber is the good times. Her sense of fun, the way she'd gossip and make me laugh and how her outrageous comments and foul-mouthed rants would make a sailor blush. And if I concentrate on the fun, then even after all the awfulness I might finally be able to forgive her. Sometimes I might even smile when I think of us together, two grown women dressed as unicorns sharing our lives – from first loves, to bad mothers and lost childhoods. We both lived through them.

And now it's up to me to break the cycle, to be one of the mothers we never had for her daughter. Mia and I now live here at number 13. Unlucky for some, but hopefully not for us. I bought the house with money from Amber's estate – and I also bought the painting back. Amber would have wanted it here, on the huge white wall, the soft pinks and oranges swirling into a Nepal sunset… the mountains topped with glittering snow. The painting is part of Amber, her first love – a memento of her past and a way of showing Mia who her mother was.

It's been over a year now since Amber and Matt died, and though there's never been any question of foul play, I can't help but wonder what really happened that night. When Amber was involved, things were never as straightforward as they seemed… but I doubt I'll ever know, because they both perished in the house that night, taking with them any story they might tell. I want a neat ending, a conclusion – to know exactly what happened: if the fire was an accident, or Amber planned something like this all along. Then again, that's the Miss Marple in me. As Matt once said, 'Life isn't like your TV crime dramas, Lucy – everything you find isn't a clue, things happen randomly and there isn't always a *reason*.' The sensible part of me knows the fire was just a tragic accident, but weird things happened around Amber, and I can't help but wonder.

Anyway, I don't have time to play detective these days. I have a demanding two-year-old who needs me, and I love to be needed.

My criminal record didn't stand in the way of me being Mia's legal guardian. My conviction didn't involve offences against children, and the fact that I'm a trained teacher helped. I hope one day more evidence will emerge and I can erase my 'stalking' conviction for good and adopt Mia properly.

I reckon Mia is Amber's way of saying sorry, and she's the most beautiful 'sorry' I ever received. And as for me, I'd rather be here with Mia than in any number of beautiful destinations around the world – one day we'll travel together, Mia and I, and I'll take her to Nepal to see the sun set over the Himalayas.

The police called me earlier. Apparently, after the accident the nanny handed a folder of Matt's to the police. There was so much to wade through it's only now the police are able to look through some of the previously logged evidence and it turns out the folder is Matt's 'autobiography.' It was his work in progress he'd called 'Matt Metcalf – A Life of Drama'. He'd always kept a diary and I can't help but feel sad that no one will ever read it now. When he gave his memoir to the nanny, he said, 'Keep this, and if anything happens to Amber or me – give it to the police.' I can't help but wonder why he did that, but I guess I'll never know.

Anyway, the police are going to look through Matt's writing and let me know later this week if there are any developments. I doubt Matt's luvvie 'memoirs' will reveal much, unless they want a detailed account of Year 10's production of *Bugsy Malone*.

As for Mia, I tell her she has another mummy in heaven, and sometimes when I look at her, the likeness takes my breath away. But Mia will have a very different childhood. Amber and I were damaged children, but unlike Amber, I'm not a damaged adult. As much as I'm here for Mia, she has saved me – I now have the future I wanted, and I'll be a good mum, making sure she's loved and supported, happy and safe here in our forever home.

I smile at my little girl, who's dancing for me now on the soft pink rug, as I lay out the cupcakes we made together earlier for our rug picnic. She's shouting 'Mummy' excitedly and clapping her little hands together and I have to stop and take it in – it's the most beautiful noise I've ever heard, as beautiful as the sound of birdsong in Miss Brownley's garden.

We're both so happy here. I try not to think about the horrible things that happened, the dead bird, the lipsticked message, running taps, baby bootees, candles smoking and all the weird phone calls and texts. I think instead about Amber and I dressed as unicorns, drinking too much Prosecco, and how she made me laugh so much it came out of my nose.

I think about her a lot as I walk barefoot around the house, just like she did. Wandering around her big, bright airy rooms, I feel her presence, hear her laughter. She once took my life, and in death, she gave me hers. And sometimes, late at night, when Mia's sleeping soundly and I'm alone, I think I smell a waft of her perfume, and hope she somehow knows that everything worked out in the end.

EVIDENCE CHAIN OF CUSTODY TRACKING FORM
Manchester Metropolitan Police
Case number 4902342

Matt Metcalf – A Life of Drama
Final Chapter

From that first time I saw her, russet hair shot through by the sun, big brown eyes, I tried not to love her. But I had to be with her, so I found her number on Lucy's phone and told her how I felt in texts. I used a different, anonymous phone, and when Lucy told me she was flirting with men I'd warn her. Later, I became more brave, more daring, it was exciting to take her spare keys from our kitchen, and go into her house following her from room to room. She never saw me. I watched from a dark corner, or behind a door, always just out of reach, but only a breath away. Sometimes, when she was out, I'd lie in her bed, breathing in her sweet fragrance, my face buried deep in her pillow. And some nights, when I couldn't bear to be without her, I'd climb in through her window, creep into her room and watch her sleep. One night, I stole her star-sprinkled scarf from the bottom of her bed. It smelled of Amber: citrus and musk. I kept it to wrap around me, and if I closed my eyes I could pretend she was with me.

Then late one night her tyre had been slashed, and I rescued her, never expecting my feelings to be reciprocated, but she was so grateful she let me kiss her. And I knew this was the love I'd been waiting for and when she became pregnant she came to live with us, and I was ecstatic, but hid it behind a facade of indifference, a performance I'll always be proud of. But I could see we weren't enough for her in our little house with our little lives and she talked of going back home to her big house. I knew then how it would end. No one ever kept a woman like Amber Young; she always got away, soon bored, looking for the next adventure. So I sent her a dead bird, wrapped in pink floral paper, a pair of baby bootees. I turned on all her taps in the middle of the night and she called our house, scared – I liked it when she was scared, because that was when she needed me most. Sometimes, when I thought she might leave me, go back to her old house, her old, promiscuous life, I would frighten her, and she'd come back to me.

But, one day, Lucy almost caught me. She was in her house, she'd been with the plumber, but I saw her looking through Amber's things. She saw the vile words I'd scrawled in lipstick on the mirror. I'd done this because I wanted to scare her, to need me again, but this time I was scared because Lucy almost saw me, so I ran out of the French doors, escaping just in time.

Lucy found a knife and Amber's pregnancy test. I told her to throw it away and then later I dug it out of the bin, and along with the knife I kept it in the scarf I'd taken from Amber's house. All the time I kept her scared and thinking someone was watching her – more texts, strange gifts, I lit candles in her home, then put them out just as she walked in. And for a while, it worked. She came to stay; she had Mia, and I was finally happy. I set Lucy up by hiding her phone until the right moment, and miraculously finding it in the kitchen drawer (where I'd hidden it). When Lucy was arrested it turned out better than I'd ever hoped. I 'found' the bundle of Amber's belongings wrapped in the scarf and Lucy was convicted – finally I had Amber to myself once and for all, and for a while it was just me and her loving each other. But it didn't last; these things never do. She went back to work full-time and the TV offers started rolling in and suddenly all she could talk about was her ex – Ben this and Ben that. I hated the sound of his name. I knew she was sleeping with him; she'd stay out later and later, coming home fawning and drunk. Disgusting.

Then she said she was leaving me and I couldn't bear it. I asked her not to go, told her I loved her, bought her a ring, but all I saw was her uncaring face laughing at me. So for a while I crushed the sleeping pills and sprinkled them in her cups of tea, the dinners I cooked, and just like my whore of a mother, they made her sleepy. She had no idea, kept complaining about feeling tired, but once she almost gave her scrambled eggs to the baby I realised I was being sloppy, so I put them mainly in her tea. The pills made her helpless. She needed me and I needed her, but no, she was never satisfied, I was never enough. So she booked her flight and told me it was over and now I know what I have to do. I have no choice, she's just like my mother after all… I thought the weather girl was different… but she's just like all the other whores.

So tonight I will make her favourite dinner, buy the Merlot she loves and sprinkle too many crushed pills in both our glasses of wine before we go to bed. And she'll lie in my arms sleepily, and as she fades I'll light the candles close to the bed, and kick them over as the pills take us away. And my weather girl will fall asleep in my arms, and never leave me again.

A LETTER FROM SUE

Thank you so much for reading *The Woman Next Door.* If you enjoyed it, and want to keep up to date with all my latest releases, just sign up at the following link. I'll only send you an email when I have a new book out, your email address will never be shared and you can unsubscribe at any time.

www.suewatsonbooks.com/email

This book started life as an idea I had while working in TV, and I wanted to play around with the idea of fame and friendship, what's real and what's fake. And however much we try, we can never really change who we are as we're all shaped by our pasts, however far we think we've come.

I asked myself what would happen if someone like you or me became friends with someone like Amber Young. Would we be impressed and in awe of her looks, her life and her way with men, like Lucy? Or would we be more cynical, mistrustful, envious? And what might happen when, into this relatively new friendship, comes trouble in the shape of a deranged stalker?

Who is he, what does he want… and who says he is a he?

I really hope you loved reading *The Woman Next Door* as much as I loved writing it, and if you did I would be incredibly grateful if you could write a review. I really want to know what you think, and it makes such a difference helping new readers to discover one of my books for the first time.

Meanwhile, I'd love to see you on Facebook. Become a friend, like my page and please join me for a chat on Twitter.

Thanks,
Sue x

www.suewatsonbooks.com
suewatsonbooks
@suewatsonwriter

ACKNOWLEDGEMENTS

As always, my huge thanks to Olly Rhodes and the wonderful team at Bookouture who are there for me every step of the way. From romcom to killer thriller, they always have my back.

Special thanks to my editor Isobel Akenhead, who brings my ideas to life with her inspiration, enthusiasm, wisdom and guidance. Thanks to Jade Craddock, a brilliant copy editor who makes sense of my ramblings, to the fabulous Noelle Holten, who puts our books out there while writing her own, and as always a huge hug and thanks to Marketing Queen and fellow author Kim Nash, who literally never stops working.

Thanks to all my wonderful friends who support and celebrate each book with me – I couldn't ask for kinder, more lovely people to have in my life – you all know who you are. And big love to my family, Nick and Eve Watson and my mum, who, provide emotional support, ideas, coffee, and laughs while enduring my obsessive murder plotting and laptop hugging until each book is finished.